To Jessie,
Enjoy!
—Nell Pope

SHARE

MERE JOYCE

SHADE

ORACLE OF SENDERS

SEVEN SISTERS
PUBLISHING

Shade
Oracle of Senders Book One

E-Book ISBN: 978-1-64255-651-3
Print ISBN: 978-1-64255-652-0

7 Sisters Publishing
P.O. Box 993
Jupiter, Florida 33458

www.merejoyce.com
www.7sisterspublishing.com

Copyright © 2018 Mere Joyce

All rights reserved. No part of this publication may be reproduced, stored in a retrieval system, or transmitted, in any form or by any means (electronic, mechanical, photocopying, recording, or otherwise), without the prior written permission of the publisher.

This book is a work of fiction and does not represent any individual living or dead. Names, characters, places, and incidents either are products of the author's imagination or are used fictitiously.

TO SEBASTIAN, FOR TAKING A NAME
AND LEAVING INSPIRATION IN ITS PLACE.

IF I CLOSE MY EYES AND CONCENTRATE, I CAN ALMOST REMEMBER A TIME when I believed nothing came after death.

I've thought about this the entire ride to Pearson International, the entire time spent waiting for my flight to board. For the past four hours I've been flying across Canada and beyond on my way to France, my thoughts endless as I try to remember if my life was ever different than this.

I think it was, for a brief moment.

If I reach to the edges of my mind, I can conjure vague memories of stormy nights where thunder bellowed, tree branches cracked against windowpanes, and a tiny version of myself believed when things died, they were simply gone. Even as a child, maybe even a baby, I understood the difference between living and dead. I just understood it wrong.

Sometimes, I yearn for those days of innocent naivety. Like now, as I sit trapped on a plane with a spirit staring me down from across the aisle.

I hold a shaky hand to my mouth, trying to stop the queasy swell of my stomach. It figures I would see a ghost on a plane. All I want to do is run, and it's like being the victim of a clever prank to know I'm locked in this cabin, thousands of feet above the ocean and unable to get away.

The clock on the screen before my seat mocks me with its sluggish progression. It's late in Ontario and early morning in France, but the plane is still flying over the ocean between continents. Which means there's no escape. Not for another three hours.

Muttering curses to myself, I close my eyes against the pinpricks of pain in my head. I should have left when I had the chance. Unease bucked in my stomach the second I stepped on board, but I chalked it up to nerves. Flying alone from Toronto to Paris isn't a trip I've made before, and I couldn't justify walking away from the cool temperature and subtle, yet unpleasant, odour of the cabin based only on a hunch. Besides, I'm on this flight for a reason, and it so happens spirits play into the destination at the other end of this nightmare trip. If I had left the plane, I would have missed my chance to get to Camp Wanagi.

When the spirit first appeared, slinking out from one of the staff only areas in the back of the plane, I was relieved to know my faint sickness came from the ghost and not a horrible premonition about the plane crashing over the ocean. Still, as soon as the spirit noticed me and made its way closer, the relief fizzled fast.

"Are you okay, sweetheart?"

The clear, living voice of the old woman sitting next

to me sounds genuinely worried. I'm grateful and bothered to know she's concerned about my well-being.

"I'm fine," I say, forcing my eyes open and wincing away from the dull light of the overhead cabin. "Just a...a bad flyer." It's a lie, but far simpler to explain than the truth.

I can't very well tell her a ghost is sitting to her right, his half-formed hands reaching over and pawing at her arm. Hours ago, she commented on how cool the plane was. I tried not to cringe when she rubbed her arm, her fingers passing through the ghost's invisible grip.

Now, she pats my shoulder and offers me a gentle smile. "We'll be landing before you know it. Try to get a bit of sleep. It will help."

I nod, trying not to grit my teeth. "I will, thanks," I say, turning towards the window and closing my eyes again.

She's a friendly lady and a good neighbor for a flight as far as strangers go. Sitting next to the teenager fidgeting in his seat and muttering curses under his breath can't be easy, but she hasn't complained. She smells nice as well—like vanilla soap and citrusy perfume. Much better than the stink of fish the spirit is giving off. I'd assume he was a fisherman in life, who maybe died from eating some bad clams, except by now I know better. If I can see him, it means this man—whether he was once a fisherman, a deep-sea diver, or a businessman with a fondness for seafood—met his end by murder.

I make a show of nestling in against my seat so the old lady will think I'm resting. All things considered,

I've done okay on this trip. But it's been four hours now, and I'm far past my breaking point.

I haven't eaten, and I can't sleep, even though I'm sure the lady's advice would be worth listening to. In a pointless effort to distract myself, I tried flipping through one of the in-flight magazines and scanned the selection of movies until I found one of those idiotic comedies where a ghost—fully formed and capable of normal speech—helps some living guy solve a mystery. I couldn't handle watching anything after seeing the movie's preview. Not with the blue-white mass nearby.

A wise-cracking ghostly companion would be fun. It might even make the pain beneath my skull worthwhile. But this spirit is confused and morose. I'm sorry I can't help him, and I'm sorry I want to shut him away so I can have some peace.

Three more hours, Cal.

The fishy stench coats my nostrils until I can no longer smell the lady's soap and perfume, and I struggle against the urge to grab the vomit bag in the seat pocket before me. I've never been around a spirit for this long before. Usually, I back away and flee the scene as soon as I get control of the nausea pooling in my gut. Now, after four hours with a spirit close at hand, I think it might be a toss-up between losing my dinner or losing my mind before the flight lands.

He doesn't talk much, this ghost. One small thing to be grateful for. My head hurts, but his silence means there's not much noise, except a small rustle of static. It pops and burbles, only occasionally bringing forth a bit of rusty sound. When he does talk, he only says one word over and over.

"Russell."

I jump, the word sounding between my ears even as I think the only saving grace with this spirit is his lack of speech.

I drag a breath in through my mouth, trying to avoid the smell. Whoever Russell is, he's obviously someone important. He might be why the ghost is still around. He might even be the one who killed the poor guy. Resolving the spirit's unfinished business is not on my to-do list, but I am curious about the unanswerable questions. Like how the man was murdered while on this airplane.

Was he stabbed? Poisoned? Shot? A major event would have been covered by the news. But I have no idea when this man was killed. He could have been here since the plane's inaugural flight. So, maybe there was a story, somewhere at some time. It could've happened a month ago, a decade ago, or more.

But I don't know what his story is, and since he can't seem to tell me, I wish he'd stop trying to say anything at all. They always want to talk, and I never know how to answer them.

I reach into the front pocket of my jeans and grip the metallic blue square of card stock I've held onto for at least half of this plane ride. My invitation to attend Camp Wanagi this summer is like a lifeline—a constant reminder of why I'm on this plane and suffering through sickness so bad I've gone to the bathroom twice to dry-heave over the toilet.

Camp Wanagi sounds so mundane, so typical. But it's extraordinary, if it's true. I'm still not convinced it won't turn out to be one giant, unfunny joke. Or worse, it won't be a camp at all, but an institution. A

SHADE

place to lock away the mentally ill who think they can communicate with spirits.

Only, I can't communicate, which is a large part of the problem. If I could, maybe this flight would be bearable.

The window is black, and the sky beyond it is an endless nothing broken only by the blinking lights on the plane's wings. When we left Toronto it was raining, but we're sailing through clear sky now. The forecast suggests the weather in Paris will be nice when we arrive, at least. I try to focus on thoughts of the city and the camp beyond it, wondering where we'll stay, what we'll do, and how I'll fit in. If I fit in at all. I never have before. It's strange to think I might now.

"Russell."

I grab my music player from the seat pocket and stick my earbuds in, pressing play and pretending I can use Paganini's "Violin Concerto No. 1" to block out the noise. The music is muted, streaming through the static thrum as if it's being played two rows away. I want to turn it up, blast it, and force it to cover the spirit's pitiful utterances. But the old lady is trying to sleep, and I don't want to disturb her any more than I'm sure I already have.

Three more hours. Three more hours until I'm off this flight and away from this spirit. Three more hours until I arrive at Camp Wanagi and finally meet others like me.

I hope.

"Russell."

I wince, covering my nose to curb the stench of fish wafting through the chilled air.

WHEN WE FINALLY LAND, I STAGGER OFF THE PLANE AND SLUMP INTO THE nearest seat inside the terminal. The warm air and solid ground help to soothe my stomach, and I breathe deep—no trace of fish attacking my senses. The lady who sat next to me gives me a sympathetic smile as she passes by, and I offer her a meagre wave before dropping my head into my hands to further calm my nerves. It doesn't take long for the sickness to fade. Once I'm away from the spirit, its effect slides off me as if I was only having a bad dream.

When I'm able to stand without shaking, I check the time and dig my itinerary out of my backpack—running my fingers over the paper's glossy black lettering. The sleek design reminds me of the lists my mom gets for her vendor conferences, not the schedule for a normal summer camp.

Although, I suppose Camp Wanagi is not normal. I'm not sure it's even a real camp. The name might be a cover-up for something considerably less casual than a summer of canoe trips and leadership exercises. In the bottom corner of the page, the initials O.O.S. are a good reminder this camp is not run by some well-renowned community group.

The Oracle of Senders is a vague and somewhat surreal concept, a name I know only from the instruction package I received after agreeing to attend this summer. It's a name with a meaning I hardly understand, though I'll grasp onto anything I can get at this point.

If the Oracle of Senders, whatever it is, can help ease the pain of seeing spirits, I don't care if Camp Wanagi is a normal lakeside camp or a secretive underground meeting place. Hell, if it gives me an explanation for what I experience and why, I wouldn't even care if it's just a bunch of people standing around in a field somewhere.

I swallow down the remnant sickness from the spirit and run my eyes along the neatly typed list of places I'm supposed to be and the times I'm supposed to be there. Customs is the first stop before I find the baggage claim and locate the bus that's supposed to take me the rest of the way to camp. Before I join the customs line, however, I stop in the bathroom to splash water over my face and fix my hair.

My little sister Rose once held an almond up to my head and happily exclaimed my hair color was a perfect match. But her observations are only accurate when my hair is clean, brushed back, and parted to one side. When it's messy, like now, it looks darker and thicker. I dislike messy hair. Raking it back with my fingers, I try to give it a neat part. I don't want to make a lazy first impression when I arrive at the camp.

When only a small fringe of hair still hangs over my forehead—the best I can do without a comb—I make my way to customs. It goes more smoothly than I expected. I tell the officer I'm in France for summer camp and hand him the paper I was instructed to provide. He doesn't ask me how long I'll be in the country, what summer camp I'm attending, or if I have anything to declare. He only nods without speaking and waves me through.

I take the paper and my passport, startled by the speed of the transaction. Trying to mask my surprise with nonchalance, I shuffle away from the desk at an awkward speed, my feet too quick for the slower stride of my legs. At least I'm alone and don't have to worry about being embarrassed. I'm too exhausted to care about any strangers snickering behind my back.

I get my duffel bag from the baggage carousel and head out to a lot full of tour buses. Gazing at the tinted windows as I pass by each row of parked vehicles, I wonder which one I'm supposed to board. But, once I pass the massive buses, I realize I've been searching in the wrong place.

At the far end, hidden from view until I'm practically in front of it, is a much smaller black van. Heaps of luggage are piled to the side, and a sign in the front window reads: Wanagi.

No driver is sitting behind the wheel, nor is anyone checking off passengers as they board. But I'm relieved to see people on the bus, teens who look my age. My heart picks up pace at the sight of the sign and the kids. It's confirmation I'm in the right place.

Dropping my bags with the others, I pat my jeans'

pockets to ensure my phone, wallet, passport, and Wanagi invitation are still tucked inside. Before I head on board, I make a final go at sweeping my fingers through my hair.

Eight people are inside the three-rowed van. Close to the door, two girls sit side-by-side, staring up at me.

"Let me guess," one of them begins before I have the chance to say a word, "you are..." She taps her temple as if she's deep in thought.

She's a short girl with thick, braided pigtails of black except for a single streak of bright pink through each one. I open my mouth to tell her who I am, but she halts me with her hand, giving me an intense stare with her small, dark eyes.

"You're Callum Silver," she finishes, her voice deep and accented.

I stare at her with blank incomprehension, too tired and unsettled to form any logical conclusions for how she knew my name. "Are...are you telepathic?" I stutter after a beat.

Both girls laugh. The pigtailed one snorts away the suggestion.

"She looked at the roster," the other girl explains. She's tall and thin, and her body is well-suited to her high voice. Her face is long and straight, as is her hair which falls in a curtain around her cheeks. The grin she wears spreads across the width of her face, lighting up her eyes and brightening her otherwise plain features.

"There's only one camper left after you," the first girl explains. "So, it was either Callum or Sabeena, and I took my best guess."

"Good odds, at least," I mumble, taking a shaky breath and surveying the rest of the van. "Do we sit wherever? I'm a little lost as to what I'm supposed to be doing here."

The pigtailed girl scoffs. "Join the club."

"All we know so far is there are ten of us in our camp group," the tall girl says. "And, since your name was on the roster, I guess that means you are part of the gang."

"There's only ten of us?" It's a small group, considering the effort they've made to get us here. As far as I can tell, the Oracle's paid for this entire trip, not to mention created a summer camp for us to attend. All that for ten kids is weird, even given the pre-existing weirdness of this whole situation.

"Well, I think we're grouped by age," the tall girl says. "At least, that's my theory. I have a feeling there are more of us, but only the ten of us are here right now. We checked. Everyone else is, or will soon be, fourteen."

I nod, confirming her unasked question. I turned fourteen back in February. And it does make sense to gather all the new campers together, though I wonder where the others are. I didn't see any other Wanagi buses in the lot.

"I'm Kornelía, by the way," the tall girl says, "and that's Mim."

"Mim?"

"Short for Maria," the pigtailed girl says with a dramatic sigh. "Well, sort of. Maria was a family name. But I think maybe Mama didn't want to call me that at all. So, she calls me Mim instead."

"Cool. It's nice to meet you, uh, both of you. I'm Cal. Short for Callum, but you already knew that." It's awkward standing here, one step on the bus without a clue what to do next.

Kornelía seems to sense my unease. She turns to motion towards the rest of the van, giving me another happy grin. "Hi Cal," she says, "Welcome to Camp Wanagi. You might as well take a seat."

"Right. Thanks." I nod again before shuffling to the back row.

The van is unlike any I've seen before. It's set up like a tiny school bus with benches to the right and left of the aisle which can fit two people each. Kornelía and Mim take up half the first row. The other front seat is empty, but a clipboard and an unclaimed sweater suggest someone plans to sit there soon. Two boys take up one side of the middle row, while a boy and a girl occupy the seat behind Kornelía and Mim. The third row has one boy per side, so I make my way back and sit next to the one with his head bent over a book.

Across the aisle, the other boy is eating a cheeseburger. The smell makes my stomach give off an involuntary growl of hunger. Without the spirit nearby, my appetite has caught up with me. What I'd really love is a bagel and a steaming hot tea, but the burger would be a concession I'd gladly make.

"Better fill that," the boy says, glancing at my grumbling stomach, "else they're going to think you're being possessed."

He smiles, his sallow complexion shadowed by the sun streaming into the window behind him. He's small and skinny with spiky black hair and dark circles around his large eyes.

"Wouldn't want that," I say, watching as he reaches into his backpack.

"Let's eat then." He pulls out a second foil-wrapped

burger. "I've been eating since I got to the airport hours ago, and I'm still famished."

He's wearing black pants and a blinding yellow dress shirt. It's a horrible color for his skin tone. I wonder if he picked it out himself or if he was forced into it by a pushy parent.

He offers the burger to me, and I almost laugh.

"I can't eat your lunch, or uh, breakfast?" I say, shaking my head while my stomach purrs in appreciation of the sight. If I hadn't been so worried about getting to the van on time, I would have spared a few minutes inside to grab a snack.

"Go on," the boy says, shoving the burger into my hand and letting go so I'm forced to take it.

He pulls open his backpack and shows me the inside pocket, which is full of wrapped burgers. I wonder if there's a burger stand open this early in the airport or if he arrived before places closed last night.

"I've stocked up," he grins. "They'll only get cold if someone doesn't help me finish them off."

This time, I do laugh. And, when the boy smiles again, I give him my thanks and tuck in.

THE BURGER'S FANTASTIC. I'M MORE RAVENOUS THAN I THOUGHT, AND I EAT the entire thing in less than a minute without even stopping to remove the pickles.

"The hunger is brutal when it kicks in," the boy says. "I couldn't eat anything on the plane, though. Don't do well with long trips." He wipes his hands on his slacks before holding one out to me. "My name's Dylan."

"Cal," I tell him, shaking his hand. "Thanks again for the burger."

"Want another?" Dylan asks, reaching for his bag.

It's tempting, but I don't want to gorge and make myself sick all over again. So, I shake my head and settle back against my seat. I glance at the boy on my other side, but his eyes are obscured by loose golden curls as he reads.

"Strange summer camp, huh?" Dylan says.

I look back at him with a laugh I hope doesn't sound

uneasy. "No kidding," I say, pressing my hand over my jean pocket where the blue invitation sits nestled beneath the fabric. "I don't know much about it, though.... I only got my invitation a month ago."

"Same. I think that's how they work. They spring it on you." Dylan grins, reaching into his bag and grabbing another burger for himself.

While Dylan scarfs down more food, I try to relax, gazing around the bus at the other campers I'll be spending my summer with. It's unbelievable to think this array of teenagers share my horrendous penchant for seeing spirits. It should be unbelievable, anyway. I rather hope it's not.

My foot starts a nervous, wishful tap as I watch Dylan take a huge bite through nearly half of his latest burger. I let him get in a few chews before I speak.

"So...can you see ghosts, too?" I ask, trying to slip the words in as if they are part of an ordinary conversation. The truth is I'm desperate to find someone to talk to about spirits. But I'm still wary enough not to assume this entire camp isn't a gigantic hoax.

"In my own unique way," Dylan says once he's swallowed. His thick eyebrows raise in amusement.

The casual way he says it makes the rhythm of my foot slow. "What do you mean?" I ask, curious to know as much about these kids' abilities as I can.

Dylan smiles. "I see the ghosts of dogs. Most people don't realize humans aren't the only ones who stick around after... Well, you know." He trails off for a moment, taking another bite of his burger. "I can't see human ghosts, or at least I haven't seen any yet. But I've been seeing ghost dogs for as long as I can remember."

"I've never heard of dog ghosts." I study Dylan, trying to determine if he's telling the truth. My initial reaction is to question his claim, but I stop myself from exploring those thoughts too deeply. I'd be quite the hypocrite if I disbelieved the first person I've ever had a friendly conversation with about seeing spirits.

Instead, I make myself wonder what it would be like to see the spirits of dogs. When I was five, my dog Sparks died of kidney failure. I wonder if he's still around somewhere.

"You see the human kind, then?" Dylan asks.

I nod, pressing my palms against my jeans to wipe away the clamminess. "My parents used to think I was crazy," I admit, smiling even though the memories are anything but fond.

I went to therapy sessions until I was ten because my parents never believed the stories I told them about the spirits I saw. Shortly after my tenth birthday, they stopped my sessions and made peace with my claims. If they hadn't changed their minds, they'd never have let me come to Camp Wanagi.

"Mine thought I had imaginary pets instead of imaginary friends," Dylan says. "I was never allowed real pets, so they thought this was my substitute for it. I guess it was. Except I didn't make the dogs up."

"No such luck for me," I say, glancing up at the front of the bus where a girl steps on board and starts talking to Kornelía and Mim. She must be Sabeena, the final camper listed on the roster.

"The ghosts I've seen have been... Well, for some reason, I always seem to see ghosts of people who have been...killed. Murdered, actually. Those don't make the best friends, imaginary or otherwise."

The boy beside me pauses midway through turning a page, but when I look at him, he finishes the motion and continues reading without acknowledging my stare.

"Murdered ghosts?" Dylan asks with a smirk in his voice. "That's weird."

"Not really," Mim says.

My eyes flick forward as she approaches us with Kornelía trailing behind her.

Sabeena has plopped down in the front. One of the boys in the middle row moves to sit with her, and Kornelía takes his place as if she had fully expected him to shift spots. Mim slides in next to Dylan, forcing him to retreat towards the window.

"Everyone has their specialty. You see ghosts of murder victims," she says, pointing at me. "I see the ghosts of the heartbroken. The ones longing for their beloveds, even in the afterlife."

"Ugh, sounds horrible," Dylan mumbles.

I smile at his unimpressed expression while Mim rolls her eyes.

"You seem to know a lot for being new," I tell her. "I had no idea people have different abilities."

"I hardly know a lot," she says. "But I've been aware of this place for a couple of years."

"How?" Dylan asks through a mouth full of burger.

Mim eyes him with distaste before directing her answer to me instead. "The camp is only run in English. I'm from Guatemala and didn't know much English before. They had to teach me first, so I could come," she explains.

"Guatemala? That's awesome," Dylan remarks.

Mim tilts her head to one side. "I guess so," she says,

sounding unsure. "Anyway, they didn't tell me much, but I do know everyone has a specialty. People don't see ghosts or not see ghosts.... It's not that simple. We all see things differently."

I nod, thinking about what she said. It makes sense there would be more than just murdered spirits still hanging around. I study Mim for a few seconds before peering past her to Dylan, who's rolling the foil wrapper from the finished burger into a ball in his fist.

"So, where are you from?" I ask. I hadn't even considered there would be people from all over the world here, even if this camp is in a foreign country. I didn't consider much in the past month, beyond getting here and wondering what I'd find once I arrived.

"The States," Dylan replies, tossing the foil ball into his bag as if he's making a basket. "Virginia. You?"

"I'm Canadian," I say. It's somehow comforting to know Dylan's American. I've been to the States lots of times—even to Virginia once. "I live in Ontario. Near Toronto."

"I have a cousin who lives in Canada," Mim says, "but she lives in Vancouver. Have you ever...?" She stops, swivelling her neck around as something hits the side of the van and a loud pounding cuts into everyone's conversations.

The other campers quiet down, and a few peek out the windows to see if someone is outside.

I follow Mim's gaze to the front, instinctively feeling for changes in the air or clouds misting through my head. Something pounds again, this time against the rear of the van. All ten of us are silent, everyone uncertain as they glance around.

"It's not a ghost if that's what you're worried about," Kornelía says.

Her high voice pierces through the tense silence, making me and a few others jump. She blushes, lowering her head in embarrassment.

"How do you know?" Dylan asks.

Kornelía shakes her head. "I just do, is all," she mumbles, folding her arms across her stomach.

"Is that your specialty?"

Mim stares at Kornelía's back, while the tall girl squirms under the attention of the entire bus. I imagine she's wishing she never spoke at all.

"Um, I guess so," she mumbles.

She raises a hand up to brush her hair back from her face, and in the seconds before it falls forward again, I notice the backs of her large ears.

"But it's nothing too special, if you ask me. I mean, I can't actually see ghosts or anything." Her English is fluent, but I'm sure she isn't Canadian like me or American like Dylan.

"So why are you here?" I ask, the words coming out half a second before I realize how rude the question sounds. I'm blushing now, and I shake my head. "Not that there's any problem with you being here," I add, and I'm happy to see Kornelía shift around in her seat with a grin on her lips again.

"It's fine," she says. "I can...sense, I guess. When a place is haunted? I mean I know whether a house is haunted when I see it, and I can usually pinpoint which rooms have, um, ghostly activity."

"Sounds special to me," Dylan says.

Kornelía shrugs. "The people at home don't think so."

"Where're you from?" I ask, too curious to hold the question in.

"Iceland," Kornelía replies, looking proud.

"Did you have English training?" Mim asks.

"No." Kornelía shakes her head again. "My parents speak Icelandic, Danish, and English, so I've always known all three languages. I never even heard of this place until a month ago. It's a good thing I didn't need extra training, anyway. My parents didn't want me to come here—even after the Senders talked with them last year. They were unhappy when I got the invitation."

The pounding on the bus has stopped. Outside people rush about, loading and unloading the big coaches. No one pays our little van any attention.

I grip my leg, feeling the hard edges of the invitation in my pocket. Oracle of Senders. The name is becoming increasingly familiar, but I still don't know much about what it means.

"Senders came to your house?" I ask, phrasing the question to make it seem like I'm not totally clueless.

Kornelía sees through my guise. She arches both eyebrows, watching me with surprise as she nods.

"The agents who came to talk to my parents," she explains, "told them all about the Oracle and my ability so they'd have the chance to get used to it. I mean I didn't know who they were at the time, but after I got my invitation, I sort of pieced it all together. I figured they talked to everyone's parents. Didn't they come to your house?"

"No, they didn't," I say. *So, I'm behind everyone else here. Great.*

Mim's had years of language training, and

Kornelía's family had a one-on-one interview with the organization. And here I sit, not even knowing what the organization's name means.

"Of course, they talked with your parents."

The voice is new. The boy with the book watches me, his finger marking his place between the pages of the novel. His curls fall to the nape of his neck, and he has a pale complexion, though not sickly like Dylan's. He's British. English, in fact. I know enough to recognize his way of speaking, even if I haven't the slightest clue which part of the country his accent originates from.

"What do you mean? Wouldn't I know if they were at my house?" I ask.

"Don't you remember a couple of stiff people in blue suits?"

His voice is a bit harsh, like I might be an idiot for not knowing this. Or, maybe, I just feel like an idiot for being so out of the loop. My brows knit together as I prepare to tell him he's wrong. But, as I open my mouth, a memory—immediate and clear—shows me he's not.

Not long after my tenth birthday, I answered a knock at the door and found two blue-suited people waiting on my front porch. They asked to speak with my parents, and I thought they were funny because they knew my name. Their suits were unusual as well, made of an almost metallic shade of blue I now realize is similar to the color of my invitation to this camp.

How had I forgotten? They arrived right around the time my parents stopped making me go to therapy. So, a conversation with the Oracle must have made Mom and Dad start believing me when I talked about spirits.

"You don't have to be a jerk about it," Mim says to the boy while I'm busy recollecting.

I blink back to the present to see him flipping open his book.

"Not my fault if some people aren't observant." He sulks, slinking back against the seat.

I want to say something in response, to either repeat Mim's retort or thank him for helping me remember. But, before I've made up my mind as to which, the noises outside resume. Three loud pounds run up the length of the van's side, and everyone tenses until, with a quick jerk of movement, two blue-suited individuals hop on board.

4

I FORGET ABOUT ARGUING WITH OR POSSIBLY THANKING THE BOY WHEN the Blue Suits step onto the bus. They look about the same age, older than us but still fitting a youthful designation. One, a guy, is tall and a mohawk adds an extra foot to his already towering height. A tattoo runs down the side of his neck, disappearing under the collar of the suit jacket. The other person is a girl. Her long brown hair is pulled back into a high ponytail, and her bright blue eyes are noticeable, even from the back of the bus.

"Hello, everyone!" the girl says in a cheerful voice as she peers around at our suspicious gazes. "I am Alex, and this is Robbie."

Alex gestures to the mohawked guy, and he waves to the group before reaching into the empty front seat and grabbing the abandoned clipboard.

My shoulders relax, a strange sensation since I didn't notice them tensing in the first place. Nevertheless, any threat I'd perceived on a conscious or subconscious level has mostly left by now. There's something official about the blue suits the girl and guy wear. Under the current circumstances, official is comforting.

"Welcome to the Oracle of Sender's camp for underagers," Alex continues, her eyes dancing with enjoyment as she takes in the sight of us. "Otherwise known as Camp Wanagi. You are the Oracle's newest recruits which, this year, means you are the newest members of the Shade Sector."

She glances at Robbie and smooths the front of her suit. "We've been keeping an eye on your arrivals throughout the day, and now you're all here, we can get started. Robbie and I will be your sector leads and guides this summer, so if you ever need anything while at camp, you can come to us."

"We attended Camp Wanagi as members of the Shade sector for four years," Robbie adds. "So, y'all can trust that we know everything you're going through."

I like the idea of finally having someone around who knows what's going on. As it is, they talk like we're all familiar with sectors, Shades, and whatever leads are. If I'm this lost already, I'm glad there are at least people around I can ask questions over the rest of the summer.

"For the next ten weeks," Alex says, "we'll be helping to run some of the camp's activities as well as supporting the oldest campers with their special projects. But, first and foremost, we're here for you."

"I bet y'all are curious about this place," Robbie says, his voice a deep and languid southern drawl. "So, we'll tell you a bit about the camp and what you'll be doing here. Then, we'll let you choose your courses for the summer."

Sector guides must be the equivalent to camp counsellors. And counsellors, plus camp activities, sounds reassuringly normal.

"But, before we do anything, we'd like to take attendance, so we can start learning who you all are," Alex finishes, taking the clipboard from Robbie and holding it out before her. She reads the first name and looks directly at one boy before saying the name aloud. "Sefa Amasio?"

"Yeah, I'm here." The boy she's already staring at waves cheerfully from the left side of the middle row.

Alex nods. She checks off the name before reading the next one down and casting her eyes about the van until they find Dylan.

"Dylan Benowitz?"

"Here," Dylan replies, his mouth full of burger again.

He wasn't kidding when he said he'd stocked up. Since I boarded the bus, he's eaten three or four burgers.

"Maria Castillo?" Alex says, her eyes resting on Mim's.

I thought Mim might be telepathic when she knew my name, but Alex's ability to fit a name with a camper is impressive. She's either got a knack for intuitive guessing, or she already knows who we are. I never submitted a picture to the Oracle, but if Senders came to my house when I was ten, it means this organization has known me for years. A picture would be one of the easiest things to obtain if they wanted it.

"Here," Mim says before adding, "but call me Mim

if you don't mind."

"Certainly, Mim." Alex smiles, making a note on her sheet. "Naasir Ereng?"

A boy with extremely dark skin raises a hand in response, and Alex doesn't even glance down at the list again before her eyes slide over to the girl sitting next to him.

"Sabeena Kriti?" she asks.

The girl who boarded the van last runs her fingers along a thick black braid of hair as she nods. Alex marks them down and shifts her gaze to the back row.

Her eyes catch mine, and her brow furrows as if she's not sure I'm the one she's supposed to be looking at.

"Meander Rhoades?" she asks in a cautious voice.

"Here," the boy beside me, the one with the book, answers.

Alex's eyes blink to Meander, and I look over at him with a smile. I guess that answers my question. She must have seen photos of us, photos she tried to memorize before our meeting. Meander and I have tripped her up for the first time, and it's a relief to know she's not an actual mind reader.

Meander doesn't meet my gaze, and my attention is drawn to the faded white-pink scar along his jaw line. I wonder if it's from an accident or a fight.

"Callum Silver?"

"Hey, Cal, isn't that you?" Dylan says from across the aisle.

I clench my fists in my lap, embarrassed to have missed my own name being called. I turn back towards the leads, but not before I catch Meander's smirk out of the corner of my eye.

"I'm Callum," I say in a rush, not bothering to tell

them I prefer to be called Cal.

"Thank you, Callum," Alex says, checking off my name and sliding her pen down to the next row.

"Lu Tong?" She glances to where a small girl with black hair and fair skin sits by the window in the middle row.

"Here," she says.

Alex turns next to face the row across the aisle where Kornelía sits beside the boy I now know is Sefa.

"Kornelía Tumisdottir?"

"That's me!" Kornelía exclaims in a rush of breath, her face reddening once the words escape. She bows her head, so her long hair hides her expression.

"Thank you, Kornelía," Alex replies, her eyes crinkling in amusement.

Forget her ability to memorize names, I'm more impressed with how easily she pronounces them. My name is fairly straightforward, but I still can't get through a single school year without at least one teacher and a few substitutes calling me Column or thinking my surname is Sliver. Alex must have studied the attendance sheet with a pronunciation guide nearby. She doesn't hesitate or stumble over anyone's name.

"And, finally, Reed Vodden."

The last camper, a boy with rusty hair and a face full of freckles, raises a lazy hand. "Here," he says, sounding bored.

"Perfect." Alex breathes the word like a sigh as she glances at Robbie.

"All right. Now, we'd like to offer y'all an official welcome to Camp Wanagi," Robbie says, picking up the role of speaker.

An older man boards the bus and takes the driver's seat while Robbie talks.

"You're here today because y'all share an uncommon talent for one thing. Paranormal abilities."

He moves into the front seat but faces backwards so he can continue to look at us. Alex joins him as the bus rumbles to life.

"First, some quick facts. There are four sectors at Camp Wanagi, ordered by age. This summer, we have a grand total of thirty-one campers. Ten in the Shade Sector, eight in Revenant, six in Wraith, and seven in Entity. Everyone at this camp has a paranormal specialty, and no two specialties are the same, though some may overlap." He pauses to let what he said sink in as we push through the stop-and-go traffic in the airport parking lot.

"At Camp Wanagi," he continues once we exit onto an actual road, "we want to help you understand and develop your talents. Our hope is you can join the Oracle in working to free the world of unresting spirits once you've finished all four Wanagi years, have turned seventeen, and have become officially certified as of-age Senders."

"You want to train us to work for you?" the red-haired boy, Reed, scoffs.

"We don't have workers," Alex replies, her smile easy and calm.

She and Robbie talk as if this is a commonplace conversation. I can't fathom how they're so unaffected by the words they're saying. I had no idea I'd be training for anything this summer, and I can't imagine spending my entire life working with spirits. Right now, I'm struggling to come to terms with the fact I'll be spending the whole summer at a paranormal camp.

"You are all talented," Alex says in her soft, airy voice, "and we want to help you use your talents to the best of your abilities. This is not a place where you fail a course because you aren't good enough. Our role as leads at Camp Wanagi is to help you explore the world of the paranormal. If, when you have finished the camp, you choose to be a part of the Oracle, we will be thrilled. But the decision is up to you. Only people with natural paranormal ability can take part in the Oracle's program. You are lucky and special. Never forget that."

Thinking about the spirits I've seen, and the pain I've endured, I don't feel particularly special. Or lucky.

How do other people experience ghosts? I could be the odd one out, feeling sick when a spirit is near. Maybe it is like a ghost-buddy comedy for some of the campers here.

"You'll be with us until the middle of August," Robbie explains. "And, during these ten weeks, you'll be taking four courses. Basics of Paranormality is required for all first-year campers. The other three courses are up to you. Each one of you will also have a mentor from the most senior group of campers. Which, this year, is the Entity Sector. Since there are more of you than there are of them—" Robbie glances at Alex with an expression I can't quite make out from the back of the van "—some mentors will be doubling up. But don't worry, you'll all have dedicated time with your mentor to discuss your experiences and your talents."

"And, at the end of the summer, you will all get a real chance to work with a spirit," Alex says. Her eyes shine while she talks. "This will be a paranormal case given to you to solve. You'll be assigned your case halfway through the summer and will complete it before you leave." She gazes at everyone on the bus, and her face takes on the expression of someone trying to hold in a laugh. "Don't worry! You'll have plenty of help," she assures us.

My shoulders ache with stiff tension again, and my forehead prickles with the first cool beads of sweat. This is a camp for kids who can see ghosts, so I guess I shouldn't be surprised to hear I'll be facing a real spirit. But the news is still unpleasant. I hope Alex is being honest when she says we'll have help. I don't want to do this alone.

"Don't worry about it yet," Robbie says. He pulls a stack of papers from his clipboard. "For today, we'll focus on course selection. Alex and I will hand out the course sheets, and y'all can select which three courses you'd like to join. Take your time. You've got the entire four-hour bus ride to pick."

Hearing we have another four hours of travel ahead of us makes me weary. I knew we weren't staying in Paris, but I didn't realize we'd be driving quite so far out of the city. At least there are no spirits around anymore. They could've got our summer off to a grand start by shoving us on a haunted bus.

Robbie hands back the sheets, and Alex sends around pens. Then, they face forward and talk to the driver while we're left to select our courses.

"The entire way over here," Dylan mumbles, glancing over the sheet he's given, "I swore to myself I wouldn't take an archery class. But I'd be glad to take one now if it was offered."

"No such luck," Mim replies, tapping her pen

against her cheek. "What good would archery be? We'd be pathetic if we went about trying to attack ghosts with bows and arrows."

"Okay, okay, no archery," Dylan agrees, "but something relatively normal would have been great. Everything here is so...*weird*."

"It's all normal," Kornelía says over her shoulder. "*Para*normal."

Dylan rolls his eyes, but he smiles as he continues reading the course selections.

I look down at my own sheet. "What is everyone else taking?" I ask, glancing over the choices. There are fifteen courses in all, but a lot of them have markings denoting only older years can take them. Courses like Channelling and Hostage Arts. I'm glad I don't have to think about those yet.

"Spirits of the Non-Human, obviously," Dylan says.

I'd like to take the same courses as Dylan, but I'm not interested in a whole class on non-human spirits. I want to learn more about the spirits I *can* see, not the ones I can't.

My eyes slide over the selections until one course name catches my attention.

"Basics of Gadgetry?" I ask aloud.

"Tech-stuff," Mim says, flipping one pigtail over her shoulder. "You know, using tape recorders and stuff like that."

"It's a bit more complex than *stuff like that*," Meander scoffs from beside me.

I didn't realize he was listening, but then again, he'd be fairly deaf if he couldn't hear me talking right next to him.

"More complex? How?" I turn to face him, but he

doesn't answer.

Like almost every other time I've looked at him, he keeps his eyes fixed downward. Even so, I'm intrigued. I go back to my own sheet and mark Basics of Gadgetry as one of my course selections.

"Ooh, Introduction to EVP sounds interesting," Mim says, more to herself than to anyone else.

"EVP?" Kornelía asks.

"Electronic Voice Phenomena," Mim replies. "Like when you pick up ghost voices in white noise."

"I think there was a movie about that," Dylan says.

"I think you're right," I agree. Once, when I was around eight years old, I had an experience with EVP. But I'm not sure I want to learn more about it now. I decide to keep Intro to EVP as a maybe and continue down the list.

It's an incredibly strange process, picking out courses like these. None of them sound real or like anything I ever thought I'd be signing up for. Eventually, I settle on Basics of Gadgetry, Introduction to Imprinting, which is supposed to be about how spirits attach to physical objects, and Emotional Entities. I think it's a good course for me. My experiences with ghosts tend to be emotional ones.

My eyes sweep over the course sheet a final time before I hand it in. Marking down what I'm taking seems more final than flying here or even getting on this bus did. It's like I'm truly locked in to this camp now. There's no turning back.

Three more hours is nothing. Now it's ten weeks until I can escape.

5

WE FINALLY ARRIVE AT THE CAMP AFTER HOURS OF A DRIVE PEPPERED WITH conversation, music, and staring past Meander out the window, and I discover we're staying at what I think the French call a château. Although a more accurate description would be to call it a simplified castle. It's small as far as castles go, I guess. No sweeping courtyards leading to towers an hour's walk away or anything. It's a single building of white stone, surrounded by water. It's like the whole place was built in the middle of a lake. On the far side of the water, a forest creeps up to the lake's edge. Directly before us, a lone walkway connects the mainland to the château's grounds.

It's a grand place, but unkempt. Bushes grow wild along the château's front, half-obscuring the large windowpanes of the first-floor rooms. There are cracks in the stone, visible even across the long stretch of water. And the lake is too close to the edge of the house. Almost as if the property is slowly sinking and will, one day, collapse into a rotted, soggy wreck.

I expected a hotel or a dormitory. It never occurred to me I'd be spending my summer in a dilapidated manor house.

"A place like this has got to be haunted," Sabeena says from the front seat as the château rolls into view.

"No," Sefa says, shaking his head, "they wouldn't do that to us."

"We hope," Dylan mumbles.

The bus pulls to a stop and our new leads beckon us towards the narrow, half-crumbled walkway leading to the château's worn oak doors.

"Welcome to Camp Wanagi, y'all," Robbie says, his arms making a wide, sweeping arch. "A beauty, ain't it?"

The others must look as dubious as I do because Alex begins to laugh as she surveys our expressions.

"Head on in, and we'll show you to your quarters," she says, every word a smile. "You're probably all exhausted and ready for an early rest."

"Will we make it without having to swim?" Sefa asks, eyeing the pathway across the lake.

Alex laughs again, but she doesn't respond, which makes the likelihood of the pathway flooding under the weight of our feet a real possibility.

Kornelía grabs Mim's arm and pulls her forward.

"Come on, let's go for it," she says.

I look at Dylan, who shrugs, and we join the girls. The pathway is so narrow we have to walk one at a time, but the stone is solid enough to hold us without breaking off into chunks and floating away into the lake. Still, I'm relieved when I reach the other side, even though it's daunting enough watching the others. Robbie is the last to cross, and once he reaches the house it's like we're all stranded on our own dismal island.

The leads take us into the house—which is almost exactly how I pictured it would be inside. The air is musty, but warm, which is good. Warm air is living air, and I like the way the staleness permeates my pores and makes me feel hot under my jacket.

The entryway is large, open to what was probably once a sitting room but is now a dining hall comprised of two sleek, stylish black wood tables out of place in the otherwise outdated and ragged interior.

It's obvious an attempt's been made to clean up in here, but the place is old and uncared for. The wallpaper is stained and peeling, and the once ornate ceiling is cracked in several places. The wood floors are scuffed, the windows dirty, and the hanging light fixture is missing half its crystalline decorations.

"Welcome to summer camp," Mim mutters as we file up the creaking stairs to the left of the entryway.

"At least the walkway isn't a drawbridge they can pull up," Dylan grins. "So, we know they're not planning to keep us prisoner."

"At this point, nothing would surprise me," Mim retorts.

"It's a little rough," Alex admits from where she's moved to the front of the group. "But you'll get used to it. Come on…the Shade lounge is this way."

We walk up two flights of stairs and down a short corridor before Alex leads us into another open space only minutely smaller than the one downstairs. This one is set up like a living room with two black couches, a black-wood study desk, and a fireplace alight with flame. The walls are dark and framed by white trim, and the floors are more of the ugly, old wood from downstairs. It's not an inviting space, but as my fellow Shades spread out within the room, it doesn't seem too bad.

Alex takes the girls to their bedroom, and Robbie leads us to ours. The bedroom is better than the lounge. White walls, wood floors, and three sets of black bunk beds adorning three of the four walls gives the room a simple, clean appearance. A single dresser is pushed beside one set of beds, right next to the bedroom door, and on the fourth wall is a door leading to a marbled bathroom that appears to be only a couple of decades, and not centuries, old.

"Get settled, and get some sleep," Robbie says. "Alex and I will be out in the lounge if you need anything. If you're hungry, the kitchen is on the main floor, at the back of the dining area. You'll get the grand tour of the place tomorrow, but if you're up to it, there'll be a bonfire in the backyard this evening to welcome all the sectors." He grins, bending forward in a formal half-bow before leaving the room.

"Sleep sounds beautiful," Dylan yawns, flopping onto the lower bunk of the far bed.

I smile, throwing my bags onto the nearest bottom bunk, the one across from Dylan's. I'll put away my stuff later. For now, I'm too exhausted to organize my clothes and cram everything into a single drawer in the dresser.

"I'm grabbing a shower," Sefa says. He picks up his red suitcase and hurls it onto the bunk above mine before pulling himself up and digging through it. He retrieves a small toiletries bag before hopping down and heading into the bathroom. When the sound of the shower burbles through the closed door, it's like a lullaby.

I lie down on top of the black sheets, kicking my bags to the end of the bed so they're out of my way.

"Weird place, huh?" Reed says, climbing up to the top bunk of the third set of beds.

No one answers him. Dylan's already asleep, and Naasir is lying down on the bunk beneath Reed's with his eyes closed, although I'm pretty sure he's still awake. Meander has claimed the bed overtop of Dylan. He's reading again, his pillows propped up against the wall in a makeshift headrest.

I consider saying something to fill the silence left from the unanswered question, but Reed doesn't seem offended by the lack of response. I don't really feel like talking, anyway. Not right now. I sit up long enough to get my phone out of my bag, and then I lay down facing the wall, slipping my earbuds in and drowning out the noises of my roommates with the orchestral sound of Haydn.

I'll have to text my parents later when it's not so early back at home. I sent them a message while on the road, so they know my flight arrived on time. They're not expecting constant updates. Besides, Rose will be setting off for her own summer camp today, tomorrow, whatever day it is back at home. They'll be more concerned about the twenty-minute drive to her day camp than they were about seeing me off at the airport.

Rose is only seven, and it'll be her first time attending summer camp. Mom's been obsessing about it for weeks.

I close my eyes and drift into the music, Haydn's "Farewell Symphony" soothing my nerves. The overnight flight without any rest has taken its toll, even though it's only afternoon here. Still, before I fall asleep, I spend a minute or two listening to my music and thinking about where I am.

A ghost camp. With other kids like me.

I'm glad I'm not alone, but having company doesn't wash away my confusion about this place. I want to know more about the other campers. Are any of them excited to be here? Do any of them like seeing spirits? I don't, and yet, I'm here all the same.

I know why I made the trip. To be around people who believe in spirits. To prove to myself I'm not insane. But I'm not sure my reasons are good enough. I didn't plan to study and confront ghosts all summer long.

Stupid. I never stopped to consider what I might have to endure this summer. If I had, would I have changed my mind about coming?

When I received the invitation to Camp Wanagi, and my parents said I could go, I mailed the acceptance form the next day. I thought I couldn't risk Mom and Dad coming to their senses and telling me I had to stay home, but maybe my lack of hesitation had less to do with my parents and more to do with being afraid to face the truth while I could still chicken out.

Despite my muddled thoughts, eventually I fall asleep. The next thing I'm aware of is someone shaking me awake. I pull my earbuds out and roll over to see Dylan sitting at the edge of my bed and Sefa's legs dangling down from the bunk above me.

"We've been summoned," Dylan says.

I rub my eyes and sit up. He points to the doorway where four guys who look about the same age as Robbie and Alex watch as we struggle to pull ourselves awake.

"Evening, Shade," one of the boys says to me. He's wearing a thick, black trench coat and black driving gloves. He must be stifling in the heat.

"What time is it?" I ask, standing and stretching my arms above my head. My stomach is uneasy, this time from lack of food and a messed-up sleep schedule.

"About midnight," Meander says. He's still sitting on his bed reading.

I wonder if he's been reading this entire time. If he does live in England, the time difference wouldn't be much, so the accompanying jet-lag might not be bad. Of course, if I've really been asleep for nearly twelve hours, it's quite probable he at least took a dinner break at some point.

"So where are we going? You're not going to push us in the lake or something, are you?" Sefa asks as he jumps down from his bunk. His arms are well-muscled and thick, and the t-shirt he wears stretches tight against his biceps.

I glance down at my own shirt, loose against my skinny frame. I've never been much of a fitness buff. Luckily, Sefa is the out-of-place one here, not me. Dylan is small all around, and Meander's taller than me, but lean. Naasir and Reed are bigger. Naasir is naturally wide-set and tall, and Reed is of average height with a pudgy stomach and a pair of doughy arms. Sefa's the only one with an obviously trained physique, which is good. It'd be a rotten summer being surrounded by a bunch of guys in way better shape than I am.

"Afraid of a little late-night swim?" the guy in the trench coat asks. His skin is a deep brown and pockmarked all over. His head is shaved, and part of his right earlobe is clipped.

"Come on, Benji," a girl says, pushing through the crowd and sidling up next to the guy. She looks older, too, but a bit less threatening with a lilac shawl draped over her shoulders. "Stop terrifying the newbies. The show will do that well enough."

"Show?" I say, my stomach giving a slow churn.

"They're the kids from Entity," Dylan whispers. "We're getting initiated."

I stare at Dylan with what I assume is an idiotic expression. I must have been sleeping heavier than I thought possible, because I apparently missed more than dinner.

Dylan claps me on the shoulder to set me moving. Benji and the others leave our room as we gather what wits we can manage, and I try to focus on getting my shoes on instead of thinking about what an initiation might include in a place like this.

"Where do you think we're going?" Sefa asks, once the older teens are gone.

Naasir glances up from the dresser where he's folding his clothes but doesn't respond. Sefa looks at me, and I shrug.

"No idea," I say, wishing the statement weren't true.

"Someplace haunted, I bet," Dylan says.

"Do you guys believe in this place?" Reed asks, glancing up from the shoelaces he's tying. He eyes each of us, his expression skeptical.

"Of course, we do." Meander sighs, closing his book

and putting it beside him on the bed. The flash of annoyance brightens his hazel eyes, giving them the momentary appearance of being fully green. "Why else would we be here?"

"My parents made me come." Reed sulks, standing up and crossing his arms over his chest. "I don't know why. I'd rather be at home."

"And where's that?" Sefa asks.

"Brazil," Reed replies.

Sefa responds with a skeptical look of his own. "You don't look like you're from Brazil," he says.

Reed tugs at the bottom of his ear, his face taking on the appearance of someone who's been told the same thing a hundred times before. "My parents are Scandinavian," he explains, "but they moved to Brazil before I was born. I've lived there my whole life."

"Ah," Sefa nods. "I understand. I'm Samoan, but my mother was born in Thailand."

"Did her whole family move there or just her?" Reed asks.

"Just her," Sefa says. "I'd like to visit her home someday and meet her side of the family. I know nothing about them."

"Nothing?" I ask, surprised. "Not even, like, your grandparents?"

Sefa shakes his head. "My mother left Thailand when she was young. She met my father, had me, and died a year later. Pneumonia. My dad was never around much. So, after she died, my grandparents took me in. They raised me. I'd like to meet my other grandparents someday, to see what they're like. If they're even still alive. I'm not sure."

The hairs on my neck tingle with the tragedy of

his casual statement. I can't imagine living a life like Sefa's. I know my parents, my grandparents, and all my aunts and uncles. I wonder if Sefa's family in Thailand is even aware of his existence.

"On that cheery note," Meander says, hopping down from his bed, his curls bouncing with the movement. "We'd better get going."

Dylan gives Meander a hard stare, but I think Meander's cold words were his way of dissolving the tension in the room. Sefa doesn't seem bothered by the remark. He was probably more uncomfortable waiting for the sympathetic mutterings the rest of us would have gushed had the silent moment gone on much longer.

Meander leads the way out of the room, everyone else following behind. Out in the lounge, the four guys and the girl who came to our door are waiting with two other girls the same age and the girls from our sector. Mim, Kornelía, and the other Shade girls are wearing matching hoodies, and one of the Entity campers shows us where our sweaters are—folded on the study table against the wide lounge's far wall.

"A little welcome gift," Benji tells us as the girl leads us to the table. The sweaters are black with *Camp Wanagi* stitched in blue and outlined in silver-grey across the front. A silver S, about three inches long, decorates one sleeve. Each hoodie has a sticky note with a name on it. When I first pick up mine, I moronically think the *S* stands for Sefa and I've got the wrong one. Then I notice the same lettering on all the other sweaters and realize it stands for Shade.

"All right, campers," Benji says.

I pull the warm sweater over my head. Decrepit

decorations aside, at least Camp Wanagi has comfortable bedding and soft welcome gifts.

"You're the newest Oracle recruits, and around here, we always like to start camp off in the right mood."

The older teens join and usher us towards the door. Their clothing is all different and peculiar. Benji has his trench coat, and the girl by his side has her purple shawl. The remaining outfits are as varied, including a military medic's uniform, a wraparound dress, and a fluorescent orange track suit. One guy even wears a medieval cloak.

I eye Kornelía as we head out of the lounge. She looks amused by the older campers' strange outfits, but it doesn't diminish the excitement gleaming in her wide eyes.

"To give you a proper Wanagi welcome, we're going on a little trip and giving you all a show," the girl in the shawl says as we walk down to the first floor. The house is dark and silent, except for the Entity campers' flashlight beams and the shuffling of our feet.

"I don't like the sound of this," Lu says, her voice low and tight.

"I love it," Mim says, grinning.

Outside, the sky is clouded over, and the night is as dark as the interior of the château. The lake crowds in on either side as we cross, the waters black and seemingly endless.

"I wonder where we're heading," Kornelía whispers once we've reached the other side and are headed down a side-street off the main road we took here this afternoon. Dots of light from distant houses guide our way, and the sight of more habitation within a ten-minute walk of the château is a welcome surprise.

"Don't know, don't care," Mim says. "I'm just happy to be doing something. Seemed like a lame first night here, otherwise."

We walk until we reach a stretch of road with eight or ten houses built close to one another.

"Don't believe the stories you've heard," Benji says as we move along the quiet street of houses. "Ghosts are real, and they're everywhere." His voice is dramatic, like he's telling a campfire tale and not talking to a group of people who know first-hand about the existence of spirits. "Tonight, some of you might even be lucky enough to see one."

We stop near a tall, black-shadowed house at the end of the stretch.

"Is that where we're going?" Lu asks, standing at the front of the group.

I stare at the house with its vine-draped stone I'm sure is pretty in the daylight and at the open shutters on the small, upper windows. My stomach tightens with apprehension as my eyes slide over to a particular frame of glass, and I stare as something flickers against the dark pocket of the pane.

I suck in a breath. Spirits aren't foreign to me. I saw one earlier today. But I don't fancy seeing another one right now. Not so soon after arriving here. The others move closer to the house, but I stay still, trying to convince myself the flicker in the window was only the beam of a camper's flashlight reflecting off the glass.

"Keep walking," Meander says with a quiet breath, nudging me from behind.

I let out the air I'm holding tight in my lungs and catch up with everyone else.

6

They crowd us into what I guess is the house's main room. There's nothing in it now, except for teens. Tons of teens, all older than us, most wearing Wanagi sweaters. These must be the other sectors. Entity, Wraith, Revenant. They stare at us from the shadows of the room, everyone standing back against the far walls. I can't make out most of their faces. The room is dark, the floorboards scuffed and dusty, and a cold draft seeps in through a hole in the wall next to the unlit stone fireplace.

Cold. My skin prickles as chilled air seeps through my fleecy sweater.

The night is hot, or at least it's supposed to be. This stuffy, closed-up old house is cold, and it's not because of an archaic form of air conditioning.

"This isn't some cult thing, is it?" Dylan asks as the ten of us stand side-by-side, across the room from everyone else.

A few of the older campers chuckle, and I think some of them smirk, though it's hard to tell in the darkness. No one confirms or denies Dylan's suspicions. I'm sure they're only silent to make us all more uncomfortable. If so, their plan is a success.

A flashlight flickers from outside the front door, and Robbie and Alex saunter into the room. It's a relief to see the leads, even if I know them only from a single bus ride. Robbie's dressed up more than Benji, or any of the other Entity campers. He's wearing a tanned trench coat, a striped vest, and matching trousers underneath. His right hand is bare, but his left is covered with an ornate, fingerless glove. It's made of a thick material, probably leather, and is adorned with chains. A brass timepiece is sewn squarely over the back of his palm, and around his right eye is a gold and brass eyepiece held in place by a strap of leather wrapped across his forehead and back around his ear.

Alex is less conspicuous. The only thing unusual about her appearance is the way she's twisted her hair back. The long strands are tied with a series of red and yellow ribbons that drape down over her shoulders.

The two smile at us, Robbie mischievous and Alex genteel.

"It's now time for your official welcome to Camp Wanagi," Alex says as she and Robbie stop in the middle of the room.

The other campers crowd around to close all the gaps. They stand in a crescent across from us.

"It's tradition that, every year, the newest leads get to show their sector what being a Sender is all about," Robbie begins, his eyes gleaming. "This year, we're lucky enough to get to show you in person.

Cooperative spirits aren't always close by. But this lovely house—" he motions around the ramshackle room "—has afforded us the ability to give you a true Sender experience."

"I feel like I've landed in the middle of a Vegas show," Dylan mutters to my left.

I quirk an eyebrow. "Have you ever been to a Vegas show?"

"No, but this seems fitting. Like, I'm waiting for the laser lights and the ear-splitting rock soundtrack to start."

"Ear-splitting rock is fine," I say, hugging my arms to my chest against the cold. "It's the other kind of ear-splitting I'm concerned about."

"I don't think they're going to cut off your ear, Cal," Dylan says.

I laugh before realizing he's halfway serious. I didn't think I'd need to explain the awful, brain-piercing noises created by a spirit's lamentations any further than I already have, but clearly Dylan doesn't have a clue what I'm talking about. I wonder if anyone else does.

Robbie's grin falters as a fresh gust of cold air sweeps down from above us like drops of mist—carrying a faint, yet distinct, scent. I try to place the sharp and salty smell, but it's still too vague. A nervous tremor sends my foot tapping, and I keep a close watch on our new leads as the smell continues to waft down with the droplets of cold.

"I guess it's show time," Robbie says in a far more subdued voice.

The expression in his eyes, a mix of excitement and apprehension, makes my stomach turn in time with the sharp scent tumbling into stronger focus. Cheese. Cheddar cheese, old and possibly growing mold. I hold a hand against my stomach, thinking about the spirit on the plane. I knew there was the chance of confronting spirits at some point this summer, but I didn't think it would happen so soon after arriving.

"Woah, what's going on with him?"

I glance at Dylan, whose eyes are fixed firmly on Robbie.

Our lead is doubled-over, his breathing labored and head bowed. I'm surprised Dylan doesn't understand what he's going through. I've never seen another person in contact with a spirit, but it's obvious Robbie feels the same things I do right now, or at least something similar. Dylan, on the other hand, doesn't appear uncomfortable at all. He doesn't shiver, sniff the air, or hold his stomach or head against the bucking sickness or the pinprick static worming its way through his ears.

I glance around at the campers from the other sectors and my own. Most of them are like Dylan, standing by and watching, spectators and not participants to whatever's about to happen. A couple of the kids fidget with unease, and the oldest campers all seem to be feeling the cold. But no one's in real pain. No one but Robbie and me.

My focus drifts from the unsettling knowledge of being an outsider, even among these other kids who are supposed to share my experiences. Instead, my attention is drawn back to Robbie, who stares up as a bluish-white mass begins to form in the room. Robbie's eyes are bloodshot, and small trickles of blood leak out of his ears. He looks like a low-budget film's idea of someone being possessed.

"What's wrong with him?" a girl, I think maybe Sabeena, gasps.

"Nothing's wrong with him," Alex says, raising a gentle hand to stop anyone from approaching. "He's fine." She's different now, too, though it's hard to say why. Perhaps it's the vague expression on her face or the way her eyes roll halfway into her head as if they're staring up at the ceiling while her chin remains positioned straight ahead.

"Good evening, Missus," Robbie says, but not to Alex or any other living person in the room.

The shape has distinguished itself into a woman now, and she stands, floats—whatever it is spirits do—across from Robbie. I watch her from the side, hearing the static in my head, the indistinguishable blips of muffled sound. I can't comprehend her mutterings, but Robbie can. He nods as if he's having a normal conversation with her. If it weren't for his outfit, or the bloody eyes and bleeding ears, he'd now seem totally relaxed in this spirit's presence. It's weird. And kind of disturbing.

"Well, Alex?" Robbie says after a moment of small chitchat with the dead woman before him. "Do any of our fellow Senders have a connection with Madame Roux?"

"Yes," Alex nods, her eyes still upturned, but her body pivoting towards me. "One of our own crew, in fact. Callum."

"You see her?" Dylan asks.

I give a weak nod. I do see her, but it seems like a trick question, like I'm going to pay if my answer is incorrect.

SHADE

"Let's introduce her, then," Robbie says.

Alex raises her palm in the air and closes her eyes. She presses her hand out in front of her, palm faced in my direction, and the spirit—Madame Roux—turns to me. She glides closer, and the static in my head increases. I wince, trying hard not to double-over in pain and queasiness. The woman mouths something, her face—what's visible of it—desperate. I do my best, but I fail to make anything out through the mumbling pain.

"I...I can't understand her," I say, my voice strained.

"She's telling you about her husband," Robbie says, sounding almost jovial. "She's always talking about him. He killed her, you see."

"Oh." I knew she must have been murdered, but the confirmation is still nice. It's like at least something here makes sense. "Yeah, I always see..."

"The ghosts of murder victims," Robbie finishes. "We know."

"We know all your talents," Alex says. "We were hoping you'd be able to connect. It was good luck, finding a spirit that corresponded with someone's abilities."

"Madame Roux is still here because of her husband," Robbie says, telling the spirit's tale for me and everyone who can't see her. "He killed her, and a mob killed him. We've tried to tell her he's gone, but she won't believe us. Still thinks he's out there, a danger to everyone."

The spirit is listening, or at least I think she is. When Robbie said the mob had killed her husband, she nodded, her expression solemn. But, when he said her husband was gone, she shook her head and the static blips became frantic. The abrupt change in her manner makes me think she knows something Robbie doesn't.

The floorboards above us creak, and Madame Roux lifts her chin, swivelling back to Robbie. Her voice rises, making the static in my head grow more intense. The floors creak again, and something cuts through the smell of cheese. This time it doesn't take long to place it. It's smoke. Cigar smoke.

"Madame Roux might not be as clueless as you think." I look away from the ceiling and focus on Meander instead, whose eyes are fixed on the stairs outside the room. I don't want to follow his gaze, but I do. Another smoky mass bubbles forward while the woman in the room with us pushes back as if she can sink into the walls and disappear.

The reek of cigars billows into a thick, unbreathable cloud. I choke against the heavy fumes as a new shape, darker and heavier than Madame Roux, sidles down the stairs and enters the room. Most of the others are looking around in confusion, but Meander's eyes are trained on the figure by the stairs.

"There's...there's something else," Alex says, her voice uncertain. "Something new. I haven't felt this before."

"Can you lock onto it?" Robbie asks, voice alive with curiosity.

Alex's eyes crinkle with frustration.

"I can't," she says, shaking her head. "But I can feel it."

"Another spirit?" Dylan asks.

I nod, although I can't make out much more than a large, smoky mass.

Still, Dylan shakes my shoulder, surprised. "You can

see this one, too? Geez. Must be a murder house."

"It is," I say, watching the figure as it advances towards us.

Madame Roux huddles by a wall and slides away as soon as the other spirit has passed. She's running from him—if a spirit can technically still run. She's afraid, that much is clear.

"Don't you remember what Robbie said? He killed his wife, and a mob killed him. They were both murdered. One just deserved it more."

"I guess someone doesn't believe in the purity of justice," Mim mumbles.

I'm not interested in a philosophical debate right now. The spirit, his shape almost wholly unformed with several dark spots riddling his body like shadows of the bullets once lodged in his abundant flesh, is still advancing towards the group.

No. Not towards the group. Towards one member of the group.

I'm glad it's not me. But I'd prefer Meander not to be targeted and for the spirit to head after someone with a bit more experience handling the dead instead.

"Meander," Alex says, a sharp, fearful edge to her voice, "can you hear what the spirit wants? Is it speaking to you?"

Meander shakes his head, which fits with my own experience, too. So far, the spirit hasn't made a peep. My head still thrums with static, but it's a steady stream of fuzz now that Madame Roux has gone out of range. The cheddar smell has dissipated, too—evaporated out of the air or overpowered by the stench of cigars.

"Cal, what's happening, man?" Dylan asks, nudging my side as if I'm some commentator at a sporting event.

I guess, to him, I am. I swallow hard, the saliva sticky in my throat. "He's moving," I say, watching the spirit's slow progression into the room.

He's near Alex now, and I can tell she feels his closeness but still cannot seem to latch on. For a moment, the spirit halts and peers around the room as if considering something. His eyes—or rather the blank shapes where I assume his eyes once were—rest on me for a brief pause before his focus moves back to Meander.

"Well, this is interesting—" Robbie begins.

In the flash of a second's time, something in the spirit's demeanour changes, and his slow pace snaps into a quick burst of movement. I jump back, startled by the smoky mass lunging towards Meander. At least his movements are not sluggish either. He ducks quickly, though judging by the way his hand comes to his cheek as he hits the ground, he didn't quite make it out of the spirit's path in time.

"Meander, are you okay?" Alex takes a step forward but stops when the spirit rushes through her. She shivers, her face paling as if struck with a sudden illness, but the expression fades when the loud crack of the ceiling above us distracts everyone in the room.

"What the..." Robbie cranes his neck back to watch small bits of plaster floating down like snowflakes.

He looks at Alex, and they both turn to Meander.

"What's he doing?" Robbie asks, the curiosity in his face only a little dampened by the strange turn of events.

Meander gets to his knees and watches the ceiling with a blank expression. "He's angry," he says.

His words are so nonchalant I want to laugh. Angry is an understatement. For whatever reason, grazing Meander's cheek and maybe missing the rest of him has set the spirit off into a frenzy. He swoops through the room, banging into the walls and ceiling like a steel marble in a pinball machine. He doesn't stop, doesn't even slow, but crashes downward, sending unsettling rumbles through the old floors.

"Should we get out of here?" one of the other campers asks.

"I think that might be a good idea," Alex says, glancing sideways at Robbie.

"Nah, we're fine," Robbie says, waving a careless hand through the air as the spirit makes another sudden lunge for Meander.

Meander dives forward. Beside him, Reed steps back, swatting the air like he's heard a fly but can't locate where the buzzing's coming from. He backs into Naasir, knocking the other boy over. Meanwhile, the spirit hurls upwards again, hitting the ceiling so hard the entire floor above us whines. Small cracking pops go off in a line across the center of the room as bigger clumps of drywall fall.

"Okay, getting out might be the best idea, after all," Robbie corrects himself.

Alex nods and begins ushering us towards the door. We head out in a rush as the spirit hits the ceiling again, and a full section of the second story falls in a heap. Campers scream, and the rush grows more frantic, kids pushing at one another to make it outside first.

"Single file!" someone yells.

No one listens as another loud groan echoes across

the room. Something heavy thuds above our heads.

"I really hope that isn't the bathroom," Dylan mutters.

The vision of a rusted claw-foot tub crashing into the living room makes the ache in my stomach worse.

"Let's get out of here before we find out," Mim says, tugging Kornelía's arm as they veer into the front hallway.

I make it to the doorway before stopping to watch the spirit swing and catapult into the far wall. Bricks from the fireplace shatter to the floor. Meander remains low to the ground, his eyes fixed on the spirit's chaotic dance.

"Come on!" I yell.

He eyes me briefly before peering around at the now emptying room. He's the last to move, and I don't think it was an unintentional moment of frozen indecision. He's waiting for the others to leave because he thinks he caused the spirit's craziness. Hell, maybe he did. But it doesn't much matter who or what set the spirit off. Madame Roux's husband is out of control now, and everyone needs to get out of this house.

When he sees the others are clearing out, Meander stands. With a deep breath he breaks into a jog to cross the room.

The movement is a mistake. The spirit catches it, and chases after him, silent, smoky, and wreaking havoc on my guts and my head.

"Hurry!" I say, grabbing Meander's arm to help propel him into the hallway.

The spirit reaches him first, and Meander clutches my wrist to pull me down, out of the way. We fall in a heap as the spirit roars over our heads and rams against the narrow walls in the hallway. The campers shriek as the ceiling above the entryway cracks, and I scramble up, grabbing Meander's hand to help him back to his feet.

His palm is clammy—as clammy as my own. The scratches on his face and thin streaks of blood on his cheek where the spirit first grazed him are visible now I am standing this close.

"Are you all right?" I ask.

He doesn't waste time answering. Instead, he pulls me forward, and we dive under the spirit's form to reach the front door. We trip over the doorway, stumbling until we reach the grass out front. The air is mercifully warm and fresh, but my head still pounds with the sounds of dull static and the groaning structures inside the house.

"It's going down!" Dylan says.

I drop Meander's hand and lean forward to help ease my sloshing stomach. We stare at the house as the blackness inside is filled with the loud, destructive sounds of the living room collapsing in on itself.

"Is everyone here?" Alex yells.

A chorus of chatter breaks out in the group.

"Revenant's all here!" someone says.

"Entity, too."

"Everyone's safe from Wraith."

"Shade's all here, too." Robbie nods, counting us all for the third time.

He and Alex look at each other for a long, serious moment, their expressions drawn and sickly. I think they might apologize for putting us in such a dangerous situation until the corners of their lips turn up. As suddenly as the spirit's attack began, Robbie's stony eyes brighten and his mouth cracks wide with a laugh.

"Well, welcome to Wanagi, Shade," he says, slumping to sit on the porch step with a satisfied, gleeful breath. "You won't find another summer camp like it."

7

Despite having a lengthy nap after our initial arrival, I sleep through the night once we're back at the château after the "show" and wake around nine the next morning. I'm not the first one awake. Naasir and Reed have already vacated the room by the time I sit up and stretch my stiff limbs. The others are still asleep, though. Sefa's left leg hangs over the edge of his bunk, Dylan's sprawled on his stomach, and Meander is wrapped in his sheets, loose curls the only part of him visible.

I maneuver my way around Sefa's leg and spend a quiet moment dumping the contents of my bags into one of the empty drawers in the dresser. Then, I grab an outfit and my toiletries and head for the shower.

By the time I step back into the room, everyone is up, except Dylan.

"I feel like I've been hit over the head." Sefa moans.

Meander brushes past me to claim the bathroom

next.

"Didn't sleep well?" I ask, sitting on my bunk to pull on my sneakers. The walk back to the château had my mind reeling with questions about Robbie and Alex and the way they smiled after the house nearly collapsed on top of us. But, when we got back to our room and my head hit the pillow, I was out cold.

"Never do when I'm not at home," Sefa replies, hopping off his bunk and going to his drawer. "Gran says I'm connected with the ocean. Says I'm squeezed too tight inland." He laughs to himself, his smile one of fondness. "Mostly, I miss my comfortable bed. But I do miss the sound of the waves and the smell of the water."

"You live on the coast then?" I ask, lacing my shoes and standing. "I've only seen the ocean a couple of times. Must be nice to live there."

Sefa nods. "It is."

"Is it morning?" Dylan mutters from his bed. He wipes a hand across his mouth before burying his head under his pillow. "I need another eight hours."

"Suit yourself," I say, heading for the door. "I'm going to get some breakfast."

Dylan mumbles something incomprehensible but makes no move to get up, so I leave without him. The lounge is empty, but when I head downstairs to the dining hall, I find Kornelía, Mim, and about fifteen other campers spread along the black tables.

Kornelía waves me over. "Morning!" She beams.

Mim doesn't even bother to glance up. Steamed milk foams at the top of the mug she grips tight. Her glower is fierce. If I had to make an easy guess, I'd say she's not much of a morning person.

The girls have black folders open in front of them, and without even asking, Kornelía directs me to the kitchen.

"It's your schedule," she says, taking a sip from a bottle of water. "The folders are in the kitchen. Your name will be on the front. You can help yourself to breakfast, too."

"Thanks," I say, wondering how she knows all this. If it weren't for Kornelía and Mim, I'd be totally lost so far this summer.

The kitchen is empty of people when I step inside, but it's not void of food. Oatmeal, cereal, bread, and pastries line the counters, along with a coffee maker, a kettle, and a selection of teas and hot chocolates. I wander over to the fridge and take a bottle of water and an orange from inside before I fill the kettle in the sink to make myself a cup of tea. The smell of the pastries is enticing, so after I've found a mug and picked out a tea bag, I grab a cinnamon bun and take a bite before stepping over to the stack of black folders on the kitchen table.

By the time I find the folder labelled with my name, the kettle's boiled, so I make my tea and load everything onto a tray to take out to the dining hall.

"Well, last night was certainly entertaining," Kornelía says as I sit next to her and open the folder.

I raise my eyes, my mouth too full of soft pastry to respond right away.

"Is that what you'd call it?" Mim says. She gives Kornelía a dubious glance over the rim of her cup. "I wouldn't say nearly being crushed to death was entertaining."

Kornelía smiles at Mim. "Yes, but it was so

interesting!" she exclaims. "Two spirits in one house, and even our leads were surprised by the second one. Cal, you got to see them both. That's amazing!"

I exchange a glance with Mim. She shakes her head as if she has no idea what Kornelía's talking about.

"Amazing's not the word I'd use," I mutter, looking back down at my folder. My muscles are sore after running, diving, and flat out falling in the house last night. And I'm still in shock over the way a lot of the older campers followed Robbie's lead and began laughing after the house came crashing down.

"Well, I thought it was amazing." Kornelía shrugs. She points to my folder, changing the subject as quickly as she started it. "How is your schedule, Cal?" she asks, leaning into me to get a glimpse.

A welcome letter, a sheet explaining the orientation scheduled for this afternoon, and an itinerary for a mid-summer day trip to Paris are inside. I flip through the papers, skimming the contents of each and stopping when I reach my course timetable.

"I've got Emotional Entities from twelve to four on Tuesdays, Basics of Paranormality from twelve to four on Wednesdays, Basics of Gadgetry from one to five on Thursdays, and Introduction to Imprinting from two to six on Fridays." I look up at Kornelía, whose freckled face is radiant next to Mim's dark hair and deep frown. "Saturday and Sunday, I'm with my mentor from twelve to two, and study time is from two to four. It says Mondays are free."

"I've got the same." Kornelía nods. "On the weekends, I mean. Mentor and study time, and Mondays off. We've got Emotional Entities together, and Basics of Paranormality, of course."

"What about you, Mim?" I ask, watching as Mim takes a long drink of coffee.

"It's her third one," Kornelía stage-whispers as if Mim can't hear her.

"Paranormality," Mim says with a sluggish grumble. She sits up straighter, grabbing her sheet and reading over it again. "That's it for us. I'm with Korni on Friday."

"Families and Their Spirits," Kornelía says with a happy sigh.

Mim groans at her cheery tone, but I appreciate her enthusiasm. It's nice to know at least some of us are enjoying our time here so far.

Dylan makes it down by the time I've finished my breakfast, and Mim has started on her fourth coffee of the morning. He, too, shares our Wednesday class. I'm guessing everyone in Shade does. And he has Introduction to Imprinting with me on Fridays. But I'm on my own for Basics of Gadgetry.

"I can't believe classes start tomorrow," Dylan complains, sitting across the wide table from us. "We just got here. Isn't this supposed to be a summer vacation?"

"No, it's not." Lu appears next to the table, her folder clutched to her chest. "This isn't meant to be a fun way to spend a couple of months. It's not even summer for everyone, you know. We're spread across the world. Some of us have to miss school to study here."

I never thought about the fact some of these kids were here over the winter instead of the summer. I'm missing the final two weeks of classes, but I took my exams early so my grades wouldn't be affected. Missing months of school is more serious. And all for the Oracle. There's so much I don't know about this camp, this entire organization.

"This bites." Dylan studies his schedule with a morose sigh. "I should have stayed home and relaxed by the pool all summer."

"You'd like that better than being here?" Kornelía asks, sounding surprised by his indifference.

Dylan shrugs. "I only came 'cause it sounded fun," he admits. "I don't plan on being a ghost hunter or whatever for the rest of my life."

"What do you want to do with your future, then?" Lu asks.

I expect him to say he doesn't have a clue what his future plans are yet, but instead, Dylan gives Lu a confident smile.

"A vet," he says. "Not a total waste of my talent, is it? I want to specialize in working with dogs. Just, you know, the living ones."

"Interesting," Lu says. She considers Dylan for a few seconds before turning to Mim. "Maria, can I talk to you for a moment?"

"It's Mim," she snaps. She doesn't look at Lu. "And, no. You can't. I'm busy."

"I need to talk to you," Lu urges, but when Mim ignores her, she huffs. "Fine. We'll talk later." She gives us all a hard stare as she walks away from the table without another word.

"What was that all about?" Dylan asks.

"Nothing." Mim sulks.

Kornelía presses her lips together, and I can tell she knows. But Mim gives her a stern look, shaking her head to warn her not to talk. I glance at Dylan, but he only shrugs again.

Mim stands, leaving her mug on the table and squashing any further attempts to discuss the topic. "Come on. Let's get some fresh air."

We follow her outside, and her dark hair hangs down in a curtain of black and pink, shining in the light of the sun. She storms ahead of us, but Dylan races forward, nudging her in the side as he slides up next to her.

"*Vete!*" Mim pushes him away.

Dylan bounces back and nudges her again. Mim gives him a more forceful push, but there's a smile at the edge of her lips. When Dylan comes back and nudges her a third time, the remnants of her scowl slips into a quiet laugh.

Kornelía steps next to me, waiting until Mim is distracted before she speaks.

"It's Lu's talent," she whispers close to my ear.

I slow, letting Mim and Dylan get ahead. They don't notice the two of us lingering behind.

"What *is* her talent?" I try to think if I heard her mention it last night, but the only time I've even heard Lu speak was this morning.

Kornelía watches Mim, even as she leans her head towards my shoulder, so we won't be heard.

"She sees people's auras. The energy around them. And she knows when spirits cling to the living…. Lu described it as residual energy worn like a cloak around a living person. I saw her staring at Mim when she told us that last night. She's been trying to talk to her ever since, but Mim won't have anything to do with her."

"You think Mim has the, uh, residual energy of a spirit?" I ask.

Kornelía sighs, standing straight again. "I don't know what else it could be. She got along fine with Lu until she explained her ability."

Dylan and Mim are heading towards the pathway to the mainland, but before they reach the first stone steps, a voice calls out from our right.

"Shade!"

Our heads turn to see Robbie sitting on a bench surrounded by overgrown shrubberies a short distance away. He's eating an apple, the crunch of its skin audible as we walk to meet him. He grins at us as he chews, his mohawk tall and stiff beneath the morning sun.

"I see y'all are still here. That's good!" he says cheerfully, surveying us. "Didn't get scared away by last night, then."

"You kidding?" Dylan asks. "Last night was awesome!"

Last night was awful, but I don't try to voice my opinion. Robbie looks too pleased with Dylan's response for me to dampen the happy mood.

"Glad to hear it," Robbie says. "We expected things to go better than that, but you know...ghosts aren't too predictable."

"Is that what all the new sectors do?" Mim asks, her voice milder now the subject's been moved away from her spat with Lu. "Do they all get an, um..."

"Initiation?" Robbie finishes.

Mim nods.

Robbie mimics the action. "Yup, sure do. It's the best when one of the leads can interact with a local spirit, but even if they can't, there's always something special the first night. When I started as a Shade, one of my leads passed out and fell down a staircase." He chuckles. "Like I said, things don't always go as planned."

"What about the clothes?" Mim asks, giving Robbie's plain jeans and t-shirt a once over. "Why was everyone dressed so strange? Was it part of the ini… the *show*?"

Robbie takes another bite of his apple and chews it while he considers her question. A bit of the fruit juice drips onto his finger, and he sucks it off before finally responding.

"You'll learn that Senders have a habit of… collecting," he says, smiling at his own choice of word. "Tokens, trinkets, even costume pieces."

"But why?" Dylan asks. "We're not expected to wear uniforms or anything, right?"

Robbie grins again, his teeth white and straight. "Nah. But it's… Well, it's complicated. Some Senders pick up…" He pauses, trying to pick the best phrasing. "Well, you know when you go on vacation, and some people collect a fridge magnet from everyplace they visit? It's sort of like that for some people. Alex, for instance. She's got a hair ribbon for every spirit she's helped release. But everyone's different. Sometimes, collections aren't about spirits at all. They're personal mementos. Some Senders have only one or two pieces. Others create an entire persona out of it."

"Like you?" Kornelía asks, and Robbie nods.

"Yeah, like me," he says, obviously proud of his impressive attire. "The first time I saw a ghost, it scared me so bad I peed my pants," he admits without a hint of embarrassment. "It was a relative of mine, not someone I knew, but some distant cousin who died in 1846. That's how my journey to become a Sender started.

"It used to be spirits who died in the 1840s. Quite precise and quite dull. With so narrow an ability, I hardly ever saw spirits. But, eventually, it grew. Now, it's anyone born in the 1800s. Not 1799 or 1900. Still precise. But much more to work with, all things considered.

"Anyway, after my first ghost, I found an old heirloom necklace my mother kept safeguarded in her jewelry box. I don't have a clue when it was made, but I reckon it must be around my era 'cause I stole it first chance I could. I kept it under my mattress for years until I came to Camp Wanagi. Then I started to understand.

"I wear it like a bracelet whenever I know I'll be up against the otherworldly. I like the way it makes me feel. More powerful. Less afraid. I didn't feel the need to pee my pants when I had that necklace nearby, and that was a very good thing indeed. So, I started collecting other things. Some things from my era, and some things I just liked. And, now, I have a full-on ghost-hunting suit."

"Do we have to collect a bunch of crap and wear it all the time?" Dylan asks, sounding dubious.

Robbie laughs.

"You don't have to do anything," he says, looking straight at Dylan. "But you might be surprised. I don't know why it happens. Lots of campers have theories, but I'm not one of them. I only know Senders collect. For whatever reason, in whatever way. Besides, it's not like we wear our costumes under our normal clothes. Sometimes, we're surprised, and there's not a damned thing we can do then. But, when we know what we're going to face, it's nice to have a little bit of comfort."

Dylan studies Robbie's mohawk as if it might be one of the lead's trinkets, while Kornelía asks follow-up questions about Robbie's process for collecting. Mim stares off over the lake, her fingers caressing the beads of a necklace she has tucked under her shirt.

I wonder if it's possible for a coat, a pendant, or anything else to make seeing spirits more comfortable. If I had a collection of my own, would I have been laughing along with the others after the initiation? It seems unlikely. Then again, all this seems unlikely. So, maybe I would. Maybe, someday, I will.

For now, I'm more concerned with surviving the next ten weeks. I can worry about family heirlooms and jewelled accessories after I've seen if Camp Wanagi is even worth my time.

8

After orientation and a free night spent writing emails home and watching movies on Dylan's laptop, courses begin Tuesday morning. The first week of Camp Wanagi passes in a blur of instructor introductions and vague course descriptions. There are no more spirits or crumbling houses, despite Dylan's conviction our lounge is about to tumble down onto the floors below. But there are outlines and promises of lessons to be learned, and by the time Friday rolls around, I'm already working on my first piece of summertime homework.

"I've got the dictionary," I announce, carrying a large, worn book over to the library table Dylan, Kornelía, and Mim are seated at.

"Good start," Kornelía mumbles, preoccupied by the pages of another book.

Our first assignment is to choose one of the four sector names and find an example, either historical or

SHADE

from popular culture, of the phenomena. I don't know what the sector names mean, though. So, I've grabbed a paranormal dictionary from the shelf while the others research, trying to find examples to go along with the definitions.

"All right," I say, more to myself than anyone else. "Let's start with Shade."

"I don't think you know your alphabet," Dylan remarks.

"I want to know what our sector means first." I rifle through the pages of the dictionary until I reach the S section.

Across from me, Kornelía raises her head. "You don't know what Shade means?" she asks, sounding surprised.

I ignore her since, two minutes ago, she ignored me when I asked if anyone at the table *did* know.

"Here," I say instead, putting my finger on the page and running down it until I find the word. "It's a...a ghost." I look up at the others, who stare back at me blankly. "That's disappointing, isn't it?"

"I could've told you that's what it meant," Kornelía says as she turns a page in her book.

Dylan smirks. "Not all of us study this stuff in our every spare moment," he says, grabbing the book from under Kornelía's gaze and pulling it away.

She narrows her eyes at him, but her lips twitch in a smile.

I look back at the definition. *The spirit of a deceased being, residing in the underworld. So, our sector is the ghost sector?* It makes sense, though it's a tad unoriginal. I wonder if there's anything to the underworld part. Maybe shades are spirits who have been somehow damned.

I flip through more pages, searching for another definition before I dwell too long on the first one I've found. "Entity," I say, landing on the next sector.

"It's a general term for a thing," Kornelía says, more interested now she doesn't have her book.

"Why aren't you doing the definitions?" Dylan grins.

Kornelía makes a grasp for her book in response.

"Entity is...a thing." I read, nodding. "Like a person or a being. Sometimes, it refers specifically to ghosts." I glance up and shake my head. "Sheesh, Kornelía, do you know *all* this stuff?"

"Certainly not," Kornelía replies.

"Then how come you seem to know so much of it?" Mim asks.

Kornelía leans closer to the table, her voice low. "I did an unusual thing," she says, her tone conspiratorial. "On our first night here, before I went to sleep, I..." She pauses, giving us each a moment of careful consideration as we lean in to match her crouched stance. "I looked up the definitions."

I roll my eyes, sitting back in my chair. Dylan and Mim groan in unison.

Kornelía's satisfaction is immense. "It's not complicated, you know," she shrugs, giving Dylan a pointed stare.

"Yeah, yeah," Dylan grumbles, handing back her book.

"Wraith?" I ask next, and when Kornelía doesn't answer, I turn to the dictionary. "It's...like a ghost, but like a spirit that appears right around the time someone dies. Sometimes, even while they're still living." I glance up and catch Mim's gaze.

Her bottom lip protrudes in a contented pout as she listens to my explanation. "Creepy," she says, her fingers twisting the frayed fabric at the edge of her turquoise shirt.

"So how about Revenant? It's the grand finale," Dylan says.

I turn the pages again. "It's another ghost, but one that's bent on revenge." I stare at the definition and grimace. "Sometimes, it's thought these are not even ghosts but reanimated corpses."

"Like zombies?" Dylan asks. I nod uncertainly.

"Guess so."

"You mean we don't only have to worry about ghosts, we have to worry about the living dead, too?" Mim asks. "*Great.*"

"I think I've found an interesting historical case involving a wraith," Kornelía says, her voice piqued with excitement.

"I can't believe you're choosing history," Dylan says, sounding offended. His hair isn't spiked today, and it hangs dark and limp over his hollowed eyes. "We have the option to pick something from a movie or TV show, and you're researching historical events?"

"I happen to like history," Kornelía says, sighing as if she's explaining something to a stubborn child. "And I happen to dislike movies and TV."

"I'm not sure we can be friends anymore, Kornelía!" Dylan continues, sounding hurt.

Kornelía smirks.

Dylan turns back to me. "So, all in all, that makes four sectors with names that mean..."

"Ghost," Mim finishes. "I bet it took a lot of effort to

come up with those."

Kornelía shrugs. "Even the camp's name means spirit."

"Is that what Wanagi means?" Mim asks.

Kornelía laughs. "Didn't you read into this camp at all before you came?"

"I thought the camp was a secret," Dylan says. "How were we supposed to find it?"

I never even considered researching the camp before I came here. From the short letter sent by the Oracle, along with the invitation for me to come this summer, I learned enough to know the camp is a government-funded initiative. Although I'm not sure *which* government. And it is more or less a secret to those not involved with it.

We're supposed to keep it hushed, or at least explain it in as vague a manner as possible to anyone curious about our ten-week absence. I wonder what the kids missing school had to tell their teachers. One of these days, I'll ask Sefa how his school board even let him miss so much class time.

"You could have at least searched the name," Kornelía scolds. "Wanagi is a Native American term. Like I said, it means ghost or spirit."

"So, Camp Wanagi is Camp Spirit," I say, smiling. It's clever, if not a little on the nose.

"Okay, smart girl," Mim says, crossing her arms on the table. "If you know so much, then tell us why it's called the Oracle of Senders?"

"Well, Senders are paranormal agents," Kornelía explains, averting her gaze.

Mim is quick to pick up on her unease.

"And the Oracle part?" she presses.

Kornelía sighs. "I-I don't know *everything*."

"It's called the Oracle because of the Ancient Greeks," Mim says with a smug smile.

"They had ghost trackers in Ancient Greece? I must have missed that day at school." Dylan scoffs.

"No." I shake my head, happy to have something to add to the conversation. "They weren't ghost trackers. Oracles were…fortune tellers, sort of. Like, they talked to the gods, told the future, and stuff."

"Ah, except, it's all wrong," Mim says.

She pauses, and I think she's trying to translate what she wants to say in her head before she attempts to say it aloud.

"The Oracles were Senders. They didn't speak to the gods…. They spoke to spirits. People thought they made predictions, but…no. They didn't. They talked to spirits."

"That makes no sense," Dylan says.

Kornelía's perked up again, and she smiles her wide smile, eyes bright with curiosity.

"Yes, it does," she says.

The squeak of her voice is so eager Dylan looks almost awestruck as he listens to her speak.

"It would be like, well, say someone died because of, um…" She catches my eye, and puts a hand on my shoulder, using me as an example. "If they were murdered. They could warn their family about it. Tell them they might be attacked next. Wow, Mim, that's amazing! How did you learn that?"

"Well, you don't do language training for two years and learn nothing." Mim shrugs, leaning back in her chair.

"Okay, but shouldn't we all be called Oracles, then?"

Dylan asks. He shifts his weight so his whole chair rocks back on its hind legs.

"I don't think the term always refers to a person," I say, thinking back to my sixth-grade history class. I didn't pay much attention back then. I never thought Ancient Greek prophets would relate to my life. If my former teacher could see me now, she'd be ecstatic. "Oracles were also the names of the temples where the prophets did their, uh, prophesying."

"So...do we have a temple?" Dylan rocks forward again, dropping his elbows onto the table as the chair thuds against the hardwood.

Kornelía and Mim share an uncertain glance.

"It would make sense," Kornelía says. "Not an actual temple, perhaps. But there's got to be some kind of headquarters."

She's right. There has to be headquarters. All this can't come from nowhere. I wonder if it's one single place, or if there are small oracles hidden in pockets all over the globe. Robbie and Alex might know. They may have visited some of them. Or, if there is only a single headquarters, our leads are probably at least aware of its location. Maybe we all get to go there if we make it through this camp and become of-age Senders.

"Well, all I know is," Dylan begins, crossing his arms over his chest as he leans back once more, "I wish I was in Revenant. At least you could argue the zombie angle there. How great would that be?" He pauses, thinking. "Hey, do you think a zombie flick would count as an example for the assignment?"

"I think the idea was to stick with ghosts," Mim says, tilting her head to one side as she regards him.

"I'm branching out," Dylan grins. "Exploring new territory. Now, if you'll excuse me, I've got a paper to write." He stands and walks across the library to the computer station.

"Can we get kicked out of Camp Wanagi?" Mim asks, watching Dylan retreat. "Because, if we can, I have a feeling one of us might not make it a full month, let alone four whole years."

9

It doesn't take long to decide what I want to write my paper about. It may be boring compared to living spirits and reanimated corpses, but I'm choosing my own sector as my topic. And, like Kornelía, I'm going to pick a historical event.

I've never researched real spirits before. It didn't occur to me I could. Some kids grow up reading ghost stories and being told tales of hauntings passed down through generations of parents and siblings delighting in a good scare. But I wasn't allowed to learn those kinds of stories. Dr. Buchanan, my psychiatrist, told me they would be too impressionable for a child with my imagination. My parents agreed. Even after I left therapy, they avoided talking about ghosts unless they had to. I was so busy trying to be normal, I never thought about looking this stuff up on my own.

Now, I have the chance, and I want to take it. Though I'm not sure where to begin my research. The library takes up most of the château's basement, and is comprised of shelves and shelves of paranormal books. I would never have guessed so much literature existed about people with abilities like mine, and I'm sure I'll have an easier time finding something among the books than I will online. But there are so many options for me to choose from. I'm not even sure what kind of shade I'm hoping to find.

I spend a long time browsing through the books. Dylan finishes his paper within the hour, and Mim leaves soon after with five pages of handwritten notes she plans to type up later. Kornelía sticks around, taking notes and reading about her wraith. After a while, Sefa shows up to work on his assignment as well.

"What are you doing your paper on?" I ask when he joins me in the stacks.

Sefa studies the book spines, hunting for the call number Dari, the librarian, gave him.

"I want to write about the oldest known spirit." He pauses and shakes his head. "I don't mean the spirit that's been around the longest. I'm interested in the spirits of people who died when they were old. I want to know the oldest person to cling to our world after death."

I stare at Sefa, intrigued by his topic choice and wondering how he came up with it. He must notice the interest in my eyes. A beat after he stops talking, his thick lips curve in a smile.

"I see the ghosts of the elderly," he explains.

"Oh." I nod, but soon my brows furrow as I think of the logistics of such a talent. "How does that work? Is it like ghosts sixty-five and older?"

Sefa lets out a deep, gravelly laugh. "I'm not sure," he shrugs. "The youngest I've seen, that I know of, is seventy. But I'm not sure it's a hard and fast rule. It's the same with Sabeena. She sees children. Well, children who died of illness, anyway. There's no set age for her, either."

"Do you think...?" I want to prod him for more details, but a nearby sound in the library cuts my question off. The noise is surprising and out of place in the otherwise quiet room. It's someone crying.

I close my mouth and turn around, creeping along the shelf to my right until I've reached the end and can see two girls sitting on the floor in a corner of the adjacent stacks. Not wanting to be seen, I keep back, curiosity driving me to eavesdrop. Sefa stands a step behind me, watching the scene as well.

One of the girls wears a Wanagi sweater with an E on the sleeve. I recognize them from our first night here, when the Entity Sector gathered us for initiation.

"Ada, you have to," the girl in the sweater says.

The other girl—Ada—convulses with sobs. Her face is puffy, and her eyes are red-rimmed and surrounded by the glistening stain of teardrops.

"I know, but..." She brings a trembling hand to her face to wipe away tears which are immediately replaced by fresh ones.

"The first summer we came here, the first *day*, you told me you were going to release him," the first girl says. She holds Ada close, rubbing her back as she speaks. "It's time, my sweet girl. You have several weeks still to prepare. You can do it, and I'll be there to help."

"I-I know," Ada repeats. She takes a deep breath and

wipes her eyes again. "But he's my brother. My twin. I lost him once before. I—I don't want to lose him ag—" She breaks into a gasping sob.

I turn away, my stomach tight. Even I can guess the topic of their conversation. Entity is the oldest year this year, and I've heard enough talk to gather final year campers get to choose their own spirit to release. Ada must have contact with her twin brother's spirit.

"Some of the campers aren't serious about being Senders," Sefa says, his voice grave. He crosses his arms over his chest, looking like a security guard about to tell off would-be trespassers. "They think this is for fun, and it's not. We were given these abilities, and we cannot waste them. They're gifts. We have to appreciate them."

I watch Sefa as he returns to the shelves and scans each row until he finds the book he's after.

"Do you really believe that?" I ask as he pulls out the book and flips through a few pages. "That they're gifts?"

"Of course." Sefa glances up at me in surprise. "Don't you?"

I listen to Ada's crying, remembering the scratches on Meander's face the night of the initiation. I think about the expression my parents wore when they told me I had to get help because of my "visions".

"I think they might be curses," I mutter, slumping back against the shelf.

Sefa studies me, but he doesn't say anything. He doesn't need to.

Sefa takes his book and leaves me alone. I stay put for a long time, staring at the rows of books across from me—many of them written by Senders. I wonder how the authors felt when they first became acquainted with the Oracle. A week at this camp has been enough to answer one of my questions about the other kids here. Some love their abilities. Some take the talents they've been given and use them as a guide for everything they do. But I still don't know if there are others here like me. Others who feel cursed. Ada might. Meander might, too. But I can't be sure, and being clueless sucks.

The mere existence of the Oracle of Senders is incredible, and I'm grateful to finally know others who share in what I've experienced. But incredible is not always a good thing, and for every second I feel included at Camp Wanagi, there's another second where I'm still waiting on the wrong side of the door—wondering if anyone will ever turn the lock to let me in.

10

"CALLUM?"

I look up from the book laid out before me on the dining table. An older teen stands on the other side of the table, his hands full of study materials.

"Uh, Cal," I say with a wave.

"I'm Daniel," the teen replies.

I never did settle on a topic for my Basics of Paranormality assignment. Any interest I had in the project fizzled out after hearing Ada cry last night. I'll pick something tomorrow and write the paper, quick like Dylan. They won't fail me for a half-assed attempt. Even if they did, I'm not sure I'd care.

I close my book, a volume on the history of paranormal studies Kornelía suggested I read, as my mentor sits down across from me.

"Hi," I say with a forced smile, watching as Daniel lowers his stuff onto the table.

He has light brown skin, wavy black hair, and light

blue eyes. He wore the army uniform with the medic band during the initiation. His English is tinged with an accent, and I think Spanish might be his first language.

"It's nice to meet you, Cal," Daniel says, reaching a hand across the table.

We shake, and then he goes back to sorting through his things.

"You're the only camper I'm mentoring this summer, and we have six weeks together."

My fingers drum against the closed cover of my book. "Why only six weeks? You're not here for the whole summer?" I'm not disappointed to know I won't be meeting with Daniel every week. I hadn't expected mentoring sessions, and I'm not convinced they'll be of any use. But it seems rude not to ask.

"No one from Entity is," he says. "Our final projects take us all over the world. I'll be heading back to Argentina for mine."

"*Back* to Argentina?" I force my fingers to stop tapping out their frenzied rhythm and open the notebook I brought downstairs with me. I don't know if I'll need to take notes, but it doesn't hurt to be prepared.

Daniel smiles, clicking a pen in an automatic gesture.

"My home," he explains. "There's a spirit there I plan to work with."

"Oh." I nod, studying him. "So, what is your specialty?" It's an ice-breaker here, like I'm asking him what school he attends or what he does for a living.

Daniel considers the question for longer than I expect, pursing his lips as he forms a response.

"I'm not sure," he says at last.

I thought all Entity kids would have a strong grasp on their talents by now.

He laughs, clicking his pen again. "We all have our talents," he continues, "but you'll come to realize it's not so black and white as you might think. Everyone has different levels of abilities. Some people can only glimpse a small part of the supernatural world. Others can grab at a much bigger piece. In simple terms, I see the ghosts of women who died in childbirth. But it goes beyond that. Sometimes..." He pauses, watching me for a moment. His gaze is intense and slightly unsettling. "Sometimes, I see more. Sometimes, it is not only the mother who suffers."

"Not just the..." I consider what he said until it makes sense in my mind. "You see babies' spirits, too?"

"In a way."

Daniel hesitates, his pen clicking in a similar rhythm as my toes, which have taken up the jittery motion I forced my fingers to stop.

"Some people have the talent for seeing the ghosts of infants. I don't. But, sometimes, I can feel the presence of another being.... Not a ghost, exactly. More like an imprint on the mother. As if the baby's spirit is haunting the mother's spirit, trapping her in ghostly form."

My first Introduction to Imprinting class gave us an overview of imprinting. I know people can get so attached to an item or a place their spirit sticks to it after they die. Certain *things* can be haunted, like a music box or a rocking chair. I didn't think the concept could include other ghosts as well.

"Wow," I mumble. "I had no idea it could get so

complicated."

"That's not even the worst of it." Daniel laughs. "We can't understand the language of babies who live. Trying to understand the needs of a baby's spirit… It's especially difficult because I can only feel the presence of an infant. I cannot see it like I can its mother." He pulls a sheet of paper from one of the binders he's brought with him and clicks his pen a final time. "It takes a lot of determination. That, at least, I have."

"Well, best of luck on your final project," I say, my voice awkward. I don't know what other remark to make. I want to ask him a million questions about his time at Camp Wanagi, his abilities, and his genuine interest in dealing with the spirits left over after such horrific events. I want to know why he likes being here, which it's obvious he does. I want to know if he ever thought seeing spirits was the worst thing to happen to him.

"Thanks," Daniel replies, cutting into my rambling thoughts before I manage to vocalize even one of my endless concerns, "but we're not here to talk about me. Today is about you. We're here to talk about your talents, and what you want to accomplish during your time at Camp Wanagi."

"You mean this summer?" I ask.

Daniel shakes his head. "Not only this summer," he says. "Your time at this camp. Each of the four years will be important. You should have a goal for where you want to be at the end of it. You don't have to make any permanent arrangements yet. But try to think about it. What do you want to accomplish by coming here? Do you want to make ghosts your life? Do you want to learn how to better use your skills?"

I don't have an answer for him. I came to Camp Wanagi because seeing spirits has always made me an outsider. Once, when I was six, I went to a birthday party in an old house, and I saw a spirit. I told all the kids about it, and everyone started to panic. Simon, the birthday boy, refused to sleep alone in his room for months afterwards. His parents were furious, and my mom and dad responded to the incident by enrolling me in therapy. After the party, they also told me they were having another child, even though they'd always insisted they never intended to have more than one.

I'd seen spirits before, but after Simon's party, I realized how abnormal my sightings were.

I got what I wanted, coming to this camp. I'm not weird here. But now I've achieved my goal of meeting others like me, I'm not sure what to strive for next. It would be nice to know why I have an ability while no one else in my family has any paranormal talents. I'd also like to figure out why I see murder victims and why I was offered the chance to come here. But do I want four summers, more than four summers, of dealing with spirits? Are answers worth the torment of being so closely connected to the spiritual world?

"Don't worry about it right now," Daniel says after a moment. "But do think about it. Make it your task this summer to make a longer goal for the future. For now, we'll focus on the present and the past. Sound okay?"

"Okay," I agree, working to slow the nervous beat of my foot.

For the next hour and a half, I tell Daniel about the spirits I've seen. There's been a lot. I see ghosts far more often than I'd like. At one time, it baffled me how there could be so many spirits, especially murder victims, hanging around our world. Of course, that was before I discovered how hundreds of thousands of people are murdered every year—millions per decade.

There have been a lot of decades in the history of time, which means there have been a lot of murders. I think even the people who believe in ghosts underestimate how many spirits are still around us. Of course, I'd guess murder victims have a higher rate of unfinished business than others. Or maybe most of us here see ghosts all the time, and I'm as clueless about the quantity of spirits as non-Senders.

It feels good to talk, to relate the incidents I've told no one except for Dr. Buchanan. It feels even better to know Daniel believes what I tell him, to know he's probably had similar experiences himself.

I tell him about the old man with the gun shot in the stomach near the downtown bank at home, and the woman I saw at Simon's party. I recount the select spirits I've seen on several occasions, the various spirits I've seen only once, and the many spirits I may have seen, the ones so quick or unformed I've never been sure if they were even real. I tell him everything, right up to the spirit on the plane ride over here and the husband and wife I saw our first night.

Then I tell him about Maggie.

"Who was Maggie?" Daniel asks, taking notes while I talk.

The dining hall is quiet despite the early afternoon hour. Since breakfast is served until eleven, lunch isn't until three, so only us and a few other studying campers are present.

I clear my throat, fidgeting in my seat.

"Maggie was a little girl who lived in my

neighborhood," I begin, my voice tight and thin. This is the hardest story to tell. The words struggle in my chest, fighting against the pressure of my lungs.

"When I was eight, and Maggie was four, she was killed by a hit-and-run driver." I pause, breathe, and continue with more strength. "About a week after she died, I saw her playing on the street. Right where she'd been struck. I watched her every day after school for two weeks. She never went away. I even saw her once at night, before I went to bed. She stayed there all the time. Running up and down the street, playing hopscotch, and skipping with invisible jump ropes."

"So, what happened?" Daniel asks, the question a gentle prod. He stops his note taking and sits with his arms folded across the table as he listens.

"After a couple of weeks, I got up the courage to approach her. I thought she couldn't be too scary because, when she was alive, she was always sweet." I smile, remembering the day I walked up to her and offered an uncertain hello. I don't expect I'll ever forget. Of all the spirits I've encountered, Maggie was the liveliest. Her face and body were well-defined, her features were prominent, and her expressions were easy to distinguish. She smelled like oranges.

"She seemed happy to see me. We stared at each other for a long time before she spoke to me. Even then, it wasn't like a real conversation. Her voice sounded like it was inside my head, a bit fuzzy and unfocused. As if I was only remembering something she'd said to me in the past."

"What did she say?"

I sigh. "She kept saying 'They need to know. They need to know.' But my mother found me outside and yelled at me for leaving the house without telling her where I was going, so I had to leave."

"Was that the end of it?" Daniel asks.

I shake my head. "The next day, Mom and I went to the grocery store," I continue, staring down at the table while I remember each detail of the day. "We were in the parking lot when I saw a familiar car. Turns out, it belonged to Maggie's babysitter. I'm not sure how I even recognized it, but I did. And, for some reason, I ran to it. Mom followed, angry I wasn't listening to her. But all I could think about was the car. I got up to it, and right away I noticed a dent in the front bumper."

I stop, my throat dry. I wish I'd grabbed a bottle of water out of the fridge before I sat down here. I glance at the kitchen, contemplating if I should get up.

"Go on," Daniel urges, making my decision for me.

I lick my lips and drag my gaze back to my mentor. "My mom came over, and I... I said, 'This is the car that killed Maggie.' I don't know why I said it, but the strangest part was...my mother believed me. Her skin turned kind of grey. I thought she might faint, but she pulled out her phone and called the police."

I shift in my seat, my foot tapping against the floor in time with the silent rhythm my fingertips have once again taken up. "I found out later that the babysitter did something she wasn't supposed to, and Maggie was going to tell her parents about it. So, the babysitter decided to hit Maggie with her car instead of getting fired or quitting the job."

Daniel makes a sound somewhere between disgust and pity. I nod and go on with the story.

"After the babysitter confessed a few days later, I

stopped seeing Maggie on the street. I watched for her, but she never came back. I guess she didn't need to anymore."

I let out a long breath and wait for Daniel to speak again. The Entity camper looks pained but intrigued.

"It is terrible to have a talent like yours at such a young age," he says with sincerity. "But to release a spirit with so little effort while so young, it bodes well for you. You must be very attuned with the spirits you see to communicate so clearly and be guided by their will."

"Guided by their will?" I ask, startled. I never thought Maggie had guided me. And I don't see why Daniel says it like it's a feat to be proud of. Being guided sounds more like being manipulated. Like being possessed.

"You're funny, kid," Daniel laughs. He studies my furrowed brow and my worried eyes as he leans forward, his arms on top of his notebook. "Don't turn away from your talents. Seeing spirits can be, well... frightening at times. But it can also be rewarding. You have the possibility to do great things. Don't be afraid of what you have been given."

"Sure," I mutter, unconvinced.

Daniel smirks as if he knows I don't believe what he said. But how can I? Everyone talks about these abilities being gifts. Everyone refers to them as special talents. All things considered equal, I'd rather have an aptitude for math or a killer pitching arm.

I DIDN'T THINK I WOULD FEEL BETTER AFTER MY MENTORING SESSIONS, but as the remainder of the weekend dwindles away, I realize my meetings with Daniel helped clear my head. I still don't know what I think of Camp Wanagi, but it's a relief to have shared my experiences and to have someone fully accept them as fact for the first time in my life.

After our time together on Saturday and Sunday, an objective for the summer worms its way into my mind. I don't like my talent, and I don't see what good it will ever do anyone. But Daniel appreciates his, and so do a lot of the other campers here. I want to understand why they're happy to be at this camp. I want to compare their experiences with my own to see if I'm missing something vital about my own ability or if I'm destined to forever hate the "gift" I've been given.

I make an honest attempt to write my paper for

Tuesday's class. I pick a shade from the 1700s, and I spend Sunday afternoon through to late Sunday night writing. The second week of courses goes by fast, the days slipping away like the fog hanging over the lake outside our lounge window on muggy evenings. Being here becomes routine faster than imagined. The following Monday night, I sit in bed, writing an email to my family as my sector mates fill the room with already familiar noises that mingle with the soft sounds of Vivaldi's "Guitar Concerto in D major".

"I don't care what you say," Dylan argues, one leg bent behind him as he completes his post-run stretches, "when I get to choose my final task in four years, I'm picking somewhere with beaches and five-star resorts."

"That's not the point," Naasir says, his voice low and quiet. He gives Dylan a disapproving frown while the shimmering black beetle on his arm inches towards his wrist. Naasir has a weird connection with insects. They flock to him, swarming around his head or slinking over his skin whenever he's outside.

Yesterday, a dragonfly *followed* him into the house. Reed hates the bugs and complains every time Naasir brings one inside. I don't mind, so long as he takes them back out before we go to sleep.

"Yeah, Dylan," Sefa agrees from the floor, where he's doing a round of push-ups. "We're supposed to pick the spirit, not the location."

Dylan scoffs. "There are spirits everywhere. Including beachside."

"You can come with me," Reed says from his spot on his bed. He's curled against the wall to keep as far away from Naasir's beetle as he can while still lounging on the same set of bunks. "I have to go to the ocean if I want to find someone who drowned."

I quirk an eyebrow and glance up from my email. "What about people who drown in bathtubs?"

"Or swimming pools," Meander adds from his bunk.

"Oh, yeah, I guess," Reed says.

"Or lakes," I muse.

"Ponds," Meander continues.

"Rivers."

"Marshes."

"Moats?"

"At least a handful in the loo."

"Okay, okay!" Reed mutters.

I smirk and share a knowing look with Meander. The scratches from Madame Roux's husband have gone now, and in the warmth of the room, his cheeks are tinged with pink. He looks as if he might say something else. But, in the space of a blink, his hazel eyes cloud, and he turns back to his book as if he'd never been a part of the conversation.

"Anyway, I expect I'll go to the ocean," Reed continues in a haughty voice. "That's the only place I've ever seen a ghost."

"How can you go your whole life seeing only one ghost?" Sefa asks.

Reed shrugs. "I live inland. Apparently, no one's drowned in my village. At least no one who turned into a ghost."

"But only one sighting...? How did you even get the Oracle's attention?" Sefa finishes his push-ups and flips over to start a set of crunches.

"No idea," Reed says. He puts down the assignment

he's working on for one of his courses and runs a hand through his frizzy, orange hair. "I barely even remember the one time I did see a ghost. The Oracle must have scouts everywhere."

I've never thought much about it, but I suppose Reed is right. There must be legions of people around the world searching for reports of kids like us. I wonder how they found me. The only obvious link I can come up with is Dr. Buchanan. Did my psychiatrist give someone my files? Or does the Oracle of Senders have access to whatever information they want, regardless of patient confidentiality?

"Well, whatever, I'll tag along with anyone going somewhere nice," Dylan remarks. He finishes his stretches and sits on his bed, unlacing his running shoes and peeling off his socks.

"Aw, man, I'm right here!" Sefa complains from the floor beside him.

Dylan smiles and wriggles his rank feet in Sefa's face, who pushes them away with a half-groan, half-laugh.

"Aren't you planning to pick your own ghost, though?" Reed asks.

Sefa sits up and begins his own stretches. Dylan runs twice a day, and Sefa works out any spare moment he can. I've gone running with Dylan a couple of times, but mostly watching these two exhausts me. I could be more active, but I prefer spending my time in other ways. When Dylan heads outside or Sefa turns the lounge into a makeshift gym, I yearn for the comfort of my violin.

I considered bringing it with me this summer, but figured it wouldn't be worth the stress of ensuring its safety. I wish I'd brought it, though. Listening to music helps me concentrate, but playing it smooths the creases in my life and revitalizes my mind whenever I'm worn down. I've been playing since I was four. My grandfather played, and he left me his violin when he died. I'm not sure what I would do without it.

"Pick my own?" Dylan shakes his head. "I see the ghosts of dogs. I can't do anything for them. So, I'll go with someone else. Carry the luggage or something."

"It's too early to plan your final task," Sefa says. "Haven't you heard? Everything changes when we turn sixteen."

"Yeah, what's that all about?" Dylan asks. It's been mentioned several times over the past two weeks, with leads, instructors, and campers alike offering vague hints about changes we won't see until our third summer here. I'm not convinced there's any change at all. I think it might be a big inside joke at the expense of the new kids.

"No one will offer up any details," Sefa says. He climbs up to his bunk and sits on the edge, his legs dangling down. When he speaks again, his deep voice is serious. "But have you noticed? The Wraith kids are... I don't know, different. Like, they're... This is going to sound stupid given the circumstances, but like they're bothered. They're haunted."

Naasir nods, eyeing Sefa before turning to study his beetle. I look at Dylan, who's pushed back on his bed and sitting with his feet stretched out in front of him. He returns my uncertain gaze. At least I'm not the only one who hasn't spotted the other campers' odd behavior.

"How can there be a change at sixteen?" Reed asks,

incredulous. "It's not like someone's got a spell on us or something. Nothing miraculous just *happens* when you turn sixteen."

"I don't think it's an exact science," Sefa replies. "I think it's like a second puberty. It hits us around sixteen, but that doesn't mean it's going to be a birthday present. Besides, there's no guarantee you'll even be here to make use of whatever the changes are. There are a lot fewer kids in the older years."

"But why?" Reed puts away his assignment and fishes out his phone. "If you've come here, why wouldn't you come back?"

"Things happen," Naasir says.

My fingers hover above the laptop's keyboard as I pause to take in Naasir's quiet words.

"Like what?" Reed asks.

"Like all sorts of things," Dylan replies. "People move, join other camps, meet someone not worth spending a summer apart from…"

"And some people might decide they don't want to hunt spirits for a living," I add in a mumble. I glance up to Reed's bed, but he's engrossed by something on his phone. I doubt he even heard me. I think I catch Meander staring from the corner of my eye, but when I turn to him, he is back to his reading.

The conversation ends, and for a while, the room settles. I focus on my email, drifting into answering my family's latest questions about camp and asking various questions about summer at home in return. I forget the others are in the room, so much so that I turn up the volume when my computer starts playing Mendelssohn's "Violin Concerto in E minor." One of my favorite pieces.

"Cal, seriously." Sefa's groan is instant, and I jump with a start. "Can't you put on some better music?"

"Better music?" I ask, feigning indignation. I'm used to having this argument. Not many people appreciate classical music. Especially not when they're fourteen. "There's nothing better than this."

"Everything is better," Sefa replies. "You're not eighty."

"What does being old have to do with appreciating good music?" I ask.

"It's not good," Sefa complains. "It's boring."

I turn the volume up to spite him. "How can you say it's boring?"

"Like this. It's *boring*."

"The music *is* lame, Cal," Dylan says with an apologetic shrug.

I roll my eyes. "Anyone else?"

Naasir shakes his head. "Leave me out of it," he mumbles.

"It's all horrible. I hate music, any kind," Reed says, slumping farther over his phone. "Just a lot of noise."

"What about you, Meander?" Sefa asks.

I tilt my head up to see Meander surveying me and Sefa in turn. He doesn't look as if he really wants to be a part of the discussion, either. But, to my surprise, he offers a few words in my defense.

"It's better reading music than anything you ever play," he says, flipping the page of his book and nestling against his pillow as if he's enjoying the ambiance of the orchestral performance.

I smile, glad at least one of my roommates is on my side. Sefa mumbles something I can't make out, but once I lower the volume a couple of slots he doesn't make any further complaints.

I play my music for another forty-five minutes, writing my email and catching up on social media. I scroll through endless messages and photos of my schoolmates on their summer vacations—some of them at beaches or cottages and some lazing about at home. I stay informed, but I don't participate. It's not like I can post a picture of the Shade Sector and give it some caption like: *Ghost Hunting FTW!* Besides, even if I could talk about my camp, I wouldn't. The people I know from school wouldn't care, and I wouldn't want to waste my time trying to get them interested. I guess I'm not supposed to, anyway.

It's not like I'm unpopular. Well, okay, maybe I am. But it's not like I'm totally alone day in and day out. I have people I talk to in classes, people I eat lunch with or sit with on the bus ride home from school. Most of them are acquaintances, and there are the occasional ones I might venture to call pals. But there's no one I'm close with. No one I stay in touch with over the summer. Usually, I go to camp, and meet new people there as I forget the people from school. When summer ends, the process is reversed. I could stay in touch if I wanted. I've just never had the desire.

I wonder if this year will be any different. When I leave this camp, will I stay in touch with my friends? I think so because I *do* think of them as my friends, a strange feat in itself.

Only when I shut down my computer for the night do I notice how quiet it's become and how dim. There are individual lights over each bunk, and when I'm ready to turn mine off, I realize the only other boy still awake is Meander.

"Night," I say as I reach for my own switch.

Meander doesn't reply—he never does—so I turn off my light and crawl under the covers. Snuggling down into the sheets, I smile as I close my eyes, the sounds of breathing, snoring, and rustling book pages remarkably like home.

12

"GATHER, YOUNG SENDERS, RIGHT HERE."

I crowd in with everyone else as Mr. Olenev beckons us to join him in the open air of a steady fall of rain. We've already spent the first twenty minutes of this *Basics of Gadgetry* lesson braving the flooded pave stones leading away from camp and tramping through endless puddles until we reached the outskirts of a nearby neighborhood. I appreciated the fact our instructor liked to send us outdoors for part of our lessons until now. Today it seems like a colossal joke to make us all stand under the rainfall, soaked through and shivering as we wait for him to explain himself.

"This, my dear campers," Mr Olenev calls once we're all settled.

His thick Russian accent carries over the pattering of rain, but as always it takes a moment to catch the rhythm and make sense of his words.

"This is an exceptional day for testing our thermal

readers."

"How is this an exceptional day for testing anything except the power of indoor heating?" Sefa mumbles, wiping a wet arm across his nose.

There are four Shades in this class, including me. Sefa, Lu, and Meander make up the rest, and in the first three and a half weeks of camp, I've yet to talk to Lu. She stands on the other side of the group, next to a Revenant girl whose name I can't remember.

I stay close to Sefa and Meander. I haven't socialized much with anyone else in the course. It's different with the other sectors. They've had time to get to know one another, and we're still trying to take it all in. I feel better being close to my roommates, even if Sefa is surprisingly serious when it comes to his schoolwork, and Meander is devoted to reading before, during, and after studies.

Right now, it's just nice to be close to other bodies. The July heat is masked by the biting rain, and we all huddle close to try to stave off the cold.

"We understand the theory of thermal readers," Mr. Olenev continues. His eyes smile as he talks, amused by our sour faces as we wait for more information. "They can tell us rises and dips in temperature, which can help determine areas of spiritual activity."

"So, why are we standing out in the rain?" Meander asks with annoyance.

I nudge him with my elbow, a caution for him not to interrupt. Mr. Olenev doesn't seem to mind, though. Our instructor never even flinches when a student talks out of turn.

"A good question, Mr. Rhoades!" He bends down to open the now soggy cardboard box he's carried outside with him. "One of the trickiest things for anyone using a thermal reader to determine is whether the readings are true representations of a spiritual presence or natural rises and dips in a location's temperature." He pulls out two identical thermal readers, the black handles leading up to small camera-like screens with a lens and a trigger on the front. "This is an old neighborhood," Mr. Olenev continues. "And a good place to hunt for spirits. So, today we will be splitting into two teams to use our thermal readers in an attempt to determine what's formerly living energy, and what's only a cold pocket or perhaps a cold bout of rain."

Mr. Olenev hands us the thermal readers as we split into two groups. I end up in the wholly unoriginal group of boys while the girls take the other reader. There are seven of us in total. Aside from the Shades, there's a Wraith named Connor, A Revenant named Ralli, a kid I still don't know, and a big, stony-faced boy named Tomas. Connor takes the device, and together, we set off in the opposite direction of our other course mates.

It's a nice neighborhood, and it'd be relaxing to wander around here on a sunny day. But the dreary weather is making us all miserable as we track the constant temperature changes of the air.

"Are we supposed to go into the buildings?" Sefa asks while Connor smacks the reader with his palm after it starts fluctuating near some house's front garden.

"Who cares?" Connor says, hitting the reader again. "This assignment is bogus. This whole camp is becoming more ridiculous every year."

I bury myself inside my Wanagi sweater, bracing against a gust of wind as Connor growls in frustration and drops the reader to his side.

"No kidding," the guy I don't know replies. "I don't think I'm even going to bother coming again next year."

"Aren't we supposed to be hunting ghosts? This classroom stuff is pointless, and everything else is even worse."

"What the hell do you think we're doing out here?" Meander says, his voice quiet but cutting through their conversation as if he'd shouted the words. "Going for a nice afternoon stroll?"

"We're not going to find any actual ghosts out here," Connor replies, rolling his eyes. "They always take us to these supposedly haunted places and try to scare us with a fake act. I think initiation this year was the worst. A complete joke, just a way to scare you newbies. Sad part is it worked, too. You're all so pathetic you start shaking in your boots as soon as someone mentions the word ghost."

I think about the night of the initiation, with its raging spirit and collapsing room. I can't believe someone could think it was fake. Staging all that would take way more effort than an initiation prank would be worth.

"I don't even know if I believe in ghosts," the other kid scowls. "I was sent here 'cause I'm supposed to have this power since when I was little I told my parents I saw people in our house or something. But I was a kid. Kids make stuff up all the time. Sometimes, I doubt if anyone here has ever seen an actual ghost."

I quirk an eyebrow and glance at Meander. He

walks hunched over, his arms crossed tightly against his chest in a useless attempt to keep warm. With the older boy's sour remark, he turns his head, and for a quick moment he catches my gaze. I don't know about most of the campers here, but I've seen plenty of spirits. And, from the first night of camp, I've been certain Meander has, too.

"If you hate it so much, leave," a solemn, heavy voice breaks in as Tomas stalks over to the others and grabs the machine from Connor's hands. "You may not see ghosts, but some of us do. For some of us, this is important."

His voice is so slow and purposeful, no one says anything in response. He considers the stunned boys, and then heads in a different direction, taking the reader with him.

I smile and follow along after Tomas.

"Idiots," Ralli says, once we've rounded a street corner and have left the two behind.

Everyone else from our group has come along as well, and now the five of us continue with our project.

"Some people never get it. Some people never have a clue."

"And some people can't even make their way back to camp on their own," Sefa chuckles, looking over his shoulder.

Connor and the other boy skulk a block behind us, keeping their distance but also keeping us in sight.

"Don't bother yourself about them," Ralli sighs, stepping up next to Tomas. "Let's get on with the assignment. The sooner we find something worth talking about, the sooner we can go back inside."

It's a task easier said than done. We wander for

another fifteen minutes with no luck, the reader's continuous dips and rises insignificant. By the time we reach a short street with a butcher's shop and a small café, the rain picks up, and the steady stream of the day turns into a torrential downpour crashing around our ears.

"Sod this!" Meander calls, veering off towards the café. He heads inside, out of the rain, and it only takes a second for the rest of us to hurry after him. The café is bright and warm, and the smell of coffee and bread are so nice I wish I'd brought money, so I could get something to eat or drink. Still, I'm happy to settle for sitting by the window until the rain lets up a bit. Although the older man standing behind the counter, the only other person in the café, isn't pleased to see five teenagers dripping all over his floor.

He says something to us in French, which I think might be along the lines of "buy something or get out", and with a sigh Meander heads to the counter and orders a tea. Sefa and Ralli join the line while Tomas and I sit at a table and watch as Connor and the other kid head towards the café as well.

I shake my head, glancing down at the table where Tomas has placed the thermal reader. The screen is showing temperatures far lower than the warm air of the café should suggest.

"Hey, look at this," I say, moving the reader over so Tomas can see it.

His hand shakes against the table top, and when I raise my eyes, I realize his face has turned a bloodless shade of white. His whole, massive figure is trembling, and I don't think it's from the rain.

I stand up and turn around, rushing into Meander

who only just manages to get his tea out of the way before I knock it out of his grasp.

"It helps if you look where you're—" Meander begins.

I cut him off, pointing at Tomas.

"The reader's showing cold," I say.

Meander's quick to understand, and his gaze darts around the room, a panicked expression giving way to one of confusion. I wonder if his bewilderment is because, like me, he expected to feel the temperature difference. Being on this side of things is unusual. I've never knowingly been around a ghost without being able to detect it. It's unsettling, maybe more unsettling than seeing the spirit would be. At least I don't feel sick, and my head is calm and clear. But Tomas's appearance is disturbing, his eyes glazing over and his body beginning to convulse.

"Is he having a seizure?" Sefa asks.

Ralli puts his drink on the table and kneels at Tomas's side. "No, this is how he changes," he says.

I don't understand what he means, but I'm glad one of us has a clue what's going on. Ralli leans in close and starts speaking to Tomas in a low whisper. I can't make out what he's saying, but the words don't seem to have any effect, anyway. Tomas continues to convulse until, all at once, his skin begins to bloom purple and his eyes roll back in his head.

"Oh, shit," Meander says.

I nod in agreement, the sentiment summing up my feelings perfectly. When the overhead lights start to blink and whine, the café worker comes roaring around the counter, shooing us towards the door and yelling in French.

"Cool it!" Sefa tells him, standing tall and making himself as bulky as possible. "He's in trouble!"

The man doesn't care. His mustache twitches as he motions for us to leave again.

"Let's get him and go," I say, moving around the far side of the table to approach Tomas.

He's big, and I'm not sure I can lift him. But, when I reach out to grab his arm, Ralli grabs hold of his other side, and between us we manage to get him on his feet.

"Come on Tomas, let's go," Ralli says, but with a single step Tomas falls forward, landing on the table and knocking it over on his way to the ground. Beverages spill everywhere, and Tomas begins to whimper as the café worker screams at the mess we've made.

"No, no, no," Ralli says, leaning down to Tomas. "This isn't good. This is *not* good."

"What's going on?" I ask. "Is this how he sees spirits?"

"He doesn't see them," Ralli says, sitting up on his knees and raking his fingers through his wet hair. "They overtake him."

"What, are we talking possession?" Meander asks.

Ralli winces. "Not exactly," he says, the words uncertain. "It's more like...they use him to give themselves power."

Tomas's whimper becomes louder, working itself into a high-pitched groan. I think the café worker is threatening to call the police now, but none of us care. Tomas's skin goes from purple to black, and the groan drops in pitch as it rises in volume. All at once, the temperature in the room plummets, and a heavy smell of yeast explodes in the air as Tomas's back arches and a misty form presses outwards from his body.

I stagger back, the stench so complete it's like being in a building constructed of raw dough. I cover my nose, and watch in awe as the spirit breaks loose of Tomas and makes a mad dash around the café.

Meander's managed to keep hold of his tea thus far, but the spirit goes for it, knocking it from his grasp and sending hot liquid flying through the air. Then it heads for the counter, its voice an inaudible whine of static that's coming not from within my head but outside of it. The spirit pushes and pulls at whatever it can, sending cups and saucers crashing to the floor, making the man in charge of the café cower in the corner.

"Help me get Tomas up!" Ralli calls.

The three of us who are still standing break our stupors and help pull Tomas to a sitting position. He's regaining consciousness now, and it only takes twenty or thirty seconds before he's well enough to stand and survey the damage being done by the wild spirit.

"It's using the energy too fast," Ralli says, his tone mild, like the café is not in a state of total destruction. "It won't last long."

He's right. Almost as soon as it appeared, the spirit's frantic figure begins to dissipate. It continues its tirade around the café, but soon it can no longer manipulate the plates or utensils. The yeast smell dissolves into the normal scents of coffee and properly baked bread. The static disappears, and in a blink, the spirit does, too. The whole episode is over in less than a minute, and the horrendous mess in the café is all that remains.

"We should go," Ralli says, eyeing the café worker who's still cowering in the corner. "We'll tell Mr.

Olenev what happened. He'll help us deal with…" he motions around him, and shrugs. "With this."

"Shouldn't we stay to help clean up?" I ask, but when the café worker overhears our words, he raises his head and begins another streak of loud French I'm sure is not full of the politest language.

"I think leaving is the better option," Sefa says, and with apologetic stares we sidle to the door and push our way back out into the rain. As soon as our feet hit the pavement, we break into a run, going about three blocks before we slow down to catch our breath.

Only once we're stopped do we realize Connor and the other kid have followed us again. They gawk at Tomas in terror, like he's a demon who just threw a few curses.

"Real enough for you now?" Meander asks in the driest voice I think he could possibly manage.

I smirk, glad the two have the decency to avert their gazes in embarrassment.

13

"WAS HE REALLY POSSESSED?"

Mim sits on the edge of one lounge sofa, her voice swaying between a whisper and a low mumble. She came into the lounge halfway through me telling Dylan and Kornelía what happened to Tomas this afternoon in the café.

"Sort of...uh, temporarily, I guess," I say, trying to remember how Ralli explained it. "They use his energy."

"He's like a power-boost," Dylan says, sounding stuck between being impressed and being horrified.

"And he's okay with it?" Mim asks, incredulous. "Is he honestly sticking around even after something like that?"

"As far as I know." I shrug. "He didn't seem too bothered by it. But, of course, we were more worried about getting away from the man working the café to dwell on his feelings about what happened."

"He's crazy if he hangs around," Dylan says from beside me. "If that happened to me, I'd be out of here as soon as my bags were packed."

"I'd stay," Kornelía muses, pressing a sketchbook to her chest while she considers the possibility of having a talent like Tomas's. "I'd want to use my ability to help."

"Help the spirit who possessed you?" Dylan scoffs, shaking his head. "Tomas could die from something like that."

It's not true, at least not as far as Dylan or any one of us knows. But Kornelía's not bothered by the prospect, even if she does believe there's truth to Dylan's words.

"It's our calling," she says, sounding almost hurt by Dylan's mortified tone. "It's what we're here to do."

"You can do whatever you want. *I* didn't sign-up for getting possessed by ghosts."

"Yeah, well, Tomas must agree with Korni," Mim says. "I just saw him downstairs, working on a research paper."

"He's crazy!" Dylan exclaims.

"He's doing what he's meant to do," Kornelía shoots back. Her cheeks flush with the burst of ferocity, and she stands, walking to the fireplace and keeping her back to the rest of us.

"For someone who can't see ghosts, she sure has a strong opinion on the matter," Mim says, her words sharp.

"Maybe that's why," Dylan says. "If she ever saw what we do, she wouldn't be so quick to say it's our *calling*."

Kornelía's back tenses, and it's obvious she can hear every word they're saying.

"Guys!" I snap, annoyed my friends are being so callous. They know as well as I do how much Kornelía wishes she could see spirits. "You said it yourself, Mim. Tomas is still here and still working on course assignments. So, obviously he has the same ideas about our *calling* as Kornelía. It doesn't matter if she can't see spirits outright. At least she's here for the right reason. She's not mooching off the Oracle, enjoying the all-expenses-paid vacation with no intention of being a Sender after it's done."

I stop, surprised by my own words. I'm not sure I want to return to this camp next summer, and I have great doubts about ever wanting to work for the Oracle of Senders. I hardly have any right to make such a comment, one I'm sure Dylan knows is directed at him and his careless attitude about this camp.

I expect him to be angry, but instead he only grins.

"Woah." He laughs, slapping me on the back. "I didn't know you felt so strongly about it, buddy."

"Neither did I," I mumble.

The splintered door to the Shade lounge creaks open and Naasir and Sabeena walk into the room with smiles on their lips and an upbeat energy in their steps.

"Hey," Sabeena says, giving us a wave as she rounds the far sofa and plops down onto it.

"You're in a good mood," Mim says.

She eyes Naasir and gives Sabeena a smirk, but Sabeena rolls her eyes at Mim's suggestive glance.

"We saw an Entity contact a spirit," Sabeena says. "Experiencing a Sender making contact without seeing the ghost itself was thrilling."

"Cal here saw a Wraith kid possessed this afternoon,"

Dylan chimes in.

"He wasn't *possessed*," I try to explain again.

"I heard about that," Naasir says, his quiet voice warm and complacent.

He spins a ring on his right pinkie, an accessory I've never noticed before. The yellow rock has something black in its middle, and I squint, trying to make out what's in it. I don't need to, though. Dylan's closer, and he deciphers it before I do.

"Is that a dead insect on your finger?" he asks, his voice only a little dismayed, like he's resigned himself to the truth already.

Naasir smiles, admiring the fossilized chunk of amber. "Mrs. Buxley gave it to me," he says, running a finger over its surface. "She said I might find it interesting. She was right."

"Your first collection," Kornelía smiles, twisting around to study the ring.

Naasir gives her a quizzical stare, and she shakes her head.

"It's nice," she says instead. "Mrs. Buxley was kind to give it to you."

"Mrs. Buxley's always encouraging our talents," Sabeena beams.

Mrs. Buxley is our Basics of Paranormality instructor. It's the only class all ten Shade kids are in together.

"She said we'll be taking the next step in our studies soon." She pulls her legs up, so she's sitting cross-legged on the sofa.

"What the hell does that mean?" Dylan asks.

Sabeena shrugs. "I don't know," she says, "but I suspect it's got something to do with our final assignment. I can't wait to start seeing spirits again.

I'm not used to going this long without contact. It was a nice break at first, but now…it's strange. It's like something's wrong."

I don't think I'd ever feel that way if I stopped seeing spirits. Having no contact would be odd, and for a while I might wonder if I was sick or something. But I wouldn't miss it, not like Sabeena's obviously missing her contact.

"I still say assignments over the summer should be outlawed," Dylan mutters.

"I'm sure you'll survive a few more papers," Kornelía teases, forgetting the rude comments he and Mim made a moment ago. She returns to the group, sitting on the floor with her pad of paper still pressed to her.

"Besides, you shouldn't approach it as work," Sabeena says. "It's practice. A chance to better our skills."

"She's right," Mim agrees. "We're here to learn. We can't do that if we spend all day sleeping and running around the neighborhood."

Dylan balks at the unsubtle hint. "Hey, I need to run to burn off energy to sleep, and I need to sleep to rest up, so I can run," he protests. "It's a delicate balance."

Mim laughs and gives him a playful shove before she raises her hands above her head in a stretch. "Whatever. For now, I think I need coffee. Want to come?" she asks, pressing Dylan's knee as she stands.

"Yeah, sure," he smirks.

Kornelía raises her head like she's going to say she wants to go as well, but when she catches the look between the two, her shoulders sink in a silent sigh, and she retreats back to the fireplace.

"I'm going to write in my journal," Sabeena says, giving Naasir a smile as she stands. "I want to jot down all the details before I forget."

Naasir nods and gives her a wave.

I don't consider myself a grand conversationalist, but compared to Naasir, I'm positively chatty. He studies his ring, turning it about on his finger so the amber catches glints of light from the fireplace, and I pull out my phone and unravel my earbuds. It's nearly 11:30, but my mind's too full of what happened this afternoon, and of what Sabeena suggested might happen soon in Basics of Paranormality, to fall asleep. The hours here are shifted, everything happening later in the day. Classes start at noon, and the kitchen serves food until midnight. It's not unusual for campers to hang out in the library or out in the back garden until the early hours of morning, and I don't think I've gone to sleep earlier than 1:00 am since our first week here.

I recline back on the sofa and listen to Korngold's "Violin Concerto". After a few minutes, Naasir goes into our room. Lu makes a brief appearance, saying something to Kornelía I can't make out over my music before disappearing back out into the main part of the château. A while after that, Meander comes into the lounge with a mug in one hand and a book tucked under the same arm.

He sits on the sofa adjacent to me, resting his mug on the armrest and opening his book, a green-clothed volume with the mark of the Oracle's library on the spine. I close my eyes, trying to envelop myself in the music, but thoughts and questions won't stop tumbling through my mind. I want to talk, but it's hard with people who don't understand—who feel so differently about this place than I do.

My foot starts tapping against air, and I pull one earbud out. I don't look to my left where Meander is probably engrossed in his reading. I stare straight ahead and open my mouth as if no one will be annoyed with me disturbing the quiet of the lounge.

"Do you think he was always like that?" I ask, thinking of the way Tomas's skin turned purple and then black, and the way he convulsed on the ground, unable to even try to get away from the spirit's hold. "Or do you think that's what happened when he turned sixteen?"

There's no answer at first. From the corner of my eye I see Kornelía lift her head, but she knows the question is not directed at her. I twist the loose earbud in my fingers, and am about to give up and slip it back in when Meander replies.

"I don't know. But, if I were to guess, I'd say he's always had the ability. Only…perhaps not like that. Not so strong."

I nod, my foot losing its rhythm and bouncing in a nervous jitter.

"It's scary, isn't it?" I ask, my voice a low mumble I'm not sure is even decipherable. But, this time, there's no hesitation.

"Yeah, it is," he says in a voice just as quiet.

By the fire, Kornelía has dropped her head again and is back to whatever she's doing with the sketchpad. I slip my earbud back in, and I close my eyes once more.

What happened to Tomas today was not only surprising, it was a grim reminder that seeing spirits is anything but fun. Sabeena might be excited for Mrs. Buxley's promise of taking our studies to the next level, but for me, being assigned a spirit as coursework feels a bit like being thrown to the wolves when all the other animals have fled the forest. I don't know if Tomas was ever afraid of his ability, though I can't imagine how he wouldn't have been, at first. Even if he wasn't, at least I know there's someone here who is. A poor concession, I suppose. But comforting, nonetheless.

14

"WELCOME EVERYONE," MRS. BUXLEY SAYS, STRIDING INTO OUR NEXT Basics of Paranormality session. I pull the cap off my pen, ready to take notes, nervous about what she's going to teach us. This is the course Sabeena's been excited for. I can see her beaming at our instructor now, and it makes me uneasy.

Mrs. Buxley waits for the room to settle. The ten of us from Shade make up the entire class, which usually means this is my most enjoyable course. I know these kids better than anyone else at camp. Even Lu, who I don't talk to, is familiar.

"Now." Our instructor sits at her desk, her hands cupped together on the desk's top. "This is your fifth week at Camp Wanagi. Believe it or not, that means you're halfway through the summer."

I haven't paid much attention to the passage of time here, but as I think through the weeks, I realize Mrs. Buxley is right. This is the fifth of ten weeks of camp.

It's gone by so fast, I'm stunned. I feel like I've just arrived. I want—I *need*—to figure out so much more before I return to Canada in August.

"And, to celebrate the achievement of making it halfway through your first summer with the Oracle, I thought I would start today's course on a special topic." She wears peach-colored lipstick, a warm compliment to her dark skin and nearly shaved black and grey peppered hair. Her lips shimmer under the lights of the classroom as she talks. "Today, we'll discuss the project you've all been anxious for. Your final task of the summer, working to release a spirit."

The class breaks into excited chatter. Mim and Kornelía lean toward each other as they whisper amongst themselves. I glance at Dylan, he glances at me, and we look back at Mrs. Buxley.

"Because this is your first major project," she says over the clamour in the room, restoring the quiet with her sturdy voice, "you won't be expected to go at it alone. Your mentors, leads, other instructors, and I will be there to support you."

"What do we have to do?" Sabeena asks. Her black hair lies over her shoulder in a long, sleek ponytail, the end twirled about her finger as she waits for a response.

"Each case is different, but the general idea of this assignment is to find a spirit, discover what its unfinished business is, and if possible, release it." Mrs. Buxley's tone is conversational, but my stomach drops as if she's given us horrible news.

I guess, for someone like me, she has. Before Sabeena brought it up last week, I'd almost forgotten about the final assignment.

"We can't do that," Reed says. He fidgets in his seat. "We're not prepared to free a ghost."

"Which is why you'll have help," Mrs. Buxley replies. She smiles at us, standing from her desk and pulling a yellow folder from the desk drawer. "Trust me. You'll be fine. You're not the first set of campers to do this, and you won't be facing any spirit on your own. You'll be working with some of your fellow Shades as well."

"But—" Reed begins.

Mrs. Buxley's outstretched hand cuts him off. "First, we'll separate into teams," she says, ignoring Reed's worried frown. "Since there are ten of you, we'll have two groups of five. If you can manage it without arguing, I'll let you choose the teams yourselves. Let me know when you've made your choices."

I glance around the room, knowing the division won't be difficult. Lu and Sabeena will work together, which means Naasir will work with them, too. Sefa won't want to work with Dylan—his serious style will clash with Dylan's easy-going attitude—so he'll choose to be with the other group. Which leaves Reed and Meander, one indifferent to his team members, the other probably not caring if he has team members at all.

I can see Mim staring across the room, working the teams out for herself. She tries to make eye contact with Reed, wanting to secure him for our group. But Reed's oblivious to her stare, and behind him, Lu's frowning, her gaze spiteful as she raises her hand to steal Reed as a team member first.

I shoot my hand up, attracting Mrs. Buxley's attention before she notices Lu.

"Callum?" Mrs. Buxley asks.

Mim swivels in her seat to face me, but not without first catching Lu's angered expression. Mim grins and offers Lu a smug smile.

"Our team will be me, Dylan, Kornelía, Mim, and Meander," I say evenly.

Mim fixes me with a look of shocked indignation, but I ignore it. She doesn't like Meander. His silence and lack of reaction to anything she's ever said aggravates the short fuse of her temper. But, if I picked Reed, Lu would bemoan the fact her team lost the camper she wanted, making Meander the unnecessary loser all because of a growing rivalry between the two girls. Besides, I can't deny how much this assignment terrifies me, and when it comes to working with a real spirit, I'd prefer Meander as a teammate. Reed's only seen one ghost in his life, an event he hardly remembers. Meander knows more about experiencing ghosts first-hand, a valuable quality when two of my other teammates can't even see spirits of the human variety.

"Good," Mrs. Buxley nods, writing our names down on a sheet of paper. "Is this agreeable to everyone else?" she asks, peering around the room.

Mim looks like she wants to protest, but I suspect she knows if she does, it'll confirm Lu's got the better of her. So, she stays quiet, as do all the other campers, and Mrs. Buxley nods again before writing the remaining Shades' names for the other team.

When she's finished making her notes on our teams, our instructor places her pen on the desk and folds her arms. "Now then, let's get into the details," she says, each word smooth and deliberate like she's rehearsed everything she's about to recite.

"Each team will be assigned one potential spirit. I say *potential* spirit because, although you'll be assigned to a place with high reports of paranormal activity, it will be up to you to make actual contact.

"Of course, since each camper has his or her own unique talent, your team will have to elect one person to be in charge of making that contact. The other team members will assist, using devices and doing research to help identify the spirit and understand its needs. We'd love for you all to face your own spirit, and eventually you will all have the opportunity to do so. But working as a team is important.

"You need to develop your skills and knowledge of the spiritual world before you're ready to tackle a ghost alone. Make no mistake, releasing spirits is difficult, and I know some of you have already seen how it can be dangerous too. Lean on one another for support. Never be afraid to ask for help."

I swallow, my nerves slightly appeased by knowing I might not be the one facing a spirit. Research I can handle. But I can't release a ghost, even if I do have others helping. Maggie's image swims into focus, but I blink her away. She was different, unintentional. I can't simply find a spirit and free it as part of an *assignment*.

Luckily, I don't think I'll have to. At least not yet. Kornelía can't see ghosts, and Dylan can't communicate with the ones he does. I still don't know what Meander's talent is, but judging by his brooding manner and the scar on his face—not to mention the contact I know he had with the spirit our first night here—I'm positive he's not keen to take center stage, either. But Mim, on the other hand, likes to take control. If my guess is right, she'll jump at the chance to be in charge.

"We'll ask for volunteers from each team to be the communicator," Mrs. Buxley says.

To my unsurprised relief, Mim raises her hand without hesitation. No one else from our group follows her movement, which suits Mim well. She grins as Mrs. Buxley marks her down.

The other group takes longer to decide. Sefa, Lu, and Sabeena all want to be the leader. They argue for ten minutes without getting anywhere, so Mrs. Buxley offers the rest of us a break while they sort it out.

"What do you think we'll have to do?" Kornelía asks as we step out into the hallway.

"Hopefully, not much," Dylan replies. He kicks his feet as he walks like he's kicking at an invisible rock. "I didn't come to camp to have assignments."

"Yeah, we know," Kornelía mutters.

Dylan sulks in silence as we continue down the hall.

"Do you think we'll have to face the spirit on our own?" I ask. "Without any instructors or leads or anything?"

Kornelía tucks her hair back behind her big ears, and gives me a meek smile. "I guess that's what we're training for," she says in her light, mousy voice. "They probably think we're ready...a lot of the Shades have seen ghosts before, after all."

"Yeah, but seeing them and freeing them are two different things," I reply. I stuff my hands into the pockets of my jeans and try to smile. "We don't need to worry, though. Mim will be happy to make contact, won't you?"

"Of course," Mim says with satisfaction. "You can

all rest easy. You've got me on your team."

"Yeah, but we've also got that Rhoades kid," Dylan mutters. He turns to me, the dark circles under his eyes almost black in the dim light of the hallway. "Why did you stick him in our group, anyway?"

"So there wouldn't be a fight over Reed." I shrug. I don't mention what I know about Meander's experiences with spirits. Everyone was there during the initiation. They should remember what happened. "I just saved him the embarrassment of being the last picked."

"Shh," Kornelía warns.

The hairs on my neck prickle as footsteps come up behind us. In seconds, Meander pushes between Dylan and I, barging through our group without a word.

"What was that about saving him embarrassment?" Dylan remarks.

Meander takes the steps of the nearest staircase two at a time, and I try to keep my sigh inaudible.

15

DANIEL KNOWS HOW WORRIED I AM ABOUT OUR FINAL TASK, EVEN WITH Mim in charge. He suggests I search through the library's materials to find past Senders who had a talent like my own. He thinks it will help me connect to the world of the Oracle if I can figure out where my abilities fit into it. So, in the hour between when my mentoring session on Saturday ends and our first official group meeting for the summer's final task begins, I gather volumes of records on the history of people with paranormal abilities.

I flip through endless pages, my earbuds in and filling my head with symphonies from centuries ago. The other guys might make fun of me, but music helps me focus. It blocks out the abundant noises of everyday life and allows me to escape to a place where I can concentrate on the task at hand. Songs with lyrics distract me, and compositions with funky soundscapes or modern instrumentation irritate my subconscious.

Orchestral pieces have long been pivotal to my best moments of reflection and study.

My head bobs along to the happy rhythm of Franz Schubert's "Rosamunde Overture" as my eyes scan the pages. The index of one book directs me to a section on people with the ability to interact, in some way, with the spirits of murder victims. Not everyone listed in the section could see them, like I do. Some just devoted their lives to researching them, and some entries are for the ghosts themselves, their biographies compiled after someone else studied their presence. But there's a minute collection of people who shared a talent close to what I possess. After searching for half an hour, I've managed to find three.

The first was a man named Basil Radithorpe, who lived in England in the 1700s. He'd been put in an asylum at the age of twenty-three because he ranted about seeing the spirits of those who had been killed. But the hauntings continued in the asylum, and after insisting the warden had killed someone in his wing, Radithorpe died under suspicious circumstances. Apparently, he became a spirit but was released in the 1970s.

The second was a woman from a family called Nishi though her name is not listed in the book. She lived in Japan in the 1500s, but the book has only a vague report about her. She supposedly shared a house with a whole family of murdered ghosts for nearly twenty years, interacting with them as if they were still alive. The book doesn't mention what happened to her. If someone found out how she was carrying on, I can't imagine her story ended well.

The third entry I find is more recent, about a Polish

man named Antoni Burak, who lived until 1954. When he wasn't working on his own cases, he travelled from Poland to South Africa in an attempt to find enough evidence to support creating an organization devoted to teaching young Senders the art of releasing spirits. His contributions eventually led to the official establishment of Camp Wanagi in 1962.

Basil Radithorpe and the Nishi woman's stories make me uncomfortable. If I had lived when Radithorpe did, I might have suffered a similar fate. I had years of therapy as it was, and if it weren't for the Oracle, I'd still be visiting Dr. Buchanan every week, trying to work out why I kept "imagining" people who had died. And the Nishi account is disturbing.

Spirits make me physically ill. I can't fathom living with them day-to-day, especially if they showed the mark of their deaths. Depending on who murdered them and how, the apparitions may have been stained with distortions of blade wounds or burn patches. Seeing them would be a constant reminder of their grisly demise. Plus, I can't shake the feeling this book is leaving out certain details, like how maybe the girl killed the family herself.

But Antoni Burak's entry is interesting. He had a talent like mine, and he laid the groundwork for the summer camp I'm now attending. I didn't expect Daniel's exercise to have any real effect on me, but I spend a long time reading through Burak's entry. I don't know if I feel particularly connected to him, but it's nice to know he existed.

I read through the records for most of the hour, only giving my eyes a break and looking around the room ten minutes before our group is supposed to meet.

The library is mostly empty, except the librarian at her desk and another camper at a nearby table. It takes me a moment to realize the camper is Kornelía.

I turn off my music and stand, stretching my arms above my head as I make my way over to where she sits. Dozens of papers are spread over the table around her, and when I get close enough, I see they're pencil sketchings. Kornelía doesn't hear my approach, so I take the opportunity to study the sketches before she notices I'm near.

The drawings are of spirits, the images sort of half-present on the paper. Their outlines are smudged, their expressions sometimes clearly formed and other times not visible at all. Each drawing accents different aspects of the bodies, and a couple are so unformed they're almost like abstract interpretations of what a person might look like.

The illustrations are unlike anything I've ever seen on paper before. But they're exactly like things I've seen in person. I could never hope to explain how a ghost looks to someone who's never seen one. But with drawings like these, I wouldn't have to.

"These are incredible."

Kornelía jumps, a mousy squeak escaping her throat. The sound reminds me of the noises Rose makes when I find her during hide-and-seek. I smile and come around to sit at the far side of the table.

"Hi, Cal," Kornelía breathes. "I saw you working back there when I came in, but I didn't want to bother you."

"I didn't know you drew," I say. I take one of the many papers sprawled over the table, and glance up to see Kornelía blushing.

"I don't," she mumbles, her head bent. "I mean, I do, but...I only draw when I'm distracted or bored. I don't do it for any real reason. I don't think I'm an artist or anything. I'm not, anyway. I only draw for fun."

"You draw ghosts," I say, keeping my tone casual and pretending I don't notice how uncomfortable she is.

"Sometimes," Kornelía nods. She pushes hair back behind one ear and begins rooting through her bag for something. "Most of the time," she corrects herself with a shrug.

"But I thought you couldn't see ghosts?"

Kornelía takes an elastic out of her bag and pulls her hair up, several strands immediately falling out and framing her face. "I can't." She smiles.

"Have you seen pictures? Or, well, how do you..." I study the drawing in front of me—a sketch of a ghostly young girl. It reminds me of Maggie. I sort of wish I had a picture like this of her. She's the only spirit I don't mind remembering.

"No, I..."

I look up and Kornelía's eyes shift away.

"I take the images from my mind," she finishes, saying the words as if she suspects them to sound pathetic.

I wonder what makes her shy away from the explanation. The drawings I see here are anything but pathetic.

"These are really, *really* good," I tell her as earnestly as I can. "These spirits... They are just like the ones I've seen."

Kornelía's eyes narrow as she watches me. "Honestly?" She sounds hopeful, like she's always wondered how accurate her drawings are.

"Yeah, definitely." I peer around the table, my eyes catching on one of the pictures. I drop the drawing of the girl back onto the table, and snatch up the sketch of a woman wearing trousers, the hips billowing out below her waist. The spirit has half-formed hair set in a tight bun, a few loose wisps lying across her cheek. She also has a long mouth, and in the drawing, she's mid-word, her foggy lips open in a moan.

"I've seen this ghost before," I mumble, concentrating on the lines of the sketch. A memory of cheddar lingers on the back of my tongue. "It's Madame Roux, the spirit from the initiation, isn't it?"

The pink blush on Kornelía's cheeks deepens, her tawny eyes shining.

"Yes," she whispers like she doesn't believe her own words. "It is." She stares at me, her mouth opening and closing several times before she lets out a big puff of air. "I envision the ghosts," she says in a rush. "When I know a place is haunted, I picture what the ghosts might look like." She takes a shaky breath, her fingers straying to the strands of hair by her face. She pushes them behind her ear and bows her head.

"I've never told anyone that...I know when a place is haunted, but I also know if the ghost is a girl, a boy, a man, or a woman. And, sometimes, I know what style of clothing they have on, too. Or their hairstyle. Or how sad they seem. But that's all in my head, so I figure it's just my imagination, right?"

"I don't think so," I say slowly, staring first at the picture before my gaze shifts to Kornelía. "Maybe you *can* see spirits, after all. You just see them in your mind, instead of with your eyes."

"No, that couldn't be..." She starts to collect the drawings, her expression panicked.

"You should tell your mentor," I say, watching her hurried gathering, "or one of the instructors. We could even tell Alex or Robbie. And—"

"*No*, Cal." Kornelía cuts me off, her words surprisingly sharp. She stares into my eyes as she reaches out and snatches away the drawing I hold. "I don't have a talent like that. I can tell if somewhere is haunted, that's all. These drawings are something I do for fun. They don't mean anything. Got it?"

"But..."

"*Got it?*"

Her voice is so fierce I can only nod, despite my desire to press her further. Her ability is astonishing, and I don't understand why she's so nervous about even discussing it. If Dylan were here, he'd crack jokes and jostle her into shyly talking about it. And Mim would be relentless until Kornelía explained the details just to get the other girl to be quiet. But I'm not like my friends. I want to talk to her about it, and I want to see the other drawings she's created. But she doesn't want to share those things with me. So, I watch her gather the sketches in silence, a million questions mixing with the remembered scent of cheese until it all dissolves into nothing.

I get up and return to my own table, putting away my phone and replacing the paranormal record books on the shelf. By the time I re-join Kornelía, the drawings are gone. She doesn't acknowledge me when I sit back down. She keeps her head bent low, scribbling on a pad of paper and acting like I'm not there.

Meander's the first of the remaining group members

to arrive for the meeting. He sits at one end of the table, with a small black binder open in front of him and his pencil tapping a distracted rhythm against the table top. He's never been one for pointless conversation, but since he overheard me explaining why I picked him for our group, Meander's been especially silent. It's awkward, the three of us sitting together, no one saying a word. I open my notebook and watch the clock, waiting for Dylan and Mim to arrive. They, at least, will talk.

The two arrive together, five minutes after three. They laugh as they come into the library, their bodies close and their joke private. They grin at the rest of us as they sit side-by-side.

"All right, let's get this going," Mim says as soon as she's seated. Her black hair is pulled back, and the two pink streaks curve from her temples in towards the clip holding the hair in place.

"You're the one with all the information." Dylan smirks. "So, go ahead."

"Right," Mim says. "Well, I'm taking a trip next week with Lani. We're going to scout for a target." Lani is Mim's mentor. They've been meeting all week to talk about potential cases.

"So, what does that mean for us?" Kornelía asks.

"Well, once we have a spirit, I'll act as the, um…" She snaps her fingers, trying to come up with the right word. "The translator, I guess. I'll tell you it's problem, and we'll go from there. Mrs. Buxley suggested we divide the rest of you into two groups. One will do research on the ghost, and the other will work with the equipment on the night of the release."

Kornelía makes a note on her paper and looks back

at Mim. "So, who will be doing what?"

"I'm doing the equipment!" Dylan exclaims.

I have a feeling Dylan and Mim decided this fact long before meeting with the rest of us. It's annoying they made the decision without anyone else's input, but I'm relieved Dylan's picked the equipment group. Having him as a researcher could end up being catastrophic.

Kornelía smiles at Dylan, an adoring expression which lingers several seconds too long. Meander, on the other hand, looks at no one. His head of curly hair bends over his binder, and I'm surprised he doesn't have a novel open in front of him like the kid in school with a comic tucked inside a textbook.

"Kornelía, what do you want to do?" I ask with a sigh.

Kornelía pulls her gaze to me, her eyes wide. She hesitates for an instant, her expression suspicious as if she fears I'm going to bring up our earlier conversation. But it passes, and she pushes hair behind her ear again as she gives Dylan a sideways glance.

"Well," she begins, "I could do research or..."

Left with the distinct impression her interests lay elsewhere, I tell her, "You help Dylan with the equipment."

Dylan eyes me in surprise. "You sure?" he asks. "I thought you were into the gadgets."

I do like the technology, but there will be other opportunities to try out gadgets at Camp Wanagi if I want them. Right now, I'd rather focus on getting the groups organized, so I know exactly what role I'll play when we face Mim's chosen spirit.

"It's fine. I like research, too," I say, which is also

true. I don't like seeing ghosts, but I enjoyed searching through books this afternoon, seeking out names and reading about Sender and spirit lives.

"All right then, that settles it," Mim says, slapping the table in front of her. "I'll find the ghost, Dylan and Korni will run the machines, and Cal and Meander will find the facts. Sounds fun, huh?"

"Better than a free pass to an amusement park," Dylan says with an almost blasé smile.

Mim gives him a serious stare which lasts for about three seconds before it cracks into a laugh.

16

"RISE AND SHINE, SHADE!"

Sefa groans from the bunk above me. "Oh, you've got to be kidding."

Robbie hovers in our doorway, laughing at our collective grumbling as we're forced awake at four in the morning.

"Come on. Come on." He laughs, flicking the main light switch on and off until Sefa throws a pillow at him. Robbie catches it, throws it back, and Sefa groans again.

Rubbing my eyes, I stare at the wall until I can process my surroundings enough to know why Robbie's waking us up so early. Once the world is no longer blurry, I double-check the time on my phone and attempt to yawn my exhaustion away.

"You've got thirty minutes," Robbie says, giving the light a final switch to the *on* position.

His brown mohawk has been dyed and the tips

are now frosted a deep red like bloodied spikes. Considering Robbie is one of the best-tempered people I've ever met, it's an odd impression.

"We've got to leave by four-thirty if we want to make the six o'clock train up to Paris."

"I've changed my mind," Dylan mutters, "I don't want to see Paris that badly."

"Yes, you do," Robbie says, his voice far too cheerful for the early hour. "Now, get up."

He leaves the room, shutting the door behind him. I roll onto my back, stretching my legs and yawning again as Dylan drags himself up to a sitting position.

"Like, I physically can't get up," Sefa says, his voice heavy with sleep. "I only went to bed three hours ago."

"I told you not to stay up so late," Reed says.

He and Naasir are awake and sitting up. I sit up, too, rubbing my head and flexing my feet as I place them on the cool floor.

A sightseeing trip to Paris sounded great at the beginning of the summer, but Camp Wanagi starts late in the morning and ends late at night. Most of the year I'm up by six-thirty to get ready for school. But, for the past six weeks, I've been waking up around ten, and it's taken a toll.

We're quiet as we shuffle about, getting ready. We take turns at the dresser and in the bathroom until, one-by-one, we stumble out into the lounge to meet the girls—who look as sleep-deprived as we do. Robbie and Alex seem to be the only ones well-rested, and they usher us outside like they're herding a pack of zombies. It's a miracle no one falls into the lake on their way to the mainland. The trip across the stones feels twice as long with everyone dragging their feet.

We take a bus to the train station, and from there, it's a two-hour train ride to Paris. Most of the trip is spent sleeping, or else eating the fruit and pastries our leads brought with them from the house. I keep my earbuds in the entire time, Mozart soothing me to sleep and Bach helping to wake me up.

When we arrive in Paris, we're led off the train and into the line for another bus. There, our leads make a renewed attempt to wake us.

"Good morning, everyone!" Alex says, a bright smile on her lips as she turns around to face the crowd of campers.

"Morning," comes a sleepy reply from the group.

"Is everybody ready for our trip today?" Robbie asks from beside Alex.

There's another grumbled reply, and Robbie claps his hands together, the sound making the nearest campers jump.

"Good!" he exclaims, but in his excitement, it comes out sounding more like *Gud*.

Alex explains the agenda for the day while I try my best to stand up straight and keep my eyes open. I wouldn't think I could fall asleep standing up, but it's proving to be not an impossible concept.

"We'll be starting our tour in a few moments. The bus will take us through the city streets, past the Paris Opera House, and down the Avenue des Champs-Élysées," Alex says. "Then, we'll head over to the Eiffel Tower, past a couple of other sites and museums, and at the end of the tour the bus will drop us off outside of the Louvre at twelve. We'll eat in the gallery and tour the exhibits before we head back to the train station late this afternoon."

There's a bustle behind us as two other groups of people line up for the same bus we're about to board. I didn't realize our sightseeing trip would be so crowded. I'm not even sure there will be enough seats on the bus for us all.

"Forget this."

I hear the mumbled words coming from my left and shift my gaze in time to watch Meander slink artfully away from the group.

"Where do you think you're going?" Mim calls, her attention also on Meander's retreating figure.

Dylan and Kornelía follow our gazes to see Meander scowling at us all, his painless escape thwarted by Mim's less-than-stealthy question.

"My cousin lives here," he says in a voice thick with sleep and aggravation, his golden-brown curls hanging over his eyes. He's got a book in one hand, a hardback with a worn cover. It's either a used-copy or one he's read many times. "I know my way around. I've been on tours like this before, and I know how to get to the Louvre on my own."

His indifference is surprising. I could understand if he was from Paris, but he's not even from this country. I can't believe he's about to leave the group behind to set out on his own.

"You can't go off by yourself," I protest.

Mim grabs my arm and tries to turn me in the opposite direction, her eyes rolling in time with the pivot of her body.

"Come on, Cal. Let him go," she urges, tugging me towards the bus.

They've started loading, and Robbie and Alex are already on board. *I could dash ahead to tell them what*

Meander's up to and risk losing him in the crowds of the station. Or...

"I can't let him leave by himself," I say in my most reasonable voice, pulling away from Mim. "What if he gets lost or hurt? Then, I'd be stuck feeling guilty about it. I'd hate to have *him* haunting me the rest of my life." I smirk, trying to convince them with a joke.

"But what if *you* get lost or hurt?" Kornelía asks. She trains her eyes on mine as if she's trying to determine my true motive for leaving the others behind.

"I'll be fine," I assure her.

I give Mim a bit of a push. "Go on. Have fun. We'll meet you back at the Louvre."

Kornelía's gaze lingers on me until Mim gives a dramatic sigh and mutters something in Spanish. I don't know the language, but I suspect some variation on the word fool is used. Nonetheless, Mim hooks her arms around Kornelía and Dylan, and the three of them start towards the bus.

I watch them for only a second before running off after Meander. I don't know what Kornelía's suspicions are, but my reason for abandoning the safety of our camp group is simple. I'm not sure if Meander is being honest about knowing the city. When I was a kid, I once lied to my visiting cousins about knowing my way around Toronto despite only having been there a handful of times in my life. We got separated from our parents, and I got us more lost than ever by trying to keep up the pretense I knew where I was going. I'm not sure why Meander would risk leaving the group if he isn't comfortable in this city, but I don't want his going missing on my conscience.

It only takes me a moment to catch up with the other

boy's slow walk. When I do, stern green-brown eyes turn on me, and Meander heaves a heavy breath.

"What are you doing?" he asks, sounding weary as if he half-expected me to do this—which is odd because I've never done anything like this before.

"Coming with you." I shrug, trying to appear casual.

"Why?"

"Because I don't feel like sitting on another bus for two hours," I lie. I glance sideways at Meander and know he doesn't believe the excuse. But, since the bus is now out of sight, there isn't much he can do about it.

We weave through the crowds of the station until we step out into the street, neither of us saying a word. I'm tempted to make small talk, but I know Meander won't bother to respond if I start commenting on the weather. So, I try to keep my thoughts otherwise occupied.

I intend to study my surroundings, to marvel at the majesty of Paris. Instead, I find my mind wandering back over the conversation I had with my friends before we parted, over the lame joke I made about Meander becoming a ghost.

Slowly, my thoughts unfurl into a peculiar fantasy of trying to figure out what Meander *would* be like if he were a spirit. It's an amusing game. I'm positive his scent would be one of musty paper, the heady smell of old books full of wonder and dust. I think his scar would be prominent, even in a ghostly form. He has nice eyes, and given how much he uses them for reading, they would probably be well-defined, too. He doesn't talk much, so I imagine his mouth would be less focused.

The part I have trouble with is trying to come up

with his reason for sticking around. I can observe his manners as much as I want, but I don't know Meander. I'm clueless about his talent, his reason for attending this camp, and his plans for the future. I don't even know what his likes and dislikes are, aside from reading. Hell, I don't even know what he likes to read.

I tilt my head to the side and study him until he gives me an annoyed glance. I'd love to know where the scar on his jaw came from. The question lingers on my tongue, tingling against my teeth. I shouldn't care. I've got no right to ask about it, and I don't know why I'm even so curious.

We walk in silence until we reach the entrance for the Metro. When we get down to the ticket machine, Meander purchases himself a pass and waits for me to do the same. I stare at the machine, suddenly realizing I have no Euros with me. A wad of Canadian twenties is stuffed into my wallet, money I intended to convert while in the city. I curse myself, remembering the leftover change I have sitting in my backpack at the château. I look around, trying to spot a conversion desk nearby. The train station had one. I was stupid not to get my funds changed over then.

"Waiting for an invitation?" Meander asks after a minute. "Because I didn't even want company, if you recall."

I bite my lip and close my wallet. Then I give Meander my most naïve expression. "I, uh, don't have any money," I admit with a sheepish smile. "No Euros, anyway. I don't think the machine takes Canadian bills."

Meander sighs, and for a moment he stares away into the crowd of commuters like he's thinking of taking off and leaving me here alone. I don't know what I'll do if he hops on a subway car without me. Try to go back to the train station, I guess. Only, I wasn't paying too much attention on the way over here. I'm not exactly sure where the station is anymore.

Meander stuffs his hand in his pocket and pulls out some money. He mumbles something beneath his breath I'm sure is an insult, but he purchases me a ticket anyway.

"Here," he mutters, thrusting the ticket at me.

"Thanks," I say, surprised. I had more than half expected him to leave me sitting in the Metro station all day. "I'll pay you back," I add.

"You better," Meander replies, heading towards the gates.

We take the subway through the city of Paris and to the Philippe Auguste station. I'm impressed by Meander's confidence as he guides us to the correct platform and gets us on and off the subway car without hesitation. As we rumble beneath the city streets, I try to imagine what's going on above our heads. I wonder what Mim, Kornelía, and Dylan are up to. I wonder if Alex and Robbie have even noticed the two campers missing from the group.

Glancing sideways, I study Meander as he reads his book and wonder where he's taking us.

When we emerge out onto the street again, it's a warm, sunny day. Paris is bright and alive, full of people strolling along the streets and driving on the nearby roads. We walk in silence down a couple of streets until Meander stops at a Parisian café. I wait outside while he goes in, the smells wafting out from the entrance making my stomach growl despite the food I ate on the train ride earlier this morning.

I shake my head at my reflection in the front window, annoyed I didn't plan better and made sure I had some proper cash on hand. At least I did remember a comb. I pull it out and fix my hair where it's been ruffled over the last few hours. It's a small concession, but combing it into its usual neat part does make me feel the tiniest bit better about my current situation.

Meander returns a couple of minutes later with a cup in each hand, a small bag balanced on top of the left one and his book tucked under his right arm. He holds the right cup out to me, and I eye him curiously.

"It won't be good.... They don't boil the water," he says by way of explanation.

I hold the cup close to my nose and inhale the familiar scent of black tea. Steam snakes across my lips, and I smile.

"You didn't have to get me anything. Thanks," I say, the words more awkward than I intended.

Meander shrugs. "I think I made it the way you like. If not, too bad." He pulls a large swirled pastry from the bag and hands it to me before taking out a second one for himself. He doesn't allow me time to thank him again. He tosses the bag in the trash and takes a bite of his pastry before continuing down the street without another word.

I follow behind him, sipping my drink and nibbling at the pastry. Meander's right about the tea, on both accounts. It's not quite hot enough, and since the tea hasn't had the chance to properly steep in boiling water, the drink tastes a bit watered down. But it *is* made the way I drink it, which is by far the bigger surprise. For always having his nose in a book,

Meander's been rather observant.

We take our food and continue to walk, heading down more streets until we turn and pass through two massive stone pillars. I think we're heading into a park until I notice the headstones.

"A cemetery?" I ask as we amble past the first graves. "I thought this would be the last place you'd want to spend time."

Meander sips his tea and studies the mass of pillars and statues before us. "Cemeteries are about the only place I know I won't be bothered by spirits," he confesses. "The dead don't haunt their graves. Most stay where they died. A sorry few manage to attach themselves to some object. They don't come here, though. Here, there's nothing more than stone, bone, and dirt."

I've never given it much thought before, but what he's saying makes a lot of sense. Still, I can't resist the question that's presented itself in my mind.

"But what if someone died, you know, while they were *in* a cemetery?"

Meander's step pauses as he regards me. Then, he shakes his head and turns away.

"You are such an idiot," he mutters, but there's amusement in the words.

When he breathes out, I hear the distinct rise of a lovely, soft chuckle. I smile, pleased I was able to entertain him for at least a second or two.

We wander through the graveyard, drinking our tea and enjoying the beauty of the day. Spirits or no, the cemetery is anything but quiet. Tourists are everywhere, huddled in clusters or snapping photographs in couplets. Still, it's enjoyable.

Meander's obviously been here before. He points out the graves he finds interesting, some of them polished and strewn with flowers, others old and worn.

I recognize the lament in his gaze as he studies the most decrepit stones, and my chest constricts with understanding. I've spent my whole life being lonely, and in my bleakest moods I've wondered if there will ever be anyone to miss me when I'm gone. I suspect Meander's had similar thoughts, and when he catches my gaze after we've stared at one crooked, crumbling tomb, it's like a promise between us. Even if we never see each other again once this summer is over, we'll do our damnedest not to forget one another exists.

He never says more than a sentence or two about any grave, but the words he does say are smooth and content like he's used to my company. All in all, it's a great way to spend the morning. I don't mind missing out on the landmarks, and I don't even mind not being with my friends. Meander's quiet, but quiet is nice in a place like this. I can imagine Kornelía here, sketching headstones or something. But if Mim and Dylan were around, they'd ruin the calm atmosphere of this peaceful place.

And it is peaceful. Something I wouldn't have expected. I don't frequent cemeteries. They give me the creeps. I see enough of the dead outside of a graveyard. I don't need reminders of them lined in rows and surrounded by neatly trimmed grass. But Meander made a good point. This place isn't full of spirits. In fact, it's quite the opposite. The people walking around are full of life.

Some of them are sad, but most of them aren't. They're untroubled, even happy. At first, I don't get it until Meander points out Frédéric Chopin's grave, laughing when I grab his arm and pull him to a stop, so I can admire the beautiful sculpture and the mass of fresh flowers left by recent visitors. I'm not sad about his death. Why would I be? I am, however, excited to be so close to one of the world's greatest composers, and I'm grateful to see there are others who still appreciate him, too.

This isn't a place to mourn, not completely. It's also a place to cherish and unite with others celebrating lives and legacies. I've been thinking about cemeteries all wrong. It's like making peace with a small part of the universe. Maybe being here isn't going to be a pivotal moment in my life, but it's made a tiny fragment of it more comfortable. I don't get many nice changes thrown at me these days, so I'll take what little comforts I can get.

Despite where I am and who I'm with, I forget all about ghosts and Camp Wanagi as the morning dwindles away. I relax into the energetic calm, counting myself lucky to be here and not stuck on an over-crowded bus racing through the city. The cemetery suits me better, and I'm happy to stay here until we have to meet the rest of the group.

Maybe that's why I'm so bothered by the unexpected and unwelcome words Meander utters a long while later, after we've slunk into the safety of each other's company and have shared in the simple joy of our rebellious day.

"There's a flat nearby that's supposed to be haunted," he says after a lengthy silence.

The words startle me from a hazy daydream about playing my violin in a warm, sunny place like this. I blink away the serene thoughts and stare at Meander in confusion.

"Haunted?" I wasn't planning to ghost hunt today. And Meander's not too interested in spirits, anyway. We share a common trait there. At least, I thought we did.

He looks uncomfortable, like he's bracing himself for something horrid. "There's an old story about it," he says, his head bent low enough his golden curls obscure his eyes once more. He tilts his chin in the direction of the exit closest to where we're sitting. "There's nothing else to do. Let's go check it out."

"I-I didn't think..." I splutter, failing to come up with a cohesive sentence, let alone a decent argument against leaving the cemetery. Dejection quashes my attempts at speech when Meander stands, taking several steps towards the exit before glancing back over his shoulder.

"Don't tell me you're afraid," he says, challenging me with his voice. "I thought this was supposed to be our destiny or something."

"I'm not afraid," I grumble, standing.

Meander waits for me to catch up before continuing forward at a brisk pace. "Let's get going then."

I follow behind, trying to figure out his sudden change in manner, trying to understand what happened to ruin our pleasant day.

17

ONCE AGAIN, MEANDER LEADS THE WAY WITHOUT AN OUNCE OF HESITATION. I wonder if he's got a knack for directions or if he's more familiar with this area than I expected. We leave the cemetery a different way than we came in, heading up and to the right until we reach a street lined with shops. White exteriors with wrought iron flower beds on second-storey windows adorn every building, and people come and go, oblivious to the dismal quest the two of us are apparently on.

Meander approaches one of the doors, fishing in his pocket until he pulls something out, and begins messing with the knob. For a minute, I think he's picking the lock, and I'm curious how he even knows which door to pick until I see the flash of a silver key and realize he's not breaking and entering.

"Okay, seriously. What are you doing?" I ask as he swings open the door. "This looks like someone's house."

"It is," Meander replies. He steps inside a dim entryway, turning back once he realizes no one's following behind. Then he heaves another of his great sighs. "It's my aunt's house," he says finally. "She borrowed a book from me last time she was in England, and she still hasn't mailed it back."

I roll my eyes to stop myself from sighing with relief. "I should've known you'd break into someone's house to retrieve a book," I muse, joining him in the entryway.

Together, we head up a set of stairs. When we reach the upper floor, Meander unlocks a second door, and we find ourselves in a small two-bedroom Paris flat. I'm still uneasy, but I trail behind as Meander heads to his aunt's room and begins pushing around piles of magazines and books on a small set of shelves beside the bed.

I stand in the doorway, listening to the quiet bumps and thuds of the shop on the ground floor below us. The apartment is nice, but it's unfamiliar, and I feel weird lingering around like a trespasser. Plus, the shades are drawn, and it's cool in here. I miss the warmth of the bright sun outside.

I'm glad when Meander finds the book he's after—a thick, black, cloth-bound volume. He offers me a triumphant grin when he picks it out of the mess, and I smile as we go back into the main living area.

"Why did you say this place was haunted?" I ask.

Meander makes a tired *tisk*ing sound and begins straightening the living room, tidying stacks of papers and taking a few empty cups to the small kitchenette. It's a weird reaction in a place he shouldn't even be, but it's amusing to watch him work.

"Why didn't you just tell me where you wanted to go?"

Meander kneels by the entertainment system and shuffles some CD cases until they're in an order he can live with.

"It is haunted," he says with a glance over his shoulder. He mumbles something about taking proper care of CDs before he stands. "At least, I always thought it was as a kid," he continues. He looks at the short hallway leading to his aunt's room and beyond, to what I imagine is his cousin's room. "I haven't been here in about five years, but I remember the place well. I spent a whole summer here then, and there were always noises in the..."

As if the memory has brought his old nightmare to life, Meander's eyes widen, and he trails off at the same time a sound clunks against the floor in the back of the apartment.

"What was that?" I ask, following his gaze to the hallway. The clunking continues, followed by a soft screeching which fades into a brief silence before the clunking begins again.

"I always heard noises in Rory's room," Meander mumbles, more to himself than to me. "I couldn't sleep in there, so I spent the summer out here on the sofa. But I was half-convinced I'd imagined it."

"Are you sure no one is home?" I ask. There's a loud thump, and the delicious pastry from earlier begins a grotesque dance in my gut. I don't know why we didn't hear anything until now. If the place is haunted, we should have known right away. But maybe my unease thus far has not simply been from being in a stranger's home. The cool air might not be from the drawn shades or an air conditioner set too high, and the noises I thought originated from below us might actually be coming from somewhere much closer.

"Positive," Meander replies. "It's just my aunt and my cousin Rory. He's visiting his dad in Ireland right now, and she's on a business trip in Germany."

Another thud is followed by more screeching, and a current of frigid air snaking out into the living room.

"Then it might not have been your imagination," I say as bumps rise over my flesh and a shiver pulls at my bones.

"We should go," Meander suggests, his voice and his expression unsure. He takes a jerky step forward and stops, staring at the hallway.

"What if it's a burglar or something?" I ask.

I hate the question because I know it's not true. There's no burglar here. Burglars don't chill my skin, cloud my head, and make me feel nauseous. I look at Meander, and know the same idiotic questions are pushing at him, drawing him to the source. One more piece of the terrible puzzle of being able to see spirits. Even when we know nothing good is going to happen, we can't seem to help investigating.

"Let's find out, but let's get weapons first," Meander says, stalling.

I nod, and together we retreat to the kitchenette. Meander grabs two knives out of a drawer and hands one to me.

"We're going to *stab* them?" I ask with a strangled laugh.

Meander offers me an impatient glance. "*No*," he says sternly, "but it'll scare whoever it is."

Except it won't. Because, whoever it is, they aren't

someone who can be hurt with a sharp blade. I know it, and Meander does, too. But, nevertheless, he leads the way back towards the hall, and I shuffle after him, knife in hand. I hold onto the stupid hope the sounds are really coming from the shop beneath us. But, as we pass the first bedroom and the small bathroom one door over, a sharp pain flares inside my ears.

It'd be nice if we opened the closed door now before us and only found a home intruder, after all. It's a strange desire. A thief would be alive, though, and probably startled by our presence and our weapons. Such a situation, however unpleasant, still sounds better than what we're likely going to face.

Meander approaches the door with cautious steps. But, when something thuds hard against it, he jumps back, stumbling into me. I just have time to swing my arm down, so he doesn't fall right against my knife.

"Don't you think your aunt would have moved by now, if her home was haunted?" I ask, my voice laced with a tremble of nerves. I don't feel up to seeing a ghost today. I never feel up to it, really. But especially today. I'm still tired from the early morning start, and after the tense ride to the cemetery, followed by the surprising enjoyment of being there, I'm ill-equipped to deal with a wild spirit thudding and screeching about some stranger's apartment.

"Nope," Meander says, shaking his head. "They've never noticed anything weird about this place. That's why I thought it was my imagination."

He reaches for the door, but stops with his hand poised an inch above the tarnished gold knob. I step up beside him, knife gripped in one fist.

"Well, let's find out if you're crazy." I sigh.

Meander makes a face somewhere between a grimace and a smile. He reaches forward, grasps the knob, and turns it. Then, in one swift movement, he pushes open the door.

The instant the door is pushed wide, the spirit surges towards us. I barely have time to realize what the wispy, cloudy mass is before I have to duck to avoid it. I don't know what would happen if this man hit me, but I don't want to find out. I crouch low and am overwhelmed by a sickeningly sweet smell. At first, I can't place it, but my stomach lurches when I recognize the coppery undertone and meaty heaviness of the scent.

It's blood. And meat. I'm struck with the certainty this spirit was once a butcher. The disgusting scents of his morbid work have followed him beyond the grave.

Loud buzzing fills my head, like an old radio out of tune. It pops and hums in static, words sporadically flitting into focus. They're hateful words, some I don't understand, others I do and wouldn't lightly repeat aloud. I cover my ears to try to block out the sound, dropping the knife on the carpeted floor in the process.

"Look out!" I uncover my ears as Meander yells at me, grabbing my arm and pulling me down a second before a desk clock hurtles through the air. I lower my head as the clock sails above me, crashing against the wall to my left.

"What was that?" I ask again, my eyes wide. "What's going on?" This ghost is like the spirit who borrowed energy from Tomas but worse. That spirit was aimless, but I'm pretty sure this one threw the clock with intention. Nothing like this has ever happened to me. I've never been assaulted by flying objects.

"The ghost," Meander says.

The spirit rushes forward again, sending a new wave of static through my head. I cringe and see Meander do the same. Like on our first night at camp, we're now hearing and seeing the same thing.

"Let's get out of here!" I call, tugging on Meander's sleeve.

The spirit, not fully formed but only a vague, bluish-white outline of a big, beastly man, raises a framed picture. It looks like the frame is floating on a strange, misshapen cloud.

"But the flat," Meander begins, his eyes trained on the ghost. "The clock..."

The spirit hurls the frame, and it thuds against Meander's arm.

"Never mind," he groans, rubbing the point of contact. "Let's go."

The spirit screams at us, and we duck our heads. The pain is horrendous. I wish I hadn't eaten anything this morning. Bile and old food climb my throat, and if I don't get out of here soon, my breakfast will make a reappearance on the plush, cream carpet.

Meander manages to get back up first, and he drags me forward until I catch my footing and race down the hall. We leave the frame, the clock, and the knives sprawled on the carpet as we run out to the living room. I turn around to see the spirit pushing past the doorframe, and out into the hall. He bangs into the wall, smashing the glass of a framed picture.

"Oh, shit," Meander mutters.

He grabs my shirt sleeve, and we rush out the door before he slams it shut and turns the lock. Shaking and breathless, we hurry back down to the street.

"I've never seen a spirit like that before," I say, my voice uneven. I wait for him to lock the outer door before we turn back towards the cemetery. "You know, one that could actually throw stuff."

Meander says nothing, and for a few minutes, we move in silence until a new thought arises.

"Can you see the ghosts of murdered people, too?" I ask.

His hands are in his pockets, and he slouches forward as he walks. He didn't retrieve the book he'd been after, and he's left his other book behind in the apartment, too.

"No," he says, the word shaky.

I gaze at him, focus on the scar along his jawline. I'm almost certain I know how he got it, now.

"Then what *is* your ability?" I ask, but Meander only shrugs, walking faster and ignoring my question.

18

THE EASY MOOD OF THE MORNING VANISHES AS WE MAKE OUR WAY BACK to the Metro station. Meander shuts down, saying nothing and not even checking to see if I'm still following him. I have to pick up speed not to lose him in the bustle of the Paris underground, but I don't have it in me to scold him for his indifference.

I don't have it in me to do much of anything. We sit side-by-side on the subway, silent and sullen. I'm so preoccupied with thinking about what happened, I almost miss our stop. Even then, when we ascend onto the street once more, I'm mildly surprised to see the massive glass pyramid of the Louvre. I forgot all about the museum, and the other campers we're supposed to meet within it. Just as my earlier contentment had pushed the thoughts from my mind, the disturbing episode we encountered in the apartment has likewise stolen my attention.

My mind is still muddled from the spirit's attack

when we maneuver our way through the crowds until we reach the drop-off location for the tour. I don't know how we manage to find the rest of Shade. It's miraculous we don't have to page the group like a couple of lost children. There are so many people—some in groups, some alone, some piling on and off one of the hordes of parked buses. If it weren't for Meander, I probably would have resorted to begging someone for help.

When I see Alex and Robbie stepping off the bus, I want to turn and thank Meander for getting us back. But I don't. He stands away from where I wait anxiously for the campers to leave the bus. He doesn't acknowledge the group, and he doesn't acknowledge me. I have an uneasy feeling he's as lost amidst a sea of queasy thoughts as I am. I guess he just has a better sense of direction under distress.

I spot my friends soon after our leads have left the bus, and even though I have to push through a tour group to reach them, it's easy to keep Dylan's baby pink polo and blue-brown checkered slacks in sight. I move into the small group as soon as I'm near enough, the four of us conversing like I haven't been absent for most of the morning hours. Meander makes it over as well, slinking in between Sefa and Lu. I watch him for a few long seconds before I turn to my friends.

"How was the tour?" I ask.

Mim huffs, waving my question away. "Fine, fine," she says, her eyes trained on mine. "But what about you? Was it horrible? We thought for sure you'd be lost somewhere, stuck in a gutter or something."

"Do people get stuck in gutters?" I force my lips into a smirk.

Mim rolls her eyes. "You could've been hurt."

"Or mugged. Big cities are known for pickpockets and muggers," Dylan adds.

I raise a questioning eyebrow. "Are they?" I hadn't been at all concerned for my safety walking around Paris with Meander. Not until we saw the spirit, anyway.

"We kept Alex and Robbie busy with questions the whole tour," Kornelía smiles. She looks over at our leads, who are sorting tickets for the museum. Alex is flustered, but Robbie is grinning as he shuffles a stack of papers. "They didn't even notice you were gone."

"Thanks," I say, my voice weary. I don't want to get in trouble for sneaking off. It's been an eventful enough morning.

"Not a problem," Mim breaks in again. "But, come on, tell us! What did you do off by yourself in Paris? Where did you go? Did you see the sights? Did Meander try to ditch you?"

I tell my friends about taking the subway and visiting the cemetery. I don't mention the apartment, or the spirit within it. I also don't mention the tea and the pastries, or how Meander paid for my Metro ride. Dylan scoffs when he hears we went to the graveyard, and Mim makes a comment about Meander being weird due to his choice of destination.

I tell them the morning wasn't bad, but I don't tell them the morning was actually quite nice before it became quite horrid. I don't know why I keep it all hidden, both the good and the bad. It feels strange talking to them about it, like it's not something they're supposed to be a part of.

When I finish relating what I'm willing to share, a

tale which doesn't take long, we join our leads and head into the art gallery. The Louvre is impressive and busy, but neither fact is surprising. It takes a long while for my head to clear enough to enjoy the museum, but Kornelía's so excited by every work of art in the place, it's impossible not to smile as she drags us from one exhibit to the next.

My stomach never settles completely, but I am able to drink a bottle of water, and it helps. At least a little. By the time we're jostling through the crowds to catch a glimpse of the Mona Lisa, I almost feel normal again.

Almost.

"Isn't this place amazing?" Kornelía asks for the fifteenth time as we wander one of the less crowded halls.

"It's art. Big deal," Mim sighs, bored with Kornelía's endless enthusiasm. "I'd rather be at Notre Dame or Sainte-Chapelle. Somewhere I can see the angels." She smiles to herself, but her eyes are solemn.

I wonder if Mim truly believes in angels or if she's referring to a secret we don't understand.

"I'd rather be outdoors," Dylan says, walking with one arm around Mim's shoulders, the other around Kornelía's. "It's so nice out. And we've been stuck inside or on a bus the whole time. I didn't even get to go running this morning."

"What about you, Cal?" Kornelía asks, amused by everyone's lack of enjoyment. "Would you rather be somewhere else, too?"

"I'm fine here," I say, although it's not true. Honestly, I'd like to be back at the cemetery, wandering among the graves of generations past. But I don't want another discussion about my morning, so I stick to the simple lie.

"I am, too," Kornelía sighs. She beams at a painting as we pass and examines her map to see which room she wants to head to next.

We finish at the gallery and head back to the train station around three. When we finally board the train again, I slump into my seat and dig out my phone, so I can put on my headphones and try to relax. The smooth motion of the train departing from the station almost lulls me to sleep. It would have, if I didn't notice Mim sitting beside me with a ball of blue yarn in her lap and a wooden crochet hook gripped in her right hand.

"I didn't know you could crochet," I say, pulling out one of my earbuds.

Mim looks up at me with an almost sad smile, the same smile she wore earlier when talking about the churches with the angels.

"Yeah. Ever since I was little," she says, her smile growing more cheerful. "Mama taught me. Said a girl should always have many talents. Some to share with the world, and others to keep hidden." She laughs, staring at the hook in her hand.

"I don't usually crochet in front of people. But I suppose my talent for seeing spirits should be the one I keep hidden. I should start crocheting in public more often." She gives me a sideways grin, her fingers flowing into the rhythm of her stitches once more.

I continue to watch her for a minute or two before I turn back to the window and slouch down farther in my seat.

The remainder of the trip back to camp is spent dozing. My music and the train's constant sway rock me to sleep, and visions of the spirit I saw this morning startle me awake again. Meander is seated several rows behind me now. I'm tempted to switch seats with Lu, so I can spend the rest of the train ride trying to get him to spill the truth of his talent and his history with spirits like the one in his cousin's home. Maybe I would if I didn't suspect it's a pointless temptation. Meander wouldn't tell me no matter if I asked nicely or demanded it loud enough for everyone on the train to hear.

I turn my music up and focus on the melody of Chopin's "Nocture op. 9 no. 2" instead, although it takes only minutes for my efforts to fail and for the memories to come back again. But, this time, today's episode flits away and is replaced with the night of the initiation. I *saw* Madame Roux's husband, but Meander interacted with the spirit to the point of getting scratches on his face. And, all the while, Dylan and most of the other campers didn't see or feel a thing.

Meander saw the spirit of Madame Roux's husband as well as the spirit in Paris. Just like I did. I may be occasionally clueless, but I've figured out he didn't go to his aunt's apartment to get his book back. He took me there because he wanted to see if I could feel the spirit, too. He wanted confirmation he wasn't insane.

I understand the desperation of longing to let someone else in on the nightmare, and I'm happy I could help prove he didn't make the spirit up. But the whole event still doesn't make sense to me.

Meander said he can't see the ghosts of the murdered. So, what is his talent? And why do our abilities overlap?

19

I MANAGE A BIT OF SLEEP ON THE TRAIN, BUT WHEN WE'RE BACK AT CAMP and it's time to go to bed, I lay awake in the darkness. My phone is across the room, plugged into the wall to charge and holding my playlists hostage, and I struggle to keep still, my muscles too tight for the soft mattress to have any calming effect. Everyone else is asleep, leaving me with no company and no music. I'm stuck with my thoughts, and those are as troublesome tonight as they were this afternoon.

When I can no longer stand the restless silence, I get up, slipping my camp sweater over my head and stuffing bare feet into my sneakers before I shuffle out of the room. The lounge is empty as well, but the moon shines in through the windows, illuminating the whole room in shadowed blue. I stand by the windows for a while, staring out at the night sky and the black lake, counting what stars I can see through the panes.

I want my violin. I wish I'd brought it with me. How did I ever think I could go months without playing it, especially in a place like this? If I need to calm down, if I need to focus, music is my only hope. Listening to concertos and symphonies is great, but nothing beats the physical act of playing, surrounding myself with the feel and smell and sound of the violin.

My fingers tingle, desperate to hold instrument and bow, and I shove my hands into my hoodie's front pocket to keep them from tapping against my thigh. A drink of water might make me feel better. It will at least give me something to hold.

I'm surprised to find the main floor of our building occupied. When I descended the creaking steps, I expected another dark, empty room. But the light in the dining hall is on, and a group of older campers talk and laugh, their enthusiasm unaffected by the late hour. I don't know exactly what time it is, but I do know I didn't even crawl into bed until close to midnight, and it's been ages since everyone else fell asleep. If I were to guess, I'd say it's close to two or three by now.

I slink past the campers, uninterested in their discussion. Their carefree joking and happy banter aggravates me. Or maybe it makes me jealous.

"Cal?"

I stop short of the kitchen and turn back to see Daniel getting up from the table. I didn't realize he was one of the campers still awake. His friends give me a curious glance before returning to their conversation. Daniel meets me by the door and follows me into the quiet kitchen.

"Hi, Daniel," I murmur, trudging to the fridge to

grab some water.

"Hey," Daniel replies. He studies me for a moment while I do my best to ignore his scrutinising gaze. "Up late. Anything wrong?"

I shrug. "Can't sleep," I say. I take a long swig of water and try to muster up a casual smile. I can feel the bags hanging heavy under my eyes, and I'm sure Daniel can see them, too.

He leans against the wall, his arms crossed over his chest. "It happens sometimes," he nods. "Especially here. I don't think I slept for half of my second summer." His mouth twists in a grimace.

I wonder what he encountered to make him so restless those summers ago.

"Anything in particular keeping you up on this night? You can tell me, you know."

I start to shake my head but stop. The person I really want to talk about my problems with won't talk about them. But Daniel might.

"Daniel, can I ask you a question?"

He looks pleased I've decided to talk. "Of course. Ask away."

I play the words through my head, trying to figure out what I want to ask. It's hard to know where to begin. I have a million questions, and those are just the ones I can formulate into words. Daniel won't understand if I ask him about the spirit I saw this morning. So, I find a simpler way to start instead.

"What happened to the spirits in the house?" I ask. Among other things, I've been thinking a lot about those ghosts today.

"Which house? Oh, you mean the initiation place?" Daniel is silent as he works through his own thoughts.

His expression is vacant, but his light blue eyes darken with concentration. "The Oracle is studying the house right now," he says, "or what's left of it, anyway. I heard something...the woman, I think. I believe they've released her."

"She's gone?" The tiniest chunk of my tension chips away. I can almost feel it sliding over my shoulder and rolling down my arm until it vanishes into the air. I'm glad someone was able to help her. At least someone here knows what they're doing.

"What about the other one?"

Daniel taps a finger against his lips.

"The other...entity is still there," he says, choosing his words with careful thought.

Entity.

"The husband, right?" I ask. "Why did you call it an entity? An entity's a spirit, isn't it?"

He doesn't say anything for a long time, but the silence is loud. It's like he's building up to something big. Although, when he finally does speak again, his words are soft.

"Do you know why ghosts exist, Cal?" he asks finally.

The question is unexpected, and it takes me a moment to answer.

"Because they have unfinished business, I guess," I shrug. It feels like a trick question.

"That's somewhat true." Daniel nods.

I quirk an eyebrow. "Somewhat?"

He sighs, turning to the counter and busying himself with making a cup of coffee. "Sometimes, when a person or other animal dies, they can't move on because there's something they need to do before they leave here," he explains, opening the fridge and pulling out a small container of cream. "The little girl you saw...Maggie. She had unfinished business because she needed to let her parents know what happened to her, so it wouldn't happen to someone else.

"But it can be more complicated than that. Sometimes, a ghost can't move on because they want to tell their mother something, and they don't realize their mother has been dead for a hundred years. And, sometimes, ghosts have been around for so long they've forgotten what they stuck around for in the first place. Spirits who have lost their purpose or have become single-minded in their reason for staying, we call them entities. They're harder to release. Harder to help."

I wonder what unfinished business Madame Roux's husband has or had. At least his wife has been released. Maybe she felt she could move on once the Oracle finally figured out her husband was still around.

"How come some ghosts are violent?" I ask, thinking of how scared Madame Roux was of her husband, even in the afterlife.

This time, Daniel seems surprised. "Ghosts have emotions like the living do," he says. "Some spirits are angry. They're mad because they died, or they're bitter about something that happened when they were alive." He settles back against the counter and takes a cautious sip of coffee. "Every so often, a spirit harbours enough energy and bad feeling to even make its presence known to non-Senders. And other times, certain people... Well...certain people possess the ability to bring out those emotions."

Certain people. My neck prickles, and I take another long drink of water to give me another moment to process what Daniel said. Madame Roux's husband certainly seemed strong enough to make himself known. But no one noticed him, at least not until the night of the initiation. And the one in the Paris apartment? I've never experienced spirits so angry or so downright violent before coming here this summer. Is it coincidence or a side-effect of attending this camp?

Or does it even have anything to do with me? I wasn't alone when I saw the angry spirit in Paris or the violent entity in the house nearby.

I gulp down the rest of my water, the events of this summer arranging themselves into something resembling order in my mind. *Scratches, scars...* I've seen many spirits in my lifetime, but not a single one has ever left a mark on me. Yet, I've already seen how easily they leave marks on someone else.

I don't make the spirits angry. Meander does. No wonder he never talks about his ability. No wonder he's so sullen about being here. Would I want to come if my talent was like his? It's a stupid question to ask. Of course, I wouldn't.

"Anything else you want to talk about tonight?" Daniel asks after a moment.

I startle out of my thoughts and shake my head. "No. But thanks...for everything."

"No problem." He smiles and places a hand on my shoulder as he heads out of the kitchen. "We'll talk at our next meeting. If you think of anything else you'd like to know about angry spirits, we can discuss it then."

I nod. "Sure thing. Goodnight, Daniel."

"Night, Cal."

I watch Daniel leave and stand in the kitchen by myself for a minute before I follow suit and go back out through the dining hall. My mentor is still there, back with his friends, all leaning in to examine something on the table. I don't acknowledge Daniel again, and he doesn't acknowledge me. I walk past the group, and head back upstairs, my feet heavier than they were when I came down. By the time I reach the bedroom again, I'm tired, the restlessness gone now I have at least a partial answer to my confused host of questions.

The room is dark when I stumble to my bunk, kick off my shoes, and throw off my sweater. I curl in towards the wall, and in a matter of seconds, I slide off to sleep.

20

"WE'VE GOT OUR CASE." MIM SITS DOWN, DROPPING A BINDER AND A STACK of folders onto the wooden table top. The thud echoes around the library.

"You've found a ghost?" Kornelía asks.

Mim beams, her grin wide as she nods. Her black hair is braided into two pigtails again, her usual style. The streaks of pink are beginning to fade now, but they still stand out amongst the mass of dark strands.

"Yes, I made contact yesterday," she says.

I put away the assignment I'm working on for Emotional Entities, so I can listen. "You mean you saw the spirit this time?" I ask. It's been almost a week since our trip to Paris, and almost a week since any of us have had contact with a spirit. Mim's been to a haunted locale three times since Mrs. Buxley assigned her as our group's leader. So far, she's come back sour and out of sorts because she's failed to have any success.

"Sort of," she says now, shrugging her shoulders and staring down at the folders on the table.

"*Sort of?*" Dylan repeats. His thick eyebrows shoot way up on his small forehead.

"Well," Mim begins, shuffling around the papers in one of the folders, "I saw something, and I heard some noises. I couldn't make out what she was saying, but I do know that it *is* a she."

"So, you couldn't make out what she said, and you only saw *something*? How is that supposed to help us?" Meander slouches against the seat at the far end of the table, the sleeves of his white shirt pushed up to his elbows. I give him a pointed glance and wait for Mim's temper to flare. But she only rolls her eyes and continues as if he didn't say a word.

"Lani and a couple of-age Senders did some cool stuff.... They asked her questions about her life and recorded her answers. They've been working with her for a while now, but since I was able to make some contact, they've decided we can take her for our project. Lani said most young campers can't establish contact at all, so I've done well."

"What do we know about her?" I ask. I want to get started on my research. There are only three weeks left of camp this summer, and we've got to have this project completed before we head home. I still don't know if I'll want to come back to Camp Wanagi after I get off the plane in Toronto and return to my mostly normal life. But I need to complete the task I've been given, so when I make my choice, I'll at least have a complete summer's worth of memories to consider.

"Well, we think she's from the 1800s, judging by when the building was constructed and the death records they could find from the village. A few women listed in the record books might be a match, and about thirty other potential matches are not accounted for. She could be any of them, but I have a list here of the ten most likely."

Mim hands me a sheet of paper listing ten names, along with approximate birth and death dates. A quick glance shows me the spirit must have been around twenty-five when she died.

"Do they know what happened to her?" I ask.

Mim shakes her head, rifling through her papers as she speaks. "That's what we're going to find out. Cal, you can take charge of researching the history of these women. Lani said she'll have some of the record books from the village sent here soon for you. See if any of these women ever stayed in this hotel." She holds up an old photograph.

The hotel pictured is a tall, square building made of grey stone, surrounded by an equally square lawn with flowers lining a walkway to its doors. It looks like a nice place to stay.

"Korni, Dylan," Mim says next, turning to the others who sit across the table from me. "You'll be meeting with Mr. Olenev soon."

"Who?" Dylan asks.

"The Gadgetry instructor," I inform him. I wish I could join. Research is fine, but using readers and recorders would be exciting, too. If I do come back here next summer, I'll try using gadgets *and* information in a case, not just one or the other.

"Yeah, what Cal said," Mim nods, opening her binder. "You'll be my back-up at the final session. I shouldn't need any help, of course. If I've already made contact, I'll be able to speak with her soon. Then, I'll find out what she needs and free her. You'll get to record everything and, you know, help me *if* I need it."

The smirk on Mim's lips confirms she doesn't believe she'll be needing *any* help from us. We're only coming with her on the final session because we have to. If she could do it by herself, I'm sure Mim would.

"When will the final session be, do you think?" Kornelía asks.

"Depends," Mim says. "If I find out what she needs soon, then we'll meet soon. We have a couple of weeks left, but I doubt I'll need that long." She grins and closes the binder. "I have a meeting now with Ms. Lind. She's going to help me channel my concentration, so I can hear the ghost better next time."

Ms. Lind is the instructor for one of the courses I don't take. She's an expert on communication techniques. I've heard she even teaches a spirit meditation course for older campers, showing them how to focus and communicate with spirits through the energy of the mind. I've never meditated before, but I find the concept of channelling interesting. One more thing to add to my wish list if I ever find myself at Camp Wanagi again.

Mim doesn't continue with the discussion of where and when we'll be contacting our spirit. Apparently, the declaration of her meeting with Ms. Lind was supposed to be her way of wrapping things up. She snatches up the piles of papers and folders, and without so much as a goodbye, she flies out of the library as quickly as she came in five minutes ago.

"That's it?" I ask. We blocked out an hour of time to go over the details of the project. I can hardly pretend the last five minutes were sufficient to prepare me for what's ahead.

"Nothing more we can do now," Dylan says, smiling as he stretches and pushes back from the table. "Guess we'll have to take the rest of the afternoon off." He sounds pleased. He relaxes for a few seconds, and then he stands, his stature still short even while the rest of us stare up at him from our seats.

"I guess you're right," Kornelía replies. She considers me as if she's weighing her options. "We can't do anything until we meet with the instructor," she says at last, gesturing to Dylan and herself, "and you can't do anything until Lani brings you the record books. So, we have nothing to work on right now."

I frown. Tools or not, I can't believe there's nothing we can do to prepare. I'm not surprised Dylan's trying to worm his way out of any more work. But I didn't expect Kornelía's lack of interest.

"Well, I suppose," I mutter, watching as Kornelía stands as well.

"Want to get something to eat?" Dylan asks, looking between her and me.

"You ate a bag of chips before we came here!" Kornelía scolds.

Dylan pouts, rubbing his stomach. "But I'm hungry!" he says with a dramatic, fake southern drawl.

Kornelía laughs, shoving him towards the library door. "I'll get you some cold mush," she tells him as she twists back towards the table. "You coming, Cal?"

"I'll meet you upstairs," I say. I watch the two nudging and pushing each other until they're out of sight.

With a sigh, I look over at Meander.

"So, should we split the list in half?" he asks as if everyone else didn't just ignore him and walk out in the first few minutes of the meeting.

I'm too annoyed to understand his question right away, leaving me to blink like an idiot as I try to process his words.

"The list? What...? *Oh*, the list." I grab the sheet of names Mim gave me, glancing at the ten possibilities. I wonder if our spirit is one of these ladies. I wonder if we'll figure out the right one if she is.

"I'll take five, and you can take five," Meander says. "I doubt we'll find much, not until we get the record books. But it's worth checking online. We can peruse the records together when Lani brings them." He doesn't sound aggravated, exactly, but impatient like he has somewhere else to be and he's been sitting at this table for ten hours instead of ten minutes.

We haven't spoken much since Paris. I don't blame him for not wanting to discuss his talent, but I wish I could think of a more light-hearted topic to engage him with. I'd like to get to know him better, but I'm not a natural conversationalist, and social grace doesn't seem to be a strong point of his.

"Yeah. S-sure," I stammer, my mind wandering.

Meander snatches the sheet from my grasp, and with a flick of his wrist, tears the page in half. He hands me back the top of the page with the first five names on it.

"Listen, Meander—" I begin, but he cuts me off.

"I'm sorry," he mumbles, staring at the paper in his hands. "For what happened in Paris."

I place my half of the paper on the table, shaking my head. "It wasn't your fault." I tried to pay him back for the Metro pass and the café food when we returned to camp, but he refused to accept my money. I figured that was his apology for how messy our trip to his aunt's was, and now I smile, feeling daft. It hadn't occurred to me he was simply being nice.

"It *was* my fault." Meander sighs, slouching farther down in his seat. He glances up at me, hazel eyes warm despite the tightness of his lips.

"You didn't know," I tell him.

He sighs again and sits up straight, picking up his sheet and tucking it into his notebook.

"I did," he says, pushing back his chair. "At least, I should have."

"It's not..." I begin again, but he stands, not giving me time to finish my thought.

"I'll do these five, yeah?" he says, holding up the notebook with the sheet sticking out the top. He turns without waiting for a response and walks out of the library.

I spend a while staring at the empty doorway and the empty table before me. I've got my list of names, and if I want, I can spend the rest of our designated meeting time hunting for the women on the computer or in the books on the library shelves. But, with everyone else gone, I don't feel like working on my own. I've been in France for seven weeks now, and I'm not any closer to making a decision about Camp Wanagi than I was when I got off the airplane in Paris. I was worried about this task when it was assigned. Now, I'm worried we'll never complete it. How can I decide anything if I never see what our abilities can do?

I slide down in my chair and let my head drop onto the table.

21

Dylan, at least, is happy. His hunger is satiated when dinner arrives in the Shade lounge a few hours later.

"I can't believe we get pizza here," he says, grabbing his fourth slice. "I didn't think France had pizza delivery."

I'm not so vocal about my cultural ignorance as Dylan is, but I have to admit it was strange to me at first, too. Usually dinner is served downstairs, but on Saturday nights, Camp Wanagi serves pizza from some local shop right up to our sector lounge. We've had pizza once a week since we arrived at camp. And, every week, Dylan remarks that he can't believe his luck while Lu grumbles about how much she despises the meal.

"Yeah, except it'd be great if they let us order what we want," Reed says, swapping his mushrooms for Sefa's red peppers.

"If you weren't so picky." Naasir tisks.

Reed ignores the reprimand as he shoves a good third of his latest slice into his mouth.

"It'd be nice if we had healthier options," Lu says from across the room, where she's hunched over the study desk working on an assignment.

"Why do you care? You always load up on sandwiches at lunch, anyway," Mim snorts.

Lu heaves a dramatic sigh. "I only do that so I don't have to suffer through those disgusting pies."

"You're nuts. These pies are delicious," Dylan grins, finishing off his slice and grabbing a fifth.

"Okay, shush everyone," Sabeena says, waving her arms to quiet the conversation. "Kornelía's going to get this."

"I'm telling you, I can't do it," Kornelía protests, her eyes fixed longingly on one of the pizza boxes.

I reach over and take a veggie slice to hand to her. She beams while Sabeena glares.

"You're distracting her," she says.

I smile, sitting back on the couch. "She's hungry. You're starving her."

Sabeena has spent the last hour teaching Kornelía some mind trick she learned in her Introduction to Communication Techniques course. She's convinced Kornelía is on the brink of unlocking access to a "deeper plane of conscious powers." I think Kornelía is regretting her decision to spend the afternoon in the lounge instead of in the library working on our group project. I'd be smug if she didn't look like a sad puppy being denied the opportunity to play with the rest of the pack.

"I'm doing no such thing. If we could get some quiet here, we could finish this experiment, and Kornelía could eat as much as she likes."

Kornelía takes a guilty bite of pizza before handing the slice back to me for safe keeping. She wipes her hands on her corduroys and presses her palms against Sabeena's. The girls sit cross-legged, facing each other on the floor. They close their eyes, and the rest of us grow silent.

"Okay, concentrate," Sabeena says. "I'm thinking of a color. Focus on that. One color. Sense my thoughts, and tell me what color is in my head."

Mim snorts again, the sound a quiet huff of breath. Dylan kicks her ankle, and she scoots closer to him.

"I can't sense things like this, Sabeena," Kornelía says, sounding like a petulant child. "I won't get it right."

"Try, girl," Sabeena insists.

Kornelía sits up straighter, squeezing her eyes tight as she tries to envision Sabeena's thoughts. It's not a part of her ability, at least not a part Kornelía's ever noticed before. But Sabeena's convinced she's a mind reader in the making, and she's desperate to prove it.

It's a fun game to watch, whatever the outcome. I wonder what color Sabeena's thinking of. Blue, maybe. Or, not quite blue, but turquoise.

"Oh, I can't do it," Kornelía whines. She drops her hands and opens her eyes.

"You didn't sense anything?" Sabeena says, dejected. "Go on and make a guess."

"Oh, I don't know…" Kornelía waves a hand before her face. "Mahogany."

Sabeena slumps forward. "No," she says with a full, pouting lip. "That's not what I was thinking of."

"No…it's what I was thinking of."

Beside me, Meander stares at Kornelía, his book closed over one finger, his usual makeshift bookmark. His expression's hard to read, but I think he's confused. And perhaps a little impressed.

"Well, you weren't supposed to be thinking of a color!" Sabeena complains. "You're interfering with the process!"

Meander shrugs. "Sorry, couldn't help it."

Sabeena sighs. "Was anyone else thinking of a color, too?" she asks. I raise my hand, as does everyone else in the room aside from Lu, who is busy with her own work.

"Well, no wonder it didn't work," Sabeena says.

"Except…isn't this proof it did?" I ask.

Sabeena looks at me while Kornelía sits up and sneaks the pizza out from my grasp.

"She got Meander's color. And he wasn't thinking of yellow or blue. Mahogany is a specific color, and she got it."

"It was a fluke," Kornelía says, more content now she's got food again.

Sabeena watches her chew and then peers around at us. "Could be a fluke," she says. "But what if it wasn't? Let's start again. This time, everyone think of a color. Kornelía, you keep trying. If a color appears to you, say it aloud."

Kornelía's shoulders slump forward, but she finishes her pizza and resumes her position facing Sabeena. She closes her eyes again. This time she doesn't tense or say she can't do it. She sits in silence, her chin raised as if she's listening for something. Then, she takes a deep breath and smiles.

"Rose pink," she says.

Reed raises his hand. "That's me," he says with an embarrassed mumble.

Sefa chuckles until Sabeena shushes him.

"Keep going, Kornelía!"

Kornelía turns her head from side to side, her face leaning towards me when she says, "Turquoise."

"Yeah, that's right." I smile.

Kornelía smiles back before she turns her head in the opposite direction and tilts it towards Sefa and Naasir.

"Gold," she says firmly.

Naasir nods his head.

"Keep going," Sabeena whispers.

Kornelía does, turning her closed eyes confidently in the direction of our sofa.

"Black, which isn't technically a color, Dylan."

"Woah." Dylan's eyes are wide.

So are Kornelía's when she opens them.

"I knew you could do it!" Sabeena squeals.

Kornelía isn't as elated as her friend, though. Guessing random colors was neat, but her sensing a specific person's choice has freaked her out.

"Okay, let's try it again. Only this time—"

"I don't think I want to play anymore," Kornelía says. She tucks her knees into her chest and pulls her long hair over her shoulder.

Sabeena is crestfallen. "But we're just getting started!"

Kornelía shakes her head, and Sabeena deflates, slipping down until she's lying on the floor.

"All that potential and nowhere to channel it," she groans.

Kornelía rests her chin on her knees and stares at the fire.

"Oh, stop being a wuss, Korni," Mim says from her spot lounging next to Dylan. "It's just a game."

"Mim," I begin, but she waves me away before I can even start to disagree.

"She's fine. She's just weirded out by her own abilities. For someone who wants to see ghosts so bad…"

"This isn't seeing ghosts," Kornelía says, her eyes still trained on the fire. "This is something else. This isn't something I wanted."

Mim scoffs. "Why not? Reading people's minds? It's great."

"Leave her alone," Meander mumbles. He's trying not to pay attention, but it's impossible when it's all happening so close.

"You stay out of it," Mim snaps, glaring past me to Meander on my other side. "You're not involved."

"I'm in the room, aren't I?" he replies, flashing her a dark look before returning to his book.

"Who knows why? You're as bad as Lu, always reading those stupid books."

Meander's hand tenses against his novel's worn cover, and I can't help smirking. It's kind of charming he wants to defend the honour of his books, but I'm glad he doesn't make the effort right now. Mim's heated enough as it is, and this conversation doesn't need to turn into a debate over the merits of literature.

"Mim, let it go," I say, motioning to Kornelía to get the conversation back on track. "She's had enough for one night."

"Yeah, whatever," Mim says, sulking into Dylan's side.

He puts an arm around her, but his attention is

mostly focused on Kornelía.

"It was pretty awesome, though," he says.

She looks back at him, her eyes shining. She smiles a little and nods her head once.

"Yeah, it was," she agrees before she turns back to the fire.

An awkward silence follows, no one sure what to say. From our perspective, Kornelía's ability is incredible, but it's easy enough to understand why she's not too excited about it. I know what it's like to have an experience no one else shares. I'm sure almost everyone else here does, too. So far, Kornelía has been enthusiastic about the possibilities of being a Sender. But her abilities are developing in an unexpected way, and she's not sure what to make of it. All things considered, I'd rather read minds than see the spirits of murder victims. But I suspect Kornelía will be okay with this new achievement once she has a bit of time to wrap her head around what it means.

For now, she sits by the fire, and the rest of us stay quiet until Reed gets up to grab more pizza and steps on Sabeena's outspread hair in the process.

"Oh, you imbecile!" Sabeena says, sitting up and running her fingers through the sleek strands. "I just washed it."

"Sorry," Reed says, sounding anything but. He reaches the pizza box and grabs two more slices while Sabeena rolls her eyes and tries to wipe the remnants of his footprint out of her hair.

22

MIM DIDN'T SPEND MUCH TIME WITH US DURING OUR LAST GROUP MEETING, and I don't see much of her anywhere else for the next week, either. She's exempt from her courses, so she can spend more time away, working with her spirit. Dylan complains about her getting off easy, but I don't think Mim would agree. Last weekend, she was confident she'd be talking with the spirit soon. But, on Sunday, she set off with Lani again. Since then, she's grown more closed off and quiet with each passing day.

This morning, at breakfast, she wouldn't talk to me or Kornelía. She wouldn't even flirt with Dylan. Her behaviour's odd, but the others don't seem to notice. They think she's just busy, and since I've only known Mim for a couple of months, I have no reason to argue their assumption.

Still, I try to talk to Dylan about it before our next Introduction to Imprinting class, but he doesn't think it's a topic worth discussing.

"Mim's got it all under control," he says, chewing a piece of gum and playing with its wrapper.

I shake my head, frustrated I can't convince him to see things the way I do. "I don't think she's got it under control, Dylan. I think…"

The door opens, and our instructor steps into the room, cutting off my chance to press the issue any further.

"Hello, everyone!" Miss Kappel says as she strides to her desk.

I slump back in my seat, picking up my pen to take notes. Dylan's never ecstatic about a four-hour lesson beginning, but I think he's pleased I no longer have a chance to bug him about Mim, at least not until the course is over.

Miss Kappel never wastes time starting her classes. In the seconds it takes for her to walk to her desk, she's already begun her lecture. "I want you to try to remember the most emotional experience of your life," she says, placing her bag on the desk before she steps to the far wall and slides a hand over the light switch. She flips the switch to turn off all the classroom lights, throwing us into darkness and giving me no time to collect my thoughts.

I sit, pen in hand, staring into the black around me and listening to the giggles and whispers from my course mates. Miss Kappel gives us a moment to be confused before she speaks again.

"All right, quiet down," she says, her voice a strange, disconnected sound. "Take a deep breath and think about what I've said. Remember your emotions. Remember the most emotional experience you've ever had."

"Like...the most scared we've ever been?" a girl asks, though I can't tell which girl the voice belongs to without seeing her face.

"The most emotional," Miss Kappel corrects. "Often, this is a memory of fright, or sadness. But not always. We can have happier emotions, too, and they can be as strong as the bad ones, though not necessarily as easy to remember."

I let my worry about Mim fade away as I think about what Miss Kappel is saying. Remembering happiness is easy, but I understand what she means about darker emotions being easier to keep a hold of. I can *remember* the happiness, but I can't feel it. It's like watching a funny movie for the first time. Afterwards, it's easy to recall the humor, but re-watching the same scenes rarely amounts to the same level of enjoyment.

But being afraid is different. I still remember the incident at the birthday party when I was six and saw the ghost in Simon's room. The ghost was frightening, but what truly *scared* me was the realization no one else saw her. Simon's parents were angry with me, and my parents decided there was something wrong with my brain. Those were terrifying days because, for a while, I wondered if they were right. And, even now I know the spirit was real, I still shudder from the memory of fearing there was no ghost, only something broken in my head.

"It is believed that spirits are not always fully formed," Miss Kappel says, her sharp voice softer in the dark. "Sometimes, only parts of ghosts remain in a house...some of their energy is attached to an object or a place, but not all. It's like they've left an arm, a leg, a heart, or even a feeling. They've moved on, but their anger or fear has stayed behind. Not so bad for them, but not too pleasant for whoever gets the detached part."

I'm fairly sure she's smiling, but I don't know whether the suggestion of mutilated ghosts is funny or disturbing.

"We're going to perform an experiment," Miss Kappel says. "And you are all going to be the test subjects."

"I knew there was a hidden motive behind this place," Dylan mumbles to my left. "They want to use us as lab rats."

"Is that so bad?" I ask.

Dylan scoffs, but it turns into a laugh halfway through. "I could've been a lab rat for my sister's cooking at home," he replies. "And, at least then, I would've gotten some free meals out of it. But I guess I could've been poisoned, too...."

"You can learn the secrets of being a ghost here, and if your sister poisons you at home, you'll be able to haunt her," I tease.

"Eureka!" Dylan exclaims. "I've found my true purpose."

A bluish glow comes to life near the front of the class, ending our quiet conversation. A square of light sits over the dark shadow of Miss Kappel's desk.

"Some believe the spirits of the dead are not the only ones who can imprint," she says.

"What do you mean?" someone asks.

"Some ghost-hunters," Miss Kappel explains, "suggest the living can also imprint. That, strong emotions—even if those emotions come from living energy—can sometimes attach themselves to an object or a place. Today, we're going to give this idea a try."

There are confused and worried whispers all over the room, and Miss Kappel laughs.

"Don't worry, it won't hurt," she promises. "All we're going to do is to think of our most emotional memory, and we're going to direct it at this box."

The box's eerie glow is easy to stare at. It draws my focus like a hypnotist's pendulum.

"Think about your memories, and think about the box. Pretend you've stored something from your memory in the box. A letter, perhaps? An object present at the time of the emotional event? Think hard and concentrate. Direct your energy at the box, and we'll see if anything happens."

The room grows inexplicably quiet. No one was talking before, but now, no one so much as shifts in their seat, shuffles their feet, or even taps a pencil. It hardly seems like anyone breathes. A soft buzzing emanating from the box is the only sound, making it impossible to not think about Miss Kappel's instructions—even if they are ridiculous.

To stare at this box and focus on the emotions in my life in hopes I might imprint something? It's more than ridiculous. It's stupid and pointless. Unless Miss Kappel knows something I don't. It wouldn't be the first time this summer I've been surprised by the breadth of the paranormal world. Besides, it's dark and quiet. No one can see me, and everyone else appears to be doing as they're told. So, I do, too.

I think of Simon's birthday party, of how upset my claims of seeing a ghost made everyone else. I recall the hushed conversations between my parents when they believed I was asleep. They talked about therapy, and I hoped they weren't going to disown me because I was crazy. I remember the moment, three months after the party, when Mom told me she was having another baby.

The air in the classroom chills, and I shiver. My stare is vacant as I watch the box and work through the painful memories of those years ago. When I hear a noise behind me, a noise like a door swinging open and closed, I pull my gaze away from the glowing light. Spots dance before my eyes, blue and white circles blooming bright against the darkness of the rest of the room.

I blink against the spots and turn back to the box again. Every so often, I hear muted scuffling like someone's walking by my desk. *Probably Miss Kappel. I don't know how she can see through this darkness.* There aren't any windows in the room, and with the lights off, it's black as pitch—save for the glowing box. If she can see, Miss Kappel must have extraordinary powers of sight.

It doesn't take long to lose myself in the box's entrancing glow once more, and I'm so busy thinking through my memories the sound of Dylan and another camper gasping jerks me back into the present with a start. I glance in the direction of the noise to see a small tendril of blue smoke hovering in the air overtop of someone's head. The smoke twists and stretches itself forward, towards the box.

"What the..." Dylan mutters as another tendril appears on the other side of the room.

Someone else gasps, and a few campers chuckle.

"Shhh!" Miss Kappel exclaims, "It's working! Concentrate, everyone!"

The room grows quiet again, but I doubt anyone's concentrating as hard now as they were before. All over, tendrils of smoke billow into the darkness, each one filtering slowly towards the box. Even I get a tendril. I want to reach up and run my fingers through it, but I resist the urge. I don't know what it is, and I don't want to risk messing up something important because of my curiosity.

"I've never had a reaction this intense before!" Miss Kappel says from the front of the class. "This is amazing!"

"What's happening?" a girl asks, her voice unsure.

"You're imprinting your memories onto the box!" Miss Kappel explains. "You're attaching to it, connecting your emotions to it. You're imprinting!"

I wish I could see my course mates. I want to assess their expressions right now.

The lines of smoke connect with the box and grow thicker. The tendrils puff out until a giant cloud of smoke forms over everyone's heads.

"Now what's happening?" a boy to my right asks.

"I-I don't know," Miss Kappel stammers. "I... There is too much. I think... I think there's too much emotion!"

"What does that mean?" another kid asks.

The smoke begins to surround us. I don't know if I should breathe it in or not. I don't know what the hell is going on.

"I'm not sure!" Miss Kappel says. She sounds panicked. "The whole room could... Oh, dear, we have to stop this now! I think...over here..."

She fumbles with something, but all I can see is blackness and grey-blue mist. It smells medicinal and is thick in my throat. I cough, waving a hand in front of my face in an attempt to clear it away.

"Ah, yes, here we go!"

The classroom lights flicker back to life, and everyone groans at the sudden brightness. I have to blink several times before I can stare around without pain. The smoke is still around us, but it's much thinner in the light. And standing at the front of the room, four leads dressed head-to-toe in black grin at us—square smoke machines with small nozzles perfect for streaking wisps of smoke through the air in their hands.

"Wait a minute...." Dylan says when he notices.

The leads, along with Miss Kappel, begin to laugh.

"It was a joke?" one of the older girls asks in a shrill voice.

"No, it was an experiment," Miss Kappel replies. "And I suspect we all did tremendously. I don't know if this box will be the source of any hauntings, but we all connected our memories and our emotions to it while forming a new memory and a new set of emotions, too. Think about it. Whenever you see this box now, what will come to mind? Living imprints, ladies and gentlemen! We've all attached ourselves to this place, this time, and this object in an emotional way."

She smiles, patting the top of the box. The campers around me groan again, burying their heads in their hands in embarrassment.

23

"Pranks aside, living imprinting is an interesting concept."

As I walk out of the classroom, hours after the smoke-machine prank and the lesson on how living imprinting might logically work, I have to look around before I'm convinced the voice is directed towards Dylan and me.

Lu walks on Dylan's other side, her petite frame clothed in a squared, red dress. She's the only other Shade in our imprinting course, but I would have thought she'd talk to anyone else in class before she spoke with Dylan or me.

"It sounds stupid to me." Dylan scoffs, less perplexed than I am by the girl's sudden effort to make conversation.

Lu's contempt rivals any of Mim's fiercest glowers as she studies Dylan with displeasure. "It's a completely valid concept," she says, her words stern.

Even though I've heard her talk in our courses

before, only now she's so close do I notice the slight lisp of her speech.

"What do you mean, Lu?" I ask, smirking at the way Dylan's eyes widen in response to her harsh tone.

Lu offers me a congenial smile. "Well, consider my talent. I see auras, and I know when a ghost is attached to a living person."

"Yeah, so?"

Dylan's unimpressed with Lu's confident manner. I have a feeling he's sided with Mim on whatever feud the two girls have going.

"Wouldn't that be like ghosts imprinting on the living? Not living imprinting."

"You didn't let me finish," Lu snaps.

I raise my brows at Dylan, and he shakes his head, looking like he wants to bolt away from this conversation.

"Sometimes, spirits attach to the living, yes. But, sometimes, it's the living keeping the spirit around. It's like the living are so attached, the deceased can't move on."

"I don't buy it," Dylan says. "The dead choose to stay or go. The living don't force them to stick around."

"So says the guy who can't even see proper spirits," Lu mutters.

"Hey, I see *proper spirits*," Dylan shoots back, his voice brimming with annoyance. "Just because I don't see the ghosts of people doesn't mean my spirits are any less important."

I've never seen Dylan so defensive about his talent before. Apparently, he's quite serious about people respecting the spirits of non-humans as well. I smile. Being a vet is a good choice for Dylan, I think. If he can keep focused long enough to finish his schooling.

We walk into the dining hall, and the sight of other Shades gathered on the far side of the room gives me a chance to settle the tension between Dylan and Lu.

"If you're talking about living imprinting," I say, the idea occurring to me only as the other campers come into my line of sight, "wouldn't Naasir's talent be a better fit? He can visit with a dying person and know if they're likely to stay around as a spirit or not. Wouldn't that be a living imprint? If they're still alive, but they're so attached to a place Naasir knows they won't, like, move on?"

Lu thinks about what I've said and nods. "I guess that makes sense. Well thought, Callum."

"Why do you always have to call people by their full name?" Dylan asks, his jaw set in a hard line.

"Because that's what their name is," Lu responds curtly.

"Yeah, but that doesn't mean they want to be called it. Cal goes by Cal, so show him a little respect and call him *Cal*."

"Guys, it's not a big deal," I say, moving to stand between them.

"Maybe not for you," Dylan huffs, staring past me. "But Mim hates it."

"Maria doesn't *hate* it," Lu says. "She *dislikes* it. And I *dislike* when people exaggerate."

"Trust me," Dylan replies, "she *hates* it."

"There's a lot going on in Maria's life you don't understand, dog-boy," Lu sneers.

I didn't think she'd stoop to name-calling, but Dylan seems unfazed.

"Yeah, 'cause you know her better than I do," he

says.

But Lu doesn't look as if she's trying to pick a fight. At least, she doesn't look as if she's *only* trying to pick a fight. Something akin to concern glints in her eyes, and her razor-thin lips press together with hesitant caution.

She glances at me, the swift gaze revealing the honesty of her last remark. I remember the second day of camp, and the way Mim pushed Lu away. I think about the way Mim's been acting lately, distant and jittery, her efforts to appear confident and in control strained. I'm not sure the two situations are connected, but they do point to aspects of Mim's character Dylan might be clueless about.

"It's an interesting theory, about the living imprinting," I say, breaking into the argument before it becomes so fierce the entire dining hall can listen in. "I never would have taken Miss Kappel seriously if you hadn't mentioned it, Lu."

Lu's troubled expression drifts beneath a disinterested exterior. She understands I'm pushing into the discussion in order to end it, and she is disappointed I won't let the fight reach its natural climax. But seeing as this is the first time the two of us have been involved in the same conversation, I can't quite make myself care if she thinks less of me. If she *can* think less of me. I'm not sure Lu's given me enough thought to make it possible for my value to depreciate in her eyes.

"Yes, well—" Lu takes a deep breath, clearing her head "—I have to go study. Goodbye, Callum. Dylan." She gives us a stiff nod before turning away, her strides long and quick as she moves in the direction of the library.

"I can't stand her!" Dylan groans after she's gone.

I don't blame him. From the little I've seen of her mannerisms and social skills, I'm not too keen on Lu myself. It's a bit disappointing. There's no rule saying we all have to get along here, but for the most part, I've found my fellow campers friendly. We're connected, all of us, and there's solidarity in the talents we possess. I enjoy the sense of belonging. Lu's the first person I've felt no companionship with. I thought it was because we hadn't talked yet. But, now, I suspect our not talking has been a blessing, not a hindrance to our camaraderie.

Still, her remarks make me think.

"Could she be right?" I ask, my eyes trailing after her before they slide over to the distractingly awful teal and brown polka-dotted dress shirt Dylan's wearing. I don't know much about trendy looks or classic styles, but Dylan has got to have the worst fashion sense I've ever encountered. "About Mim?"

Dylan lets out a frustrated growl. "She's not right about anything, Cal. Mim's *fine*. Okay?"

"Okay," I mutter, though I don't believe it. I hold in a sigh, studying Dylan's shirt before I shift my gaze to the short boy's face, a new thought making its way forward.

"Dylan, do you ever...? I don't know, feel like you're behind everyone else here? So many of the campers have it all figured out. They understand their talent and know what they want to do for, like, the rest of their life. They have their own theories about stuff that I don't even understand half the time."

"Well, that's about twice as often as I understand."

Dylan laughs, but when he notices my serious expression, he stops chuckling. He shifts his weight from one foot to the other, and hunches his shoulders in a half-shrug. "Not everyone is like us. Some of these kids have parents who actually *believed* them when they said they saw ghosts. They've had years to learn about it. Besides, people like Lu are lifers. They'll come to camp and go on to work for the Oracle as soon as camp's done."

"How do you know I'm not a lifer?" I ask.

Dylan blinks in surprise. He considers me for a second and then shrugs wholeheartedly. "Are you?"

"I don't know." I rub my right temple, a dull headache starting to throb. "I keep trying to figure it out, but I just don't know. Are you coming back? You're not a lifer, you've said so yourself. Are you going to come back to camp next year?"

Dylan grins. "Of course," he says. "Unless I happen to be dating my dream girl or something. It's fun here, and I'll admit it's nice to be around other freaks like me." He pats me on the back as he waves across the room where Sefa and Naasir stand by the front door, beckoning us to join them outside.

There's a beehive on the camp's property, and one of the Revenant girls is allergic. She's been avoiding the spot all summer, but when Naasir heard about her allergy, he promised to move the hive to keep her safe. For the past week he's been showing the bees where their new home will be. This evening, he's planning to move the hive itself, with his bare hands and no apparent concern about getting stung. Dylan's been affectionately calling him Candyman all week. Naasir doesn't have a clue what it means, but I think he appreciates the nickname.

Dylan takes off, and I follow behind, the way I've done the entire summer. All this time at camp, I've gone along with the others on everything, never making my own decisions. I'm not confident about my talents and my future here like everyone else. People like Sefa and Lu know they'll be a part of the Oracle for good. People like Dylan know they won't. And people like me?

I seem to be the only one who's still so unsure.

24

Miss Kappel's imprinting experiment bears resemblance to the essay I still haven't started for Mr. Bujak's Emotional Entities course. I'm supposed to describe my most emotional encounter with a spirit, a recollection stretched into one thousand words. Emotional Entities is the only course I'm taking this summer that makes me feel as if I'm still in school. I've had the assignment for a week, and I can't figure out what spirit I should write about.

I took my notebook outside with me this afternoon, thinking the peace of a bright day might be enough to fuel my writing. But Dylan, Kornelía, and Sefa have joined me on the far side of the black lake, and it's hard to concentrate when no one else is doing homework.

Kornelía's lying on her stomach, her hair pulled into a precarious bun atop her head. She's sketching, her pencil stuck between her teeth whenever she pauses to consider the picture. She's so invested in the work she doesn't even realize we can all see it. Not that Sefa or Dylan notice. They're too busy arguing and laughing in turns, oblivious to anything outside of their conversation. But I notice Kornelía. She's... different, like this. Lying here in the sun, working on a picture, not nervous about saying the wrong thing and not shy about the quality of her abilities.

It's not only the setting that's changing her. It's this summer, this place. At the beginning of camp, all Kornelía could do was sense if a location was haunted. Now, she's reading minds, and even though it still freaks her out, I think she's happy to know her talents are developing.

We're all supposed to develop, eventually. The second puberty as Sefa called it. But Kornelía's the only one of us showing signs of hitting it early. Daniel said it might mean her talents have a lot of shaping up to do. I wonder if that's true, and what it means for Kornelía if it is. She can already draw spirits with incredible accuracy, and Sabeena's game proved she can pull other people's thoughts into focus, too. She may not see much with her eyes, but her mind's something to admire.

I envy her. But I also like the way she's changing. Ethereal is too strong of a word, but it's almost correct. It's like she's on her way to being ethereal, like she's transforming into something otherworldly herself.

"Oh, come on, you were never picked on for your talent growing up?" Sefa asks, unaware of the peculiar nature of the girl lying next to his feet. He throws a peanut in the air and catches it in his mouth.

"No, it never came up," Dylan shrugs. "It's pretty easy in my neighborhood. New houses, new school.

Not a lot of dead dogs wandering the hallways, you know?"

"But you must have seen some," Sefa insists. He glances at Kornelía, who's ignoring the discussion. Then he looks at me. "He must have seen some," he says again as if he's waiting for my input.

"Sure, I saw a couple," Dylan answers before I have a chance to open my mouth. "But it wasn't a big deal. My family knew, but no one at school did. I figured out pretty early it wasn't strays I was seeing, so I learned to keep my mouth shut."

"Yeah, but the pain," Sefa says. He eyes me again, this time his expression one of solidarity. He must remember what I went through our first night here.

"Pain?" Dylan asks.

For a moment, I'm stunned by his blank expression until he shakes his head and laughs.

"Oh, you mean the head pain. Yeah, I get that, but it's not bad. I don't know what it's like for everyone else, but Cal and that Rhoades kid sure seemed to get hit pretty hard during initiation."

I bristle when he calls Meander "that Rhoades kid" as if he's only heard stories about Meander and has never met him in person, let alone been his roommate for two months.

"Hell, Robbie even bled from his ears. It's not like that for me. It's like the beginning of a headache, sometimes a bit of a sore ear, too. Nothing major, though. Unless I'm a master of tolerating pain, or Cal's a big wimp."

I throw my sandwich's wrapper at his face. It hits him in the eye.

"Geez, man, take my eye out, won't you?" He

winces.

Sefa erupts in barking laughter.

"Some master of pain," he says.

Dylan glares at him before picking up the wrapper and throwing it his way. Sefa catches it and crumples it in his fist.

"I don't feel any pain," Kornelía pipes in without seeming to notice that the addition of her airy voice startles us all. She briefly raises her eyes to us before ducking back down to her work. "Maybe it's because I can't communicate, but what I sense doesn't hurt. Feels a little chilly, but that's all. And, besides, I like the cold. It's refreshing. I always feel hot and stuffy afterwards."

"Well, I get the pain," Sefa says. "Head ache and ear ache from all that awful noise. There's also the smell to deal with."

Kornelía peers up from her drawing again, one eyebrow arched. "Smell? I never smell anything."

"I do," Dylan muses. "At least, I think I do. Sometimes. Not always. Usually a bone smell or like some kind of meat. Sometimes there's nothing, though."

"There's always a smell for me," I say.

Sefa nods like the two of us understand something the others don't. This summer, I've figured out that not everyone experiences spirits the same way. It's a given when we don't even see the same things. But it's nice to know some of us overlap.

"Well, no wonder you were both bullied," Dylan says. "Wandering around holding your head and complaining about imaginary smells."

I laugh, but it's not actually funny. Dylan may have

escaped ridicule growing up, but I didn't. It's hard to act normal when you're not. Hanging out with other kids is a challenge. One I'm not often up to. Even going to the movies has proved impossible at home. On more than one occasion, I've failed to ignore the effects of the forever-teenaged employee wandering the parking lot where he was stabbed after a late shift. It's not fun trying to talk about what film we'll see while the guy follows me, crackling in my head and filling my nostrils with rotted butter so thick I can't stomach the popcorn once we're inside.

I wonder what it's like for Dylan at home, if it's as easy as he claims it is to look away and pretend there's no spirit barking at him from the road where it was run over.

"Well, all I can say is I'm glad I've got the ability I do," Dylan says, stretching himself out on his back. "I don't think I could handle the full force of it."

"I wish I could feel more," Sefa says. He stares up at the sky, his mouth drawn in a tight line. "And I would like to be better at communicating, so I could do more for them."

"I wish I could feel more, too," Kornelía adds. She erases something on her picture and starts reforming what I think is part of a spirit's face.

I'm not sure how to respond to Dylan's statement. I'd like having less pain, but there doesn't seem to be any point in having pain at all. I'm not clambering to have more ghostly interactions, and I would prefer to say I wish I didn't feel *anything* when a spirit's nearby. Complaining about my ability when two of my friends just declared their wish to experience more, however, is selfish. And, since I'm stuck with my talent whether

I want it or not, it'd be more reasonable to hope I might someday be useful to the spirits I can't avoid.

I don't mention either thought aloud. I close my notebook and stand up, tired of trying to work and uninterested in continuing the conversation.

"I'm going to go for a walk," I say, tucking the book under my arm and pulling out my phone. I unravel the earbuds and open my music, flicking through the playlists until I find one suited to the warm day.

Sefa and Dylan go back to talking about their childhoods, and Kornelía gives me a wave as I leave. I walk around the side of the château, heading towards the woods behind the house. Birds flit from branch to branch as I wander among the outermost trees, always keeping the château in sight. From behind, the whole house is lopsided, like part of it is starting to sink into the lake. I hope they do some repairs before next year, otherwise it might be a soggy summer.

I try to think about the spirit I'll choose for my essay as I walk, but I'm soon distracted by Saint-Saëns's "Le Carnaval des Animaux". The music pulls my thoughts away from coursework and pulls my feet away from the house. I wander deeper into the woods until the sun is blocked by the trees and a pocket of cold prickles against my skin. I shiver, trying to shake off the coolness as I take in my surroundings. The forest is green and quiet, and I'm tempted to continue farther in. But the shade makes my head feel a bit foggy, and I don't want to risk getting lost in the dimness.

I take out my earbuds and concentrate on navigating my way back to camp. When I'm nearly out of sight of the spot where I stopped, I turn back. I thought I was surrounded by trees, but when I look again, I realize I was standing in a small clearing. It's picturesque from afar, birds swooping overhead and a small bush of yellow flowers blossoming under a beam of sunlight I would have discovered if I'd ventured a little bit farther. It looks like the perfect spot for reflection, but the idea of returning makes my heart patter with apprehension.

I have an uneasy feeling that, if I zone out again, I'll regret it. So, I turn around and hurry back the way I came, thinking the library might be the best spot for my essay writing, after all.

25

"I HATE IT WHEN THE LIBRARY'S BUSY," MEANDER GRUMBLES AS WE WALK into the basement room full of books, tables, and right now, people. It's crowded in here with campers studying or working on projects at the tables and several more kids roaming the small set of stacks or sitting in groups on the floor.

I laugh at Meander's expression, his eyes disappointed like he was promised a treat and has been presented with a chore instead. "Do you like any place when it's busy?" I ask.

He huffs. "No, but the library is the worst," he complains.

I never did come here to work on my essay this afternoon. I still haven't even started the damned thing. But, tonight, I'm happy to put Mr. Bujak and Emotional Entities out of my mind so I can concentrate on our final project instead. I twist around bodies and chairs to make my way to a far table. This one is void of people, but full of old books and decorated with a handmade RESERVED sign.

"I guess this must be us," I say, dropping my bag beside the table and surveying the mound of thick, old books. "At least Lani saved us somewhere to sit."

"Look at these," Meander says, losing his melancholy expression as he takes one of the books in hand. They're ledgers, bookkeeping records on special loan from some regional archives. They've been taken out for us, so we can determine the name of the spirit Mim has been trying to contact.

Meander opens the book. It's filled with rows and rows of a small, tight scrawl of faded handwriting. "I think we're in this for the long haul," he says, not sounding too sorry to be faced with such a mountain of reading materials.

"We'd better get started then." I slip into my seat and dig my notebook out of my bag. "How do we want to tackle this? Should we search randomly, or should we tackle each name one-by-one?" Our search efforts up to now have been fruitless. I was hopeful we'd have better luck tonight, but I wasn't expecting to have quite so many volumes to go through.

Meander doesn't respond to my question. He's absorbed in the book already, his eyes making their way down the ledger columns, and his fingers sliding along the old text.

"Meander? You with me?"

When he still doesn't answer, I kick the side of his shoe. The fabric's remarkably white next to the grubby former-white of my own sneakers.

"What?" Meander startles, glancing up in surprise. "Sorry, Cal. What'd you say?"

I want to give him a snarky look of annoyance, but I can't help smiling as he sits down beside me. I recognize the concentration, the way he falls into his reading. It makes me miss my violin. It makes me glad to know I'm not the only one who can lose himself in something so completely.

"How should we start searching?" I ask again, this time with his full attention. "Should we go name-by-name, or book-by-book?"

"Neither way is the most efficient, is it?" Meander sighs. He pulls out his notebook, and his half of the list of names. "Unless you possess an outstanding memory, I doubt we'll be able to remember all ten names as we go along. But searching one at a time will take forever."

"We each have half the list. We could keep it split and each work on five names," I suggest. "I guess that's still not effective if I have the book with one of your names, though."

"No, but it's not a bad place to start," Meander says. He reaches across me to grab my half of the list, which I've laid out beside my notes. He places the two halves side by side between us. "Focus on your five," he says, "but keep your eye out for the other names as best you can."

I nod, studying the five names beside me and glancing over the names on Meander's list as well before I grab a book at random and open it. For a full two or three minutes, I stare at the page, trying to make sense of the scrawling handwriting that, long ago, marked the paper with words from another language. Lani gave us a sheet with some basic words in French that might be useful, and since the ledgers are mostly in list form, I can make out where names and dates are. Still, anytime there are notes, it's impossible to decipher, despite my years of mandatory French lessons taken in school. For those first frozen moments, I'm sorry I didn't steal Kornelía's spot in the equipment camp with Dylan, after all.

"These records are insane," Meander mumbles, already jotting down notes. "What are you looking at? I've got death records. Fitting."

"I got..." My eyes sweep over the page without a clue as to what I'm supposed to be reading until I notice the words "Château de Rouseville" in the top corner. Reading the title causes my perspective to shift, and at last, the ledger starts to make a bit more sense.

"I've got records from the hotel," I say, carefully pulling out more pieces of information. Check in and out dates, registered guests, and comments. It's a relief to understand the layout, even if I don't understand anything written in the comments section.

It's enough to get me going, and soon the research takes on a more productive angle. I flip through book after book, sometimes exchanging ledgers with Meander and sometimes picking fresh ones off the table. There are about fifteen books of varying sizes and from varying times in all. Some of them are easy to get through, especially when they're a decade too old or new, and we know we can rule them out right away.

Others take ages. One book of birth and death records is so difficult to understand that Meander and I go over it together, our heads bent over the text as we try to make out line after line.

"Who the hell wrote this?" Meander asks after the first twenty pages.

"I don't know, but I want to tear their fingers off, so they can't write anything else," I mutter, rubbing the bridge of my nose and trying to keep a headache at bay.

Meander laughs. "Considering they've likely been dead a good hundred years or so, you've probably got your wish."

"That's morbid…and oddly satisfying," I admit.

Meander grins. "Now *that's* morbid."

I smirk. "What can I say, I get vicious when I'm tired of translating subpar cursive."

"Well, if it's any consolation, I feel the same way," he says. "We can be morbid together."

"At least I'll have company."

His eyes rest on mine for a few long seconds, and I remember the day in Paris when we held each other's gaze after studying the dilapidated tomb. I never believed staring into someone's eyes could be as meaningful as books and movies make it out to be. But looking at the sunburst of chestnut streaking through the deep jade of Meander's irises is like glimpsing an entire universe of questions I didn't know I needed answers to.

His stare is familiar, which could be because the fright and loneliness I suspect he is used to feeling are crushing emotions I know so well. But something else glints in his eyes too, something pleasant and unexpected, like a cautious invitation to explore. I don't know him well enough to venture far into his world. But the soft tremor buzzing under my skin as we continue to lock gazes makes me determined to journey further, even if I have to do it inch by careful inch.

The room is warm and slightly off-kilter when Meander at last looks back down at the book. "Come on, let's keep going. All this effort has to pay off at some point."

To our surprise, it does. The last section of the book contains two of the names on our list, one from my half and one from his. The name from my paper, Marceline Humbert, was born in Fos-sur-Mer, the French commune where the haunted hotel is located. She died from illness at the age of twenty-four, single and without children or apparent occupation. Meander's grasp of French is better than my own, and he translates that she died at home. The woman from his half of the list has an almost identical story. Born in the same year, she died two years later than Marceline, also from an illness and also at home.

"I think we can rule those two out," Meander says, drawing a line through each name.

It's good to see the fresh, black ink striking two of the ten names away. It's nice to see our efforts rewarded.

We work through another four names on the list over the next three hours. There are two more cases like Marceline, young girls who died at home due to illness or injury. Then there's Greta Hildenstrom, who wasn't born in the commune but was married there in 1867. About a year later, she died in childbirth. I wonder what Daniel would say about Greta. At least her baby survived—a boy who grew up to have a large family of his own. I get caught up in her lineage, tracking the children and grandchildren at generational intervals apart. I have to remind myself

I'm searching for a specific woman, one I'm sure is not Greta. She, like the other girls we found, died at home.

Near the end of the three-hour mark, I rule out the next girl, Emilie Blau. She was twenty-seven when she died in the street after being stuck in a wicked storm. I spend a while thinking about Emilie's story. I'm curious to know why she was out in the storm, where she was going, and why she was alone. I want to know if the storm killed her or if she died from other causes.

The records don't tell me much. It's like starting a good book only to discover half the pages are missing. It's like listening to a grand symphony only to end on a hanging crescendo. Eventually, I write her name on a separate piece of paper and tuck it into my notebook. After camp is over, when I'm back at home and have more time, plus my own computer to search with, I might try to find the missing details of the life and death of Miss Emilie Blau.

"I need a break. And tea. And biscuits," Meander says after I've crossed Emilie off the list. He stretches his arms over his head and peers around the now empty library.

I follow his gaze, realizing for the first time, how quiet it's become. I didn't notice people trickling out as the evening wore on. Now, even the librarian who sits at the small reference desk is gone.

"Better now?" I ask, smirking at Meander as I turn back to him.

He matches my expression as he stands up from his chair. "Much," he says. "What time is it, anyway?"

I pull out my phone to check the time, doing a double-take when I see it's nearly ten pm. I show the screen to Meander, who seems just as shocked.

"Well, what do you think?" he asks, folding his arms across his chest. "We can call it quits and start up tomorrow or keep working through the last names."

"I'm good to keep searching, if you are," I say, the words honest. I'm not tired, and although my eyes are a little sore from so much reading, I'm enjoying the process of hunting and finding. Plus, we're over halfway through now. I don't want to lose our places in the books or forget which ledgers we've already checked.

"Definitely," Meander says, "but not before I get some tea."

"And biscuits? Isn't that a weird thing to pair with...?" I shut my mouth as I realize the answer to my own question. "Nevermind. You mean cookies, right?"

"Yeah, what did you think I meant?"

"The plight of the Canadian," I smile, standing to follow him out of the library. "We're forever stuck between American and British meanings. American biscuits and British biscuits are two very different things."

"Oh, right. American biscuits are like...scones or something."

"Sort of. Less sweet, though, more like a dinner roll than a breakfast food. You can eat them for breakfast, too, but I don't usually. I prefer them with..." I pause near the bottom of the stairs leading up to the dining hall, aware I'm rambling. "Why are we talking about biscuits again?"

Meander chuckles. "I don't know. You thought I wanted dinner rolls with my tea?"

"Oh, right."

We head upstairs and boil water in the kitchen while Meander hunts for cookies and I find suitable mugs and tea bags.

"Are we even allowed to eat in the library?" I ask when the water finishes boiling and the tea begins to steep.

Meander shrugs. "Probably not. But no one's there to say we can't. Just try not to spill your tea all over the record books."

I pause mid-stir. "Gee, that makes me feel much better about sneaking food downstairs."

"Fine. Forget I mentioned spilling tea. Worry about crumbs instead."

"This is an old house, I'm sure there are mice living in the walls of the library, you know," I say. "They'll probably all come out at the smell."

"Won't have to worry about crumbs after all, then." Meander smiles, pouring the milk while I add the sugar. He takes his tea the opposite of how I take mine, with far more milk but considerably less sugar.

Once both cups are prepared, we take them and the snacks back to the basement.

"Okay, who do we have left..." Meander combines the remaining three names onto one sheet before surveying the pile of books on the table. "It took three hours to get seven names done... appears as though it's going to be a late night."

"I don't mind. The only thing I've got on my to-do list tomorrow is working on Mr. Bujak's essay," I say, my words nearly a groan.

"Your most emotional experience with a spirit." Meander scoffs.

He's in Emotional Entities, too. The more I see of his

ability, the more that class seems like a perfect fit for him.

"Like they're not all emotional."

"Miss Kappel, our Imprinting instructor, said the strongest emotional experiences don't have to be about fear or grief," I say, cupping my mug. "I'm trying to keep that in mind, but I'm coming up blank."

"A fine concept for some people," Meander says, "but I didn't think happy spirits were all too common."

"Have you written anything yet?" I ask. It's a nice break, sipping tea and eating cookies while we talk about homework. If I told Dylan, he'd say it sounded like torture. But I like this.

"Yeah, I wrote it a week ago," Meander nods.

"What did you write about?" I ask, realizing how personal the question is as soon as it's out of my mouth. "Uh, you don't have to tell me. I-I don't have to know...."

He considers me for a moment before he takes a long sip of tea and stares down at the book before him. I assume the gesture means he's not going to talk until he looks back up at me and runs his teeth over his bottom lip before he speaks.

"It was about a year ago," he says, eyes drifting to the library stacks. "At a classmate's house. I was there working on a group project. They didn't really want me there, though, so I went out back when they broke for lunch. Thought I'd sit in the garden until it was time to return to work." He sighs, taking another sip of tea.

"It was an old woman. And, you know, I'm used to spirits being, well, troublesome. But this one fooled me. She seemed pleasant, peaceful even. I guess she was until she spotted me. Then she changed, became really nasty, and said some things that took me by surprise. Personal things. Or, at least, they seemed personal. Normally, they don't. But whoever this woman hated, he had enough in common with me that her comments hit me unlike anything ever had."

Another sigh, another sip. He licks his lips, and my eyes slide to the scar on his jaw as he continues.

"I'm also used to spirits clanging around, but...she was the first one who ever attacked. Scratched my neck. My classmates thought I'd been in a fight with some vicious stray cat. Before that, spirits had been bothersome, but not dangerous. This woman changed that."

I thought Kornelía was the only one whose talents were starting to develop. If Meander's ability has already progressed to the point spirits can physically harm him, I dread to think what will happen over the next couple of years.

"Wow," I say, trying to formulate the best response. I'm terrible at finding good words. Music I can handle. Words are not my thing. "Well, doesn't matter what I write about, I guess. My essay's going to be pretty lame next to that."

Meander gives me a half-smirk, and with a heave of his shoulders, he turns his attention back to our project. I do the same, and together we dive back in, pouring over volumes as we try to find Mim's ghost.

For the next hour and a half, it's slow going. Meander finds one of the remaining three, Sarah Verdier, in a birth record from 1839. There's no corresponding death record, and no record of occupation or marriage, either.

"Chances are, she left the place and never returned," Meander says, his hand poised above her name on the list, trying to decide if he should mark it off.

"Probably," I agree, "but we can't be sure, can we? Not without some kind of record."

"Seriously? You're going to make me keep her name here?" He hovers the pen low across the paper, and I grab his hand to keep it from making a mark.

"Yeah, I am. At least until we find the final two."

"Fine," he moans, dropping the pen.

I grin and release my grip on his hand. "Just think. The sooner we find the last two names, the sooner you can cross off Sarah."

"And then all my dreams will have come true," Meander says, flipping to the next page.

It takes another half hour to find the next woman, a Miss Hélène Severin.

"Look at this," Meander says, pushing the record book close to me and scooting his chair over.

"She died in a private home," I say, looking where his neatly trimmed fingernail rests on the column describing the place of death.

"Yes, but look at the address." He searches through his notebook until he reaches a page of bullet points written in a careful hand. "It's right next to the hotel."

"Really?" I take his notes, impressed by his penmanship, and study the fact sheet he must have put together before our meeting tonight. I compare the address he's written with the one in the ledger book. "You're right," I say.

Meander furrows his brow, his eyes slightly squinted as he works to translate another part of the ledger.

"Damn, she died of an infection," he mumbles. He

studies the text, his lips set in a tight frown.

"So? What difference does that make?"

He gazes up at me, his eyes tired but determined. "The infection was drawn out. Over a year maybe? I can't exactly make it out, but…if it was that long of an illness and *next door* to the hotel, it's unlikely she'd be haunting it."

"It's the closest thing we've found," I say, taking Meander's pen and circling Hélène's name. "Let's not rule it out based on the length of the infection."

"I guess," Meander says. "What does that leave, one name? Who's the lucky girl?"

"Isabelle Levasseur," I say, trying hard not to butcher the name. The words slip easier from my tongue than I expected, and with them, comes the odd feeling her name is the one we've been waiting for. My eyes shift to Meander and our gazes catch.

There's something different about Isabelle. All I had to do was say her name aloud for me to realize we should have been searching for her first. Meander and I spend a frozen moment staring at each other, and when the spell is broken, we go to work. Meander takes the hotel record books while I look for the record of her death. Lani's paper says she died in 1857, and with that information, it's almost too easy to find the correct ledger.

"Here she is!" I exclaim.

Meander stands, leaning over my shoulder to read the text. "She fell down a set of stairs," he reads, his head lowered close to my own.

His hair smells like sandalwood. It's a nice scent, and I blush when I realize I'm wasting time noticing something so mundane, when our search is about to come to an end.

"Yes. She fell... She fell in a château. *The* château. The Château de Rouseville!"

He turns his head to meet my gaze, our faces inches apart. My skin tingles from his discovery. His cheeks bloom with pink from what he's found.

After a long, short moment, he swallows.

"She's the one," he says, stepping back and returning to his chair.

I nod, wiping my palms on my jeans and taking a deep breath before grabbing the book again. "Yeah, I think so," I agree, reading over Isabelle's entry and knowing without a doubt she's the one we're after.

"Well, it only took until one in the morning," Meander says, smiling. "But we did it."

"I'm glad," I say, marking down the page of the book before I close it. "To be honest, I didn't know how all this would go. You know...I didn't know if you were going to do much."

I glance up at Meander to see his jaw tighten. My stomach tenses at the sight. I didn't mean to offend him, but it's obvious I've failed at my latest attempt at small talk.

He runs a hand through his soft curls, and presses his lips together. "That's a common conception around here," he says through gritted teeth.

"I'm sorry. It's just..." I want to shut up and stop talking, but I can't seem to keep myself under control. "You know, you're always reading during our courses, and you generally don't seem too...chipper about being here."

His eyes fall, and his voice lowers into something like regret. "I never wanted to be here."

"Then why are you?" I make my voice as gentle as possible, hoping this will turn into another story, another way to restore the mood from a moment ago. But my plan backfires spectacularly.

Meander's head snaps up, and anger flashes in his eyes as he grabs his notebook and his empty mug of tea before turning away from me.

"Sometimes we don't get a choice," he mutters, storming out of the library before I can even call out after him.

26

I FEEL GUILTY ABOUT MEANDER FOR THE REST OF THE WEEKEND. I WANT TO apologize, but he's nowhere to be found. I even wait up for him Sunday night, sitting in the lounge until my eyes droop and I almost slide off the sofa, but still he doesn't come in until after I've given up and gone to bed.

By Monday, I'm tired and stressed. Between Meander's disappearing act and Mim's aggravated aloofness, I'm so confused and drained I try to skip out on the camp's activity day—a late-summer venture meant to de-stress the sectors or prove to the locals the summer camp is real. I'm not sure which. Whatever the case, today's game is not optional. Still, Kornelía has to prod my back the entire way across the lake.

"It will be fun," she assures me, grabbing my arm once we're across so she can pull me around to the forest at the rear of the château. "And, besides, you don't have another choice. So, you might as well enjoy yourself."

"Shouldn't you be trying to cheer up Mim instead of me?" I ask.

Kornelía ignores my question in favor of shoving me towards the other campers.

Ten minutes after we arrive, Robbie cups his hands around his mouth to raise his voice over everyone's chatter. "All right, everybody!" he yells with a cheerful grin. "Today, you've been divided into two teams, the Spirits and the Senders. The object of the game is simple. When I blow my whistle, both teams go into the woods and find their camp. When y'all hear the sound of the air horn, the battle begins.

"If you are hit, retreat to the *opposite* team's camp. That means hit Spirits are trapped with the Senders and hit Senders are floating with the Spirits. Whichever team survives longest wins. So always keep an eye on your team's camp. There are twelve people on each team, so your goal is to see twelve captives in your camp."

"I think this could be worse than archery lessons," Dylan mutters.

"Yeah right, 'cause you don't like holding *that* at all," I reply, nodding towards the gun in Dylan's hand.

We all have one, but Dylan's is the biggest. The plastic guns probably originated as water pistols, but they've been painted with bronze, silver, and tarnished shades of gold, giving them the appearance of something from an alternate-reality Old West. I wonder if Robbie had a hand in their design. They remind me of his collections. They probably started out behaving like normal water pistols, too. But now, instead of water, they shoot streams of foam. Dylan and I are Senders, and our foam is bright, neon green. The Spirit team's foam is bright, neon blue.

Dylan laughs and holds his gun tight. "I suppose there are some perks to this," he says, his smile mischievous.

"Okay. Ready, everyone?" one of the Revenant leads yells. There are assorted cheers from the crowd of campers, which today is made up of everyone who isn't out completing their final task of the summer.

The trilling whistle sounds, and campers rush to the forest. I start with a walk, but Dylan grabs my sleeve and drags me into a run alongside him. He is swift and agile on his feet, and it's difficult to keep up with his pace, despite his short legs. I'm out of breath by the time we reach the Senders base camp deep in the woods, which is marked by a row of green flags stuck in a bunch of trees. The Senders team gathers together, and one of the Wraith kids, a boy named Fredrick, shouts instructions at us.

"Go in pairs!" he calls. "Run together, but stay a few feet apart. That way, if one of you gets hit, the other one can hit the Spirit back. Never hesitate to hit a Spirit. We're Senders, it's what we live for!"

The campers around me laugh, all except Mim, who stands by a tree looking like she wants to be here even less than I do. When we break into groups to wait for the air horn, Dylan and I join her and Kornelía by the edge of the camp base. Dylan and Kornelía peer into the woods as if they're getting ready to attack something while Mim sulks. When the echoing noise of the horn reaches our ears, the rest of the Senders team lets out a loud cheer and runs into the playing zone.

Our group walks together for a while until the girls veer off to the left, and Dylan and I head right.

"You've got to keep quiet," Dylan explains as if he's played this game a million times before.

It's like a game of paintball or laser tag. I wonder which one Dylan's a master of at home.

"Then they can't hear you. Stay in the thick of the trees as much as possible. These bandanas don't keep us hidden well." To mark which team we're on, each of us was given a bandana to wear. Dylan's is wrapped around his forehead like he's an action-movie star while I've tied mine into a loose neckerchief. Regardless of their location, however, the bandanas are easy to spot. Our team's markers are bright green, like the foam inside of our guns. The color choice is not a subtle one.

"What if they take one of us hostage?" I ask in mock seriousness.

Dylan nods, like he truly thinks such a thing might happen.

"Never surrender," he says wisely. "If you're going to lose, go out fighting. We're not friends here. The Spirits want nothing to do with the living."

I raise an eyebrow, dubious. In my experience, spirits often want a lot to do with the living.

We continue for a few minutes before we hear distant yelling followed by loud bellows of laughter. Someone must have been hit. Picking through trees, careful not to be noticed, we sneak forward until we find the remnants of blue and green foam splattered on the ground.

"Who do you think lost?" I ask, and Dylan lets out a long breath.

"Look there," he says, pointing to a tree limb covered in a thick layer of green foam which oozes down to a puddle on the ground. "Whoever shot the green foam missed. But whoever shot the blue foam—" he turns his gaze towards the much smaller spot of scattered blue foam several feet away "—hit their target."

"Which means," I begin.

"One of the Senders was hit," Dylan finishes.

He sounds morose, and I almost laugh.

I've been spending less time with Dylan over the past couple of weeks. His lack of interest in our project, or even in Mim's well-being, has been more than irksome. But it's activities like this which make me remember why I became friends with Dylan in the first place this summer. Dedicated student and keen observer of the human condition he may not be, but when it comes to having fun, he's an excellent person to have around.

We continue at a steady pace, taking our time and paying close attention to the woods surrounding us. We only stop when, a while later, we hear a noise somewhere close by.

"Don't move," Dylan whispers.

I listen for a repetition of sound until it rustles behind us. "Move?" I whisper back.

After a short pause, Dylan nods. "Now!" he says.

I whip around, not sure where I'm supposed to aim. When I notice a bright blue dot a few feet away, I hold up my plastic gun and press the trigger, thinking of nothing else but hitting my target. I stumble back a step as green foam somewhere between the fluffy foam of a bubble bath and the compact foam of Silly String blasts out from the gun. A similar line of blue shoots towards me, and I throw myself to the left as the foam sails past my head. A short way off, a kid named Chen stands covered in green. The boy wipes a hand across his face as he licks his lips.

"Tastes a bit like watermelon," he muses.

I grin, and Dylan rushes back to me, surveying the damage.

"Good, we both managed to avoid getting hit," he says, relieved.

Another green-covered kid, a Revenant girl named Anna, sits on the ground where Dylan struck her, trying to get foam out of her hair.

"That's at least two down."

Shrill screams sound far off, but Dylan and I keep going in the direction we were already headed. We creep through a clump of thick trees and watch as two campers, a Sender and a Spirit, shoot each other at the same time and take one another out of the game.

"So at least two from the Senders, and three from the Spirits," I count aloud. We wait until the campers amble off towards the team bases before Dylan suggests we keep moving.

"Let's go now before someone else comes to investigate the scene," he whispers.

He begins to move forward as a sound echoes ahead of us. I reach out to stop him, but I'm too late. He's beyond my grasp, and he steps out from the cover of the trees, walking only a few paces before blue foam splatters against his chest.

"Dylan!" I call as I raise my own gun and blast foam at Lu.

She screams, crumpling to the ground with a sobbing pout. Dylan mutters something beneath his breath and sighs.

"The blue tastes like blueberries," he mumbles, tasting a bit of the foam on his finger.

I barely manage to hold in a laugh, but Dylan picks himself up, hanging his head as he turns in the direction of the Spirits camp.

27

I CONTINUE ALONG WITHOUT SPOTTING ANYONE FOR SOME TIME. I WEAVE IN and out of trees, stopping every few feet to listen for any nearby campers. There are more screams far off, and some yelling I can't understand. I wonder how many Senders are left in the game, and how many Spirits.

The fun I started to have dwindles as I walk by myself in the forest, spotting no one. I think about heading towards one of the camps to take inventory and see how many people have been hit. It's so quiet in the woods, there can't be many players remaining. I don't know the exact location of the camps, but I turn left, and start in the general direction I think the Spirits camp is in. I walk for about five minutes before I finally hear a cracking noise, like someone snapping a small twig and letting the break of it echo through the woods.

I survey the area and see a flash of blue from behind

a large tree trunk. Slinking over to the tree, I hold my breath and step as lightly as possible. I wait at the back of the trunk, listening for the sound of someone readying themselves for attack. When I don't hear any more noise, I ready my own weapon and brace myself before running around the tree in a sharp curve.

"Of course, you're the one to find me," Meander says through a deep sigh when I round the tree.

I'd wondered where he'd been all morning. I figured he'd snuck away from the game, heading back to our lounge to read one of his books. But here he is, sitting on the ground with his gun leaning up beside him and a blue bandana wrapped around his left hand.

"Go on then. Get it over with," he urges, waiting for me to hit him.

I hold my gun out, considering his bored expression. It would be the easiest thing to do to take him out of the game, and it's not like he's putting up a fight. He's choosing not to play, and by blasting him, I would be doing him a favor.

But I'm not feeling so generous as to make it easy on him. He said it himself. I found him, and by the wary glint in his eye, I think Meander knows I'm not going to let him off the hook.

"You have to at least try to get me." I keep my foam gun up, but I make no effort to use it.

Meander shrugs. "What's the point?"

"It's fun?" I lower the weapon and give him a hard stare. My desire to apologize has vanished. If he's going to be difficult, then I am, too.

"Not for me," Meander says, bringing a knee up to his chest and lowering his chin onto it.

"Okay.... Well, wouldn't it give you great satisfaction

to beat me?" I ask, trying to draw him into a fight.

Meander blinks at me as if I'm talking nonsense. "No," he replies. The corners of his lips twitch in what I think is almost a smirk. "I wouldn't want to waste the energy."

"Gee, thanks."

"Why don't you shoot me? If you don't, someone else will." Meander glances to the side, looking doubtful anyone will find us out here.

"I'm not so sure," I say, following his gaze. "I think we might be the last ones left. Two of the last ones, anyway. If you took me out of the game, you might win the entire thing for your team."

"Wow, how exciting."

I rest my gun against my leg, huffing with annoyance. "You're a real pain, you know that?"

Meander raises his head and glares at me. "You're the pain."

He scowls, though I don't think there's any real anger behind it.

"Everyone else ignores me. You're the only one determined to be a bother all bloody summer."

"Yeah, I'm a real sucker for punishment," I say. I don't want to make him madder at me than he already is. But I don't think being nice is the way to keep him engaged right now.

"I never asked you to talk to me," Meander says. He pulls himself up to a stand, and steps in close. "If you haven't noticed, I've never asked anyone to talk to me. You can have all the fun in the world with your damned ghost tracking. I'd be happiest if I never saw another ghost in my life."

"I know." I nod. "I understand."

He eyes me closely, trying to puzzle out what I mean. "I figured you were the most likely to," he admits. "But I haven't told anyone…"

I shake my head, cutting him off.

"I don't know what your talent is," I say. "Not exactly. But I have some idea. I was with you in Paris, remember? And at the initiation. Your spirits aren't nice. You said as much the other night in the library."

Meander bites his lip and stares down at the ground. "They're not a friendly bunch, no," he mumbles.

"I'm sorry about what I said," I tell him.

He shakes his head. "You don't have anything to apologize for, and I don't need anyone feeling sorry for me," he says, his voice stubborn.

"Yeah, but I shouldn't have suggested you were slacking off, and…"

His head snaps up, the same way it did in the library. I step back, my stomach plunging.

"Don't pity me," he says, his voice harsh.

"Right." I sigh. Even my attempt to apologize has failed. I take another step back and prepare to leave him be. But as I reach down to grab my gun, I change my mind. He can brood all he wants, and with good reason. But he can't deny me the right to say what I've been trying to tell him for days.

I catch his eyes and soften my features. "Well…I'm sorry, anyway. Whether you like it or not."

"Stop it," he snaps.

He looks like he's ready to tackle me, and I bite the inside of my cheek to stop from smiling. This is more emotion than I've seen him show all summer. I don't know why it bothers him so much, but now I've got him riled up, I'm not letting go. Even if he spends the rest of the summer pissed off at me, it will be better than him ignoring the fact that I or anyone else here exists.

"I'm sorry," I repeat, my voice cracking on the last note.

Meander picks up his foam gun for the first time. "I'm serious," he warns.

His hazel eyes are dark and dangerous, but there's something else there, too. Something I suspect is a faint glimmer of amusement. I step forward again. He's taller than me, but not by much. If I straighten my back, I can meet him eye-to-eye.

"I'm really, really sorry," I say in my most earnest voice.

Meander narrows his eyes and raises his gun. "That's it," he says. "You're dead, Sender."

I break into a grin as I hightail it away, fleeing through the forest. We keep a steady pace as I duck between trees and jump over low bushes, Meander following my every movement.

"Get back here, Cal!" he calls.

I push my legs to run faster. I swerve around an old tree stump and hop over a fallen branch. My foot slips on a scattered pile of leaves, but I catch my balance and keep from falling.

"I'm sorry, Meander! For everything. I'm terribly, terribly sorry!" I yell back.

He mutters a few curses in a growled response. I can tell he's getting closer.

I make a sharp turn to the left, the right, and then the left again. There's no one else around, and I see no signs of leftover foam on any of the unfamiliar trees. When Meander approaches from behind, I swing around so fast I fall to the ground. I land hard on my side, icy pain rocketing through my arm. I scramble up as best I can, grabbing my weapon in both hands. Meander watches my movement, and in a flash, he pulls up his own gun.

We stare at each other, aim our weapons, and pull the triggers. And I realize, far too late, my gun is all out of foam.

In the space of a second, I'm covered with cold, slimy blue all along my front and my face. I groan, my head cloudy as I sit up and wipe foam out of my eyes. Meander stands above me, his gun lowered and a smirk halfway up his lips.

"You look ridiculous," he says, his voice breaking into a soft laugh even as he taunts me.

I consider the blue foam covering my hand, and I bring a bit to my mouth. Dylan was right. I do taste a hint of blueberries.

"Yeah, but I taste delicious," I say, before realizing how awkward the words are. My face flushes with heat while cold chills vibrate down my spine and spread through my stomach.

Meander smirks wholeheartedly, but he spares me from suffering through an all-too-easy comeback. He reaches a hand down to help me up. The motion makes me dizzy, and I sway forward until he catches me by the shoulder.

"Foam take that much out of you?"

I try to roll my eyes and shake the uneasy tremor from my muscles. But the tilt of my head shifts the static as if the motion turned the volume in my brain up to maximum levels.

I lurch around to face the place I just stood from, the

one that sent cold and sickness through me. I thought this part of the forest was unfamiliar, but now I see it's not. I wandered here two days ago, stopping nearby when I started to get cold and decided to turn back.

I was too preoccupied to realize it was not the impact of the fall or the wet foam making me so uncomfortable. It was something seeping up, something clinging onto me from deep within the ground. I stare at the grass until the something thuds. It sounds like a fist against a piece of wood buried far under the grassy mound.

My first thought is of an unmarked and long-forgotten grave. But when Meander lets out a whisper of pain, I remember the cemetery in Paris, the peace and warmth of the burial site. This spot, if it is a grave, was not the site of a proper funeral.

"There's something under there," I mutter.

Meander nods, but he takes a step back from the spot, pressing thumb and forefinger to his temples. The thud sounds again, but it's quieter now Meander's stepped back. If he'd been the one to fall on the spot, I wonder how loud the spirit would be, how much force it'd be able to muster.

"We should—"

I start to kneel by the spot, wondering if I can clear any of the grass and dirt away to reveal whatever's underneath.

Meander clutches at my arm and keeps me on my feet. "Go," he finishes for me. "We should leave." His voice is a warning. He's not close enough to be pulled in.

He's stayed on the outskirts of this spirit's presence, but I'm two feet closer, and it's enough to keep me curious. Meander tugs at my shoulder, and it's like the apartment in Paris, like the last time the two of us saw a spirit together. Only, this time, I don't want to run. I'm sick of running. I'm sick of ignoring the talents I have, of trying to escape every time I encounter a spirit in need of my help.

They're the ones who are dead. So, why am I always making room for them? Why do they get free-range of my life while I'm constantly ducking out of their path?

"Cal, let's go," Meander says again.

I look at him, first at his serious eyes, then at his faded white-pink scar. Meander's had it worse than I have. Sometimes, he can't duck out of the way.

"We should investigate," I murmur. The spirit must be trapped. If it weren't, it'd be up here, probably attacking the boy fuelling its anger. Being stuck beneath the ground might even be the spirit's problem, the unfinished business keeping it on this side of the great divide.

I doubt anyone knows this spirit exists. If we don't do something about it, who will? Who knows how long it's been here. Who knows how many more summers will pass before another Sender winds up in these woods and senses its presence.

"Cal." Meander hisses my name, drawing my attention back to him.

His eyes have brightened with aggravation, but I still don't move. Motionless, I think about the spirit, frustrated because I want to run away from the pain and uncertainty of what's below the grass, even while I long to approach and face the dead head-on.

The spirit thuds again. I wince as the static spikes loud between my ears. Meander pulls hard at my arm.

"Callum."

It's enough to break the trance. With a sigh, I let Meander lead me back to the other campers.

28

I DON'T SLEEP WELL THAT NIGHT. I DREAM ABOUT THE SPIRIT IN THE woods, hear it knocking like it's trying to call to me. Three times I bolt awake, convinced I need to get up and go dig it out.

I didn't tell anyone what I experienced in the clearing, and as far as I know Meander didn't, either. Maybe if we had alerted our leads to the ghost's presence, I wouldn't feel responsible for it now. But I'm used to keeping the spirits I see a secret, and I can't seem to stop myself hiding this one away, too. Even in the middle of the night, when my breath is fast, and my head is full of muffled taps made with a dead hand, the idea of letting the authorities know what's behind the château seems strangely implausible.

I give up on sleep by seven, and drag my feet all day, my heavy eyes a constant reminder of the spirit's pesky effect.

"She'll cheer up tonight," Dylan says, although I'm

not entirely sure what he's talking about. He pushes open the door which leads out to the small back garden, the outdoor path a shortcut to the basement steps around the side of the château.

I stumble over the transition from hard tile to soft grass, banging my arm against the doorframe in the process. I wince, the muscles sore from where I fell.

Dylan watches as I rub my arm. "Don't you think?" he asks, and I blink at him, trying to remember what he's just said.

"Uh...yes?"

Dylan rolls his eyes at my pathetic attempt to fumble through the conversation. "Mim. The party. She'll cheer up then, don't you think?" he repeats, and then I understand what he's been going on about since we left the Shade lounge ten minutes ago. Yesterday's game may have broken through Meander's tense mood, but it had no effect on Mim.

As the day of our spirit contact approaches, Mim grows colder and more anxious, to the point even Dylan's starting to take notice. We've tried to talk to her, all of us together and each of us apart. We leave for Fos-sur-Mer tomorrow, and right now, we're no closer to figuring out what Mim's been so bothered about than we were a week ago.

Dylan's argument is feeble, and we both know it. But I don't have anything new to add, so I nod along.

"Yeah, maybe," I mutter, watching as two tawny blue birds swoop together near the ramshackle shed in the garden's back corner. If there was an occasion which could cheer Mim up, tonight might be a good contender. Even though it's a Tuesday, there's a party happening tonight in the dining hall.

Alex said it's an annual thing, one last event meant to bring all the sectors together so everyone can relax from the stresses of their final tasks. I'm not generally big on social events, but this place is familiar, and most of the people here are friends or at least friendly acquaintances. It should be fun. It should at least be bearable. The leads have started setting up, and after the last course has finished this afternoon, we'll go down as a group to have one more free night before our big ghostly event.

"It'll be fun, tonight," Dylan says, his voice not enthusiastic enough for me to take him seriously. "We need a break, is all."

I want to shake my head and warn him an evening's break won't fix everything, especially after yesterday's game made no difference to Mim's mood. But I think he knows. So, I smile instead, pulling open the side entrance to the basement steps and being careful not to trip over my own exhausted feet.

"I wish my break could start a few hours early. I've got Emotional Entities for the next four hours." All my other courses finished last week. But Mr. Bujak insisted we come for one final lecture today. If it were any other course, I wouldn't mind spending one more afternoon taking notes. But the idea of another Emotional Entities session feels like a punishment for a crime I didn't realize I'd committed.

"I don't envy you," Dylan grins, the flash of his teeth more honest than anything he's said since we left the lounge.

"I'd be worried if you did." I give Dylan a wave as I head down to the basement, and he crosses the side lawn to go for a run.

I finished Mr. Bujak's essay two nights ago while I was waiting up in the vain hope I'd catch Meander before bed. I gave up trying to channel Miss Kappel's notion of strong emotions being good ones. I didn't even write about the most emotional spirit I've seen. I wrote about the most emotional experience I've had around a spirit instead.

It happened when I was eleven and Rose was four. We were with my parents on vacation. When we checked into our hotel room, I found a spirit—a man who'd been hung, probably as a suicide cover-up from whatever murder took place there.

Rose and I went up to the room first, and I started freaking out because I thought I'd have to sleep beside it for the entire trip. Rose got scared, too, and when my parents came into the room, they were terrified. Not because of what I claimed to see, but because Rose was acting the same way I was. They were frightened she was like me, and when they discovered she couldn't see or sense anything and was only reacting to my freak out, they were relieved. And angry at me for making her upset.

I don't think about that spirit often. We changed hotel rooms, and the new room was far enough away the spirit didn't bother me again. But, for the rest of the vacation, I couldn't shake the image of my parents huddled around Rose, glad she was only a scared little girl and not a freak like her big brother.

I didn't want to write the essay. I rushed through it, writing it out by hand and not bothering to edit it before tucking it away so I could hand it in today. I don't care if Mr. Bujak thinks I have crappy penmanship and a bad grasp of sentence structure. The assignment was cruel.

And I wasn't lying when I told Dylan I wished I could skip the next four hours. Emotional Entities is not like my other courses. It's not useful, fun, or familiar. It's tedious and boring, and if I don't fall asleep within fifteen minutes of listening to Mr. Bujak's droning voice today, I'll consider myself a champion.

I slide my essay onto the pile of other papers on the instructor's otherwise empty desk on my way into the room. Then, I go to my usual desk and slump in next to Kornelía. Our course starts in four minutes, and I'm already dreading Mr. Bujak's grating tendency to use drawn out, complicated sentences that he feels the need to simplify immediately afterwards. An irritating habit which usually means we run over the four-hour course mark.

"You look tired," Kornelía remarks.

I drop my arms and head onto the table top while waiting for the course to start. Damn spirit. If I hadn't kept dreaming about it, I would have woken at a reasonable time, feeling refreshed and only a little sore after yesterday's game. Instead, I'm stuck two blinks away from dozing and wondering why I kept dreaming about the ghost in the first place.

"Need a nap?" Meander asks when he arrives a minute later and sits on my other side.

I turn my head to him and smile, but I don't have it in me to muster a response. I'm happy he's sitting here, though, and not in his normal seat at the back of the room. I don't even mind when he pulls out a book and starts flipping pages. The sound's become familiar over the last nine weeks. It'll be weird falling asleep without it when I get home.

Home. I can't believe it's less than a week until we leave. Tomorrow we confront Mim's spirit, after which we will have a few free days before camp is over. It's a strange concept, and I'm not too pleased about it. I need more time here. I'm still not ready to decide if I want to come back.

At least this is my last course session. It'd be nicer if the summer didn't end with Mr. Bujak, but after today, I can delight in the fact I won't see him until at least next summer.

Our instructor arrives right on schedule, as always, and takes ages to settle in his desk and organize our essay papers. I wonder what he'll do with them after the course is over. Seems pointless to read a bunch of essays for a group of kids who won't even be around to hear his remarks.

"Today, class," Mr. Bujak finally says after ten minutes have crawled by.

I haven't fallen asleep yet, but his pinched, nasally voice is ready to send me off to slumber.

"Since this is the final session of the course, I thought it might be beneficial for you all to witness the unique abilities of your instructor. That is, I'd like to show you my personal talent."

I quirk an eyebrow and attempt to sit up. Mr. Bujak's never even hinted at his abilities before. None of our instructors have. Sabeena and Lu hounded Mrs. Buxley about it once, but she only smiled with tight lips and said it wasn't relevant to the topic of the day. This is something none of my other courses covered, and it's impressive it's coming from Emotional Entities.

Mr. Bujak pulls a laptop from his bag and rests it on his desk with the oversized screen facing us. Unless the computer is actually a spirit in disguise, it's a disappointing follow-up to what he suggested we'd see today.

"We're watching a video?" a Wraith girl named Corianna asks when our instructor opens a video clip.

"Yes," Mr. Bujak replies. He doesn't beam at us or appear the least bit excited about what he's going to share. He adjusts the video's volume, and before pressing play he turns to survey us. "Unfortunately, there is no satisfactory entity on which I can actively demonstrate our lesson today. That is, there is no spirit close enough for me to show you my talents in person. But this video footage, while not of the greatest quality, highlights the key components of my interaction with spirits. That is, you can see my talent in action."

"If he ever gets around to starting the damned clip," Meander mutters.

I smirk, leaning back against my seat and crossing my arms over my chest.

Mr. Bujak brings a finger to the play button on the keyboard but pauses and looks back at us again. "The example I'll show you today has a particular relevancy to the lessons in this course. That is, the spirit you will see has a connection to our course material."

This time, when he turns back to the computer, he does manage to press the play button. He then turns off the light, allowing us a better view of the screen. The classroom is small, and it's not difficult to make out the features of the clip. In the shaded green colors of a night vision camera, a room is visible, and Mr. Bujak faces a corner with his back turned away from the camera lens. He says something unintelligible, and glances over his shoulder at whoever's filming. Then, with a jerk, he returns his gaze to the wall.

It doesn't take long for things to happen. Mr. Bujak's breath becomes labored, his head drooping forward as the camera's mic picks up a sound like a dog panting. It's uncomfortable, watching him gasp and choke as if something is stuck in his throat. But the breathing evens out when Mr. Bujak sinks to his knees, gripping his temples with a moan. With his head between his hands, he slumps into a ball on the floor.

"This is like a horror movie," someone whispers from the other side of the room.

It *is* like a movie, only instead of a bad CGI monster, a real spirit slowly forms in the air above Mr. Bujak's lowered head. The spirit is like the other spirits I've seen—partially formed and green-hued in the video, but likely smoky blue in direct contact. It comes into focus like a photo developing, each detail of its misshapen body more and more solid until, at last, it appears opaque—like a warped, human figure floating in mid-air.

Mr. Bujak pauses the video.

"That's a real ghost?" Corianna gasps.

I look at the girl across the room before turning my attention to several other campers. Everyone stares at the solid mass hovering near the side of the screen.

"Mr. Bujak," Kornelía says, her high voice frantic, "I can't see ghosts. So, why can I see this one?"

"Yeah, I don't see ghosts like this, either," Corianna agrees.

"We are all given individual talents for individual purposes," Mr. Bujak says with a nod. "My talent is to solidify the spirits I come into contact with. It is a physical connection. One that assists more than actively intervenes. I cannot communicate with spirits, but my presence can solidify them, so others can see them as clearly as I do."

"Wait, so that spirit has been...solidified?" Kornelía asks.

"Correct," our instructor answers. He takes off his large, round glasses, and cleans them with the edge of his blue suit jacket.

"But what's the purpose of that? Why would you make a spirit solid if you can't even communicate with it?" Corianna asks.

Her tone is harsh, but Mr. Bujak is unfazed.

"I cannot communicate," he repeats, glancing at the laptop, "but I can assist. There are, for example, Senders who are only able to make verbal contact. That is, they may be able to communicate, but may not be able to see. In these instances, I connect Senders to spirits through sight."

"What did this one need to be released?" a Revenant named Lee asks.

Mr. Bujak sighs, studying the screen. The spirit is a peculiar sight to behold—like someone has taken a ghost and frozen it.

"We are still unsure," he admits. "Reports of this entity go as far back as any records we can find. We located her in the northern part of Mexico. She is so ancient we cannot speak with her. Typically, language does not create a communication barrier between spirits and the living. You can speak to a spirit in any language, and they will understand."

"So, if I speak to a ghost from America, and I speak in Cantonese, it'll understand me?" Lee asks.

Mr. Bujak nods again.

"Exactly. And this works both ways. Spirits typically have no trouble communicating with us in terms of language. But, this spirit's speech patterns are so archaic that it is, fundamentally, a different way of communicating altogether. We have some language experts in the Oracle, but none were able to speak with the spirit while it was in fully spiritual form. However, with my assistance, we may be able to connect it with an expert who can understand."

"So, you solidify her in the hopes you'll be able to free her...but what if you can't?" Kornelía asks.

"If we cannot free her," Mr. Bujak explains, "she will either remain a spirit until we understand her needs or..." He pauses. "Well, there is another option."

"What is it?" Corianna's voice is sharp with accusation again.

I wonder if she's familiar with whatever concept Mr. Bujak is talking about.

"Another method for ridding the world of spirits," our instructor says. "But not one you need to worry about right now."

He doesn't elaborate, but I wish he would. I had no idea, not even the inkling of a thought, Senders were capable of solidifying spirits. If they can do that feat of seeming magic, what other kinds of impossible things can Senders accomplish?

"Language is not our only option for communication, however," Mr. Bujak continues, drawing attention back to the lesson. "Sometimes, emotions can help determine a spirit's unfinished business." Something almost like a smile flits across his face. "Take a gander at our spirit and see what you can tell me about its emotional state."

Watching the spirit from a recorded piece of footage means I can't feel a thing, but I understand what Mr. Bujak's getting at. The spirit looks sad, the half-visible expression on her face devastated and mournful. She floats with limp limbs as if she wants to drop dead on the ground but is too light to do so. She has lost all hope. Even from this quick glimpse of her I know she wants to move on.

"As I'm sure you are aware," Mr. Bujak says, his voice even more serious than usual, "emotions are powerful. What emotions did our spirit reflect onto you?"

"Sadness," Kornelía half-whispers.

"Yes, yes," Mr. Bujak replies. "And what type of sadness was it?"

"Loss," I say, staring down at my desk. I don't want to see the spirit anymore.

"Good," our instructor says. "Emotions are specific, and we can use them when other forms of communication fail. Even if we never break the language barrier for this spirit, we know her grief is over something she's lost. And that can tell us a lot. If she felt such loss upon her own death, she may have died in a time of great loss overall. During a battle or a widespread sickness. We can use her emotions to gain insight into what her energy is clinging to, and through this, we can work to establish an understanding with her and an outlet for her to be released. That is, we can work to finally free her."

I force my eyes back up to the spirit on the screen. Her face is not directed at the camera, Mr. Bujak, or anything else in the room. The spirit stares past it all, into the distance of memory. I hope they find out what her unfinished business is soon. Nothing deserves to feel such horrible pain, and for such a long time.

I think about the spirit in the woods, the one I won't have any chance of helping. And then I think about Mim's spirit, the one I do. For weeks, I've been worried about the task we face tomorrow. It may not be fun, and for all I know, our ghost might be as vicious and violent as the one in Paris was. But it doesn't matter. Regardless of her anger or the discomfort she brings, the spirit doesn't deserve to suffer, and she needs our help to finally move on.

I watch the computer screen, wide-eyed and momentarily wide awake. A Sender's puzzle is hard to put together, and I'm afraid to discover what the finished picture will be. But I want to try my hand at completing it, and I think a corner piece just fell into place. I've taken a step towards making a decision about my future with spirits at last.

And to think I wanted to skip this course in favor of an afternoon nap.

29

"I WISH MIM HAD TAKEN EMOTIONAL ENTITIES," KORNELÍA SAYS AS WE WALK back to the Shade lounge after the course has finished. "I think today's lesson could have helped her."

"Do you?" I glance at Kornelía, her long hair tucked behind her large ears, and a denim skirt hanging down beneath a close-fitted burgundy tee. She's been as unsuccessful with talking to Mim as me and Dylan, but I have my suspicions she knows more than she's telling.

It wouldn't surprise me. She and Mim are far closer than Mim and I are, and Kornelía has a knack for sensing things. Plus, there's the whole mind-reading development. None of us have a clue how much Kornelía can pull from our minds, and since the night she first discovered the talent, she's been tight-lipped about discussing the particulars of her newfound ability.

At any rate, she won't say what she knows, even if

she does have insight. Every time I ask, she changes the subject or shrugs my questions away.

"I think it would do everyone here a lot of good," she says now, once again avoiding my attempts to make her talk.

I roll my eyes, but by now, we're in the dining hall. There are enough people bustling around setting up party snacks and hooking up a sound system that I don't try to pry any more.

"You coming to the party?" I ask Meander instead.

His eyes widen in mild panic, which makes me laugh.

"I take that as a no."

"Not really my area," he says, gazing around with distaste as we head up the main staircase.

"You don't want to spend one more night with everyone who's still around?" Kornelía asks.

She gives Meander a pitying look, and I hold back a wince, knowing now how touchy he is about people feeling sorry for him.

"No, I'm good," he replies, the words clipped.

I roll my shoulders, the motion sending a wave of pain through my arm. "It's a good night to get some rest, too," I say, rubbing the tender spot and thinking a nap right about now would be fantastic. "We've got a busy day tomorrow."

"Let's not talk about that for a while," Kornelía says through a sigh. "Around Mim at least."

"Right." I nod as we reach the lounge.

No one else has returned from their afternoon activities, so Kornelía settles down with her sketchpad, and Meander puts his notes away before heading back downstairs to grab some food. I lay on one of the sofas and drift in and out of sleep for about an hour until Mim and Dylan have returned and we're ready to join the celebration.

A bass beat pulses through my feet as we make our way out of the lounge. Opening the door is like opening a portal to another world. The music and voices are loud, and the decorative party lights cast twinkling shadows on the walls as we walk down the three flights of stairs to reach the dining hall.

Only one table remains, pushed to the wall and covered with snacks and drinks. The rest of the space is open, meant as a dance floor but mostly filled with groups of campers talking and laughing. It's a lively crowd which is what Mim needs, and when we first descend, it seems like she might relax. Arm looped with Dylan's, she smiles at course mates, and the two share gossiping whispers when they notice one of the Revenant girls making out with a guy from the Entity Sector.

"This is great!" Kornelía beams, watching the room, a look of elation spreading across her face.

I wouldn't have guessed Kornelía would be into big parties like this. Maybe she's never been invited to a party before or she just likes the people she's surrounded by. Hell, maybe she's been a party girl all this time, and I was misled by her initial shyness.

We get drinks and stand together, none of us saying much. I'm still tired, and the loud music grinds on my nerves. I'll stick around for a while, wait until the others veer off to talk with more campers. Then I'll slip back upstairs and turn in for an early night.

"Hey, isn't that Sabeena?" Mim says after a few easy minutes have passed.

I watch her expression tighten as she says it, and when I follow her gaze, I wish she'd have remained oblivious to the other girl's presence. It is Sabeena, standing in the back corner of the dining hall near the kitchen with Lu, Sefa, Reed and Naasir on either side. None of them look pleased to be here, and watching them across the room makes a shiver crawl up my spine. Mim's gloomy mood is cheerful compared to what I'm witnessing now.

"They're beat," Kornelía says in a hushed voice nearly inaudible over the music.

"I'd say battered is more like it," Dylan adds.

The other half of the Shade Sector faced their own spirit a couple of days ago. I didn't give it much thought, but now they're all together, I realize I haven't seen much of any of them since the event occurred. They've been absent or asleep. Come to think of it, the girls have been absent, and the boys have been asleep.

I saw Sefa Saturday afternoon before they left, and I saw Lu at yesterday's game when she sat on the forest floor, looking like she might cry. Seeing them now, my stomach drops. I can't believe I've been so wrapped up in my own world I didn't even notice their altered habits.

"Anyone know how their task went?" Mim asks in a tight voice. She's slumped into herself again—worn and haggard, her black hair messed, her pink streaks faded, and her dark eyes dull.

"No idea," Dylan says.

I know Sabeena eventually won out on being team leader for their group, and since she sees the spirits of children, I suspect a child was their target ghost. But I don't know any of the specifics of their case. It never came up in conversation, just as they have never asked about our case. I wish I knew the details. Or maybe I don't.

I make no move to approach them, ask how things are or question what happened when they left camp and faced their spirit. I don't move, and neither does anyone else.

"Do you think they were successful?" Mim asks, watching on as the group stares past us, unaware of our scrutiny.

"Yes," Kornelía nods.

Dylan is skeptical. "How do you figure? They look pretty bent out of shape, if you ask me."

"No, Kornelía's right," I say, rubbing the sore muscles of my arm and thinking about the irritated frustration I'm still feeling over the spirit in the woods. "I think they were successful. This…this is simply the aftermath." I don't know how to explain it, but I do believe Kornelía's right. There's something satisfied in their demeanour. They're drained, yes, but they're not morose. They're stunned, bewildered even. But they're not frustrated.

"You mean this is what we've got to look forward to?" Dylan asks.

"Well, only if we're successful." I give him a wry smile.

"And why wouldn't we be successful?" Mim snaps, anger flashing into her dark eyes. "If Lu's team can finish their task, then our team can, too."

I share a look with Kornelía and make myself as meek as possible before I respond. "I was only kidding, Mim," I say, trying to appease her. "I know we'll be successful."

Only, I don't know it. With Mim acting so weird and the team not putting a lot of effort into preparing for the event, I can't begin to imagine what we'll be doing tomorrow or if what we do will have any effect on the spirit. But Mim's in a foul enough mood. I don't want to make it worse by voicing my concerns.

"Yeah, we're going to do great," Kornelía agrees, wrapping a hand around Mim's free arm. "Hey, there's Lani. Let's go say hi, okay?"

Kornelía does her best to distract Mim, pulling her away from us and over to Mim's mentor. Dylan and I stay behind, watching their progress.

"Girls," Dylan mutters, shaking his head.

I glance sideways at him, but don't respond. I doubt it has anything to do with being a girl, and everything to do with Mim being in charge of contacting our group's spirit. Maybe it's because of his canine talent, or perhaps it's his personality, but Dylan has never really understood the effect ghosts have on a lot of the campers here. It's no coincidence the other half of our sector is acting like the Wraith campers—the ones who have been turning sixteen and have had their full abilities unleashed. Dealing with spirits leaves its toll.

The Revenant kids are back after their first summer at Camp Wanagi, though. They chose to return after their first final tasks— as did the Entity campers, the ones who are now mentoring the new recruits as they finish their final year here. There has to be something else to all this, doesn't there? Otherwise, no one would ever return to Camp Wanagi.

I wish I could talk to Daniel. My mentor is in South America now, working on his own case. But, if he were here, I know I could ask him these things. I feel stupid, like I wasted our sessions together. There are so many questions I want to ask him now, things I never considered nine weeks ago.

I watch the other campers having fun at the party until I notice Sabeena sliding to the floor, her knees drawn up and her head buried. Even from across the crowded room, it's easy to see she's sobbing. Reed and Naasir sit down next to her, rubbing her back and smoothing her dark, plaited hair.

"Should we go over?" I ask, my question uncertain. It seems rude not to offer help.

Kornelía's back at my side, her attempt to keep Mim occupied already a failure. She shakes her head, her expression resolute.

"No," she says, the word quiet but firm. "This doesn't concern us."

Dylan rubs Mim's shoulder and nudges her with his elbow. "Want to go for a walk or something?" he asks, his voice as gentle as it's probably capable of being.

Mim shakes her head. "Let's go back to the lounge," she says, turning away from Sabeena and setting her sights on the staircase. "I can't take any more of this. Not now. I just want to go to bed."

It's not even time for dinner, but no one argues with Mim. As a group, we leave the party behind, retreating in silence back to the comfort of the lounge.

39

DESPITE MIM'S DETERMINATION TO GO TO BED EARLY, SHE CAN'T SLEEP, and neither can I. After a late night of hanging out in the lounge, I toss and turn for over an hour before giving up and heading back out to the couches and the fire. Our room is too stiff, the quiet too deep. Naasir, Sefa, and Reed all fell asleep quickly after returning from the party around eight, and their slumber is so complete they don't move a muscle or make the faintest sound. It's disturbing, and not even my music or my exhaustion can distract me from the suffocating silence.

By midnight, our whole group is out in the lounge. Even Meander is with us, curled up at one end of the sofa I sit on with a book open in his hands and a frustrated expression in his eyes. He can't focus on the pages before him anymore than I can focus on my music. It doesn't help, not even out here in the lounge. We're all wound up, unsettled by the other campers' appearances and stressed about being like them after tomorrow.

"If we aren't successful, I won't be able to face coming back next year," Mim says out of nowhere, long after we've all settled into the lounge. She sits on the floor in front of the fireplace, her back to us. "My father will be disappointed if I stay home, but Mama won't mind."

"My parents would be thrilled if I decided not to return," Kornelía says. "They hate the idea of this place. Think it's not right, working with ghosts. I don't know why they're so worried, though. I have six brothers and sisters. They have plenty of other children around to be normal." She lets out a breath, half-amused and half-upset.

"Do they really think you're weird?" Mim asks.

Kornelía nods. "Yes. I love them, but they're big on appearances," she admits. "Isn't good for their image to have a daughter attending a secret camp for an unbelievable purpose."

"Wow." Mim turns to her friend. "Sorry, Korni. I had no idea."

Kornelía smiles. "It's fine," she says, waving away Mim's concern. "They don't hide me away or anything. They still love me and all that. Plus, my baby brother Bruno thinks it's neat."

"I always wanted a baby brother or sister," Mim laments. "Being an only child is boring."

Dylan scoffs. "Want to switch? I'm the baby brother of two sisters, and it's way too crowded at our houses." Dylan and his sisters split their time between their mother and their father, but evidently, Dylan thinks two whole houses is not enough for three siblings.

Mim smirks, one of the few happy expressions she's worn over the last weeks. "And what do your families think of you, Dog Whisperer?"

"Dead Dog Whisperer," Dylan corrects. "And they're fairly ambivalent about the whole thing. I'm honestly not sure they believe it, but so long as I get a good education and land a good job, they don't care how I spend my summers."

"What about you, Cal?" Kornelía asks. "How do your parents feel about your ability?"

I slouch down in my seat. "They're okay with it, I guess. They used to be freaked out, thought I was crazy. But, now, they just deal with it. I don't talk about spirits around them if I can help it, and they don't ask. I think they like to pretend I'm at some scholar's camp for the summer or something. They'll let me come back, if I want to. But they'll devote most of their attention to my little sister. So far, she's showed no signs of being like me."

"None of my siblings have, either," Kornelía says with a nod. She eyes Meander, looking unsure if she should pull him into the conversation.

I take the decision out of her hands by giving his sneaker a gentle kick. "Who do you have at home?" I ask.

Meander glances up at me. I know he's been listening to us talk, but he looks uncomfortable with having to participate in the discussion.

"Just my mum and me," he says with a shrug. "I have a brother... Well, a half-brother, but he's twenty and doesn't live at home anymore."

"Is your mother okay with your talent?" Kornelía asks.

Meander stares at his book, shrugging a second time. "No, not really," he says. "But she'll make me come back next year. So long as it keeps being all-expenses-paid, she'll see it as a great excuse to be rid of me for a while."

I study Meander's profile, remembering our night in the library.

"Sometimes we don't get a choice."

I may have my secret fears about Rose and my parents' reason for having her, but at least I know they haven't shipped me overseas to get me out of their lives for ten weeks.

Kornelía isn't sure how to respond. She eyes me for guidance, but I'm not sure what to say, either.

To my surprise, Mim breaks the silence. "So, I'm the *only* only child?" she asks, sounding peeved. "When I get home, I'm having a talk with Mama about this."

"Hey, I'm serious," Dylan says, "You can take one of my sisters. I can do without the cat fights."

Kornelía giggles. "Well, I like my siblings, but you could borrow one for a while. There are enough of us at home, we can do without one for a bit."

"Siblings on-loan? I think we're onto something!" Dylan exclaims.

Mim laughs. "Well, if we do fail tomorrow, at least we have a back-up plan."

With our laughter, being together becomes easy again. We talk about anything and nothing until we're finally able to fall asleep—still in the lounge, sprawled over the sofas and the floor.

In the morning, I wake first and find my legs tangled with Meander's. Mim sleeps stomach-down on the floor, and Kornelía lays nestled against Dylan's chest.

My back hurts from the sofa, my arm hurts from the game in the forest, and my left leg is asleep from being pinned under Meander's weight. But, as the sun filters through the lounge and the stirrings of life echo from the dining hall below us, I feel strangely at ease.

The calm won't last. When the others wake, this peace will be disrupted. Mim will be furious to find Kornelía cuddled next to Dylan. She'll stalk off while Kornelía chases after her with explanations while Dylan brushes the whole issue away with a stupid joke, and Meander will skulk off by himself, ignored by everyone else. But for a few more moments, the calm will linger, and I'm glad. I like the scene before me now. And I feel, for the first time, ready to tackle this camp and face my talents—howling spirits and all.

The revelation comes just in time. We leave for our final task today.

31

"Are you ready?" Lani asks, a big grin on her face. Several hours after the tranquility of my waking moments, the serene mood of the morning feels years distant. As I suspected, Mim and Kornelía fought before breakfast, and by the time noon rolled around, everyone had once again fallen into the brooding silence lately plaguing the entire Shade Sector. Now, the five of us sit solemnly in a black van, Lani twisting back to face us from the passenger seat up front.

"I don't think it matters much, does it?" Dylan asks.

"You'll be fine," Lani says.

The hired driver starts the van and drives us away from camp. Lani gives us each a reassuring smile, one Mim doesn't see since she's already staring out the window and pretending the rest of us aren't here.

At the beginning of the summer, Daniel told me all the Entity campers would be away for the latter half of camp, but he wasn't totally correct. Lani's final task took place in the eastern part of France, so she's been nearby the whole time she's been working with Mim. Now, there's a hint of concern in her eyes as she regards Mim's dark expression, but she turns to the front again, disappearing from view behind the wide, faux-leather seat.

The drive takes about five hours. We're headed south to the French coast. Mim's been to Fos-sur-Mer before, but for the rest of us, this is new territory.

We travel in silence. Dylan spent most of the morning running along the streets of the neighborhood beyond the château's lake, and now he stares at the passing road with anxious desire and an almost content exhaustion. Meander reads, Mim crochets a sweater after she finally looks away from the window, and Kornelía draws. I slip my earbuds in and let the composers of the Second Viennese School keep me company as I watch the afternoon dwindle away.

The sun is fading, earlier now than the beginning days of camp. Next week we go home, the summer over. Regular school and Autumn weather are just beyond the horizon, at least for me and the other campers from the Northern Hemisphere. I'll be happy to see my parents and Rose, and I'm desperate to play my violin again. I'll be glad to be back in Canada, too, where I know the best place to get a doughnut in the morning, and where I can practically walk around my neighborhood blindfolded. But I'm going to miss my friends, and it is nice being surrounded by present and future Senders.

"Are we almost there?" Dylan asks Mim after a long time, nudging her from where they sit side-by-side in the back row.

"Huh?" she asks, startled by his question.

Dylan smirks. "Are. We. Almost. There?"

She glares at him, nudging him back before she peers out the window. Her fingers grip tight to the taupe yarn of her half-finished sweater while she surveys the passing landscape.

"Yes," she breathes as the distant blue of the coast comes into view.

"It's nearly dark," Kornelía comments, pencil poised above her sketchpad. She sounds surprised, like she looked up expecting the radiance of July only to be struck by the fading glimmers of late August.

"Summer's almost gone," Dylan agrees.

"It always goes by fast here," Lani sighs from the front, her voice nostalgic. This is her last year attending the camp, and it's easy to tell from her tone that she'll miss it.

Will I feel the same way three summers from now? Will I even be at Camp Wanagi then?

"We're here," Mim says twenty minutes later, sucking in a breath as she presses her crocheting to her chest.

I pause Schoenberg's "Transfigured Night" and peer out the window to see the Château de Rouseville in the last remaining light of the day. It resembles the old photograph, only it's updated now and more modern in style. I expected a beaten down, half-rotted shell of a building. Instead, I find a neat and tidy hotel still in operation. People mill around the entrance, and a man in uniform hails a taxi for an elderly couple on the street. Rows of blossoming pink, blue, and white potted flowers sit beneath windows lit from within which offer a glimpse of a crowded dining room.

"I'll let the managers know we're here," Lani says as the van comes to a stop.

We climb out, thankful for the chance to stretch our legs after the journey. As soon as his feet hit the pavement Dylan sprints off for a quick jog up and down the street. Meander offers a quiet "Cheers, drive," to the silent man still sitting behind the wheel.

"You lot take the equipment up to the room," Lani instructs once Dylan is back. "Mim, you have the key for room three-oh-eight, right?"

Mim nods.

"Good. I'll be waiting for you in the lounge when you're finished. Good luck!"

"You mean you're not coming with us?" Kornelía asks as she hefts a bag over one shoulder.

For being so thin and spindly, Kornelía's arms are full of easy strength. I wonder if it has anything to do with her having so many siblings. I remember how heavy Rose seemed when she was born, even if she was only a tiny baby. Kornelía's probably spent years carrying infants and toddlers around at home.

"No," Lani smiles. "This is your task, not mine. I'll come up to check on your progress after you've had a chance to work for a while. And, if you're successful, tomorrow some of the of-age Senders will be here to sweep the room and ensure the spirit has left. But the task itself, that's up to you." She gazes at our bewildered faces and laughs. "Like I said, good luck!"

The hotel lobby is draped with red velvet, and dark floors clack under our heels as we pass the concierge desk and head to the stairway. There's no elevator in the Château de Rouseville, so we have to walk up all three flights. Dylan and Kornelía each carry a duffel bag of equipment while Meander and I haul up the more than two dozen record books we used for our research in case we need to do any fact checking once contact with the spirit is established. The stairs are steep, and the books are heavy. Mim walks before us, carrying nothing, but she's so nervous none of us bothers to mention it.

We make our way up slowly, our movements sluggish under the weight of our accessories. Mim leads the way, but her steps are so hesitant she never gets far ahead.

The hotel lobby was decorated in deep shades of reds and browns, but when we reach the third floor of the Château de Rouseville, the palette is much brighter. Thin, beige carpeting covers the floors, and the wallpaper is comprised of pale green and beige stripes. After every third or fourth room, landscape paintings are hung on the walls, and golden plates adorn each door, marking the room number. All in all, it's an average hotel up here, and that realization is both disappointing and relieving.

Even on the third floor, we're not alone. Guests of the Château murmur in their rooms, watching TV or chatting as they prepare to go out for dinner. It makes what we're about to do less frightening, and more surreal.

"This is it," Mim says as we approach room 308.

She pauses, standing still until Dylan pushes at her back. Then she nods and slides the key into the lock. We're all so quiet I can hear the lock clicking open as the key turns. Mim grips the door handle and pauses for another long beat before she turns the knob and pushes the door open.

There's nothing odd about the room. Even after seeing the normal state of the rest of the hotel, I guess I still expected there would be something special about our destination. But it's an ordinary hotel room, at least by its appearance. There are two beds separated by a wooden night table, a TV, a wardrobe for clothes, and a window on the far side of the room with its drapes pulled shut against the view outside.

"This is where we've had the most luck contacting her," Mim explains as we pass the small ensuite and set our bags down on the beds.

The room looks ordinary, but it doesn't feel that way. I'm cold by the time I reach the first bed, and nauseous when I set my bag down on the second.

"This is where she stayed," I mumble without thinking. The room number seemed familiar when Lani mentioned it out by the van, but only now do I remember why. This is the room Isabelle Levasseur stayed in when she fell down the hotel's stairs. I shudder. The stairs she fell down were probably the same ones we just climbed up.

"How do you know she stayed here?" Mim asks.

She sounds angry, and I have a bad feeling my answer's not going to calm her down. Me and Meander were in charge of research, but Mim hasn't asked a single question about what we found. I mentioned Isabelle at our final meeting, but the annoyance in Mim's squint makes me think she doesn't remember.

"One of the names you gave us. The list we researched? Well, one of those women stayed in this room. I told you about her. I told you she was the one."

"I don't remember you telling me that," Mim snaps.

I appeal to Dylan and Kornelía, but they shrug,

averting their gazes. I *did* tell Mim. I told the entire group. But Mim's been so obsessed with figuring things out on her own, and so worried about making sure she does this whole task better than anyone else, she didn't bother to listen.

"I told you Monday afternoon, Mim. After the game in the woods, when we met for our last project meeting," I say, trying to keep my voice steady.

"No, you didn't," Mim says, her own voice heated. Her face is flushed and her stance defiant.

"Yes, I did." I'm getting angry now. I don't want to make the situation worse, but I'm losing patience with Mim's refusal to admit when she's wrong.

"You *didn't!*" Mim turns to Dylan and Kornelía, tilting her head to one side. "Did he tell us anything?"

Dylan says nothing, busying himself with the zipper on his duffel bag.

"He may have," Kornelía starts, but a sharp look from Mim makes her lower her head. She's still trying to get back on Mim's good side after this morning's episode on the couch, which means she now only hunches her shoulders. "But I don't really remember."

"See?" Mim says with a triumphant flash of teeth. "No one remembers you saying anything about a woman staying here."

"I do."

The dry, English drawl makes it impossible for me not to smile. I glance behind me to where Meander sits on the edge of the second bed. He stares at Mim straight on, his face stony.

"He told you all on Monday. We met at *your* insistence, and you spent the whole time reviewing your own notes and not listening to what anyone else had to say."

"I...I..." Mim looks like she's going to yell at Meander, but as she stutters, the fire in her eyes dims. "I...don't remember," she says at last. Her jaw tightens, and with a sudden flail of her arms, she begins walking in circles and muttering to herself in Spanish. She paces in a loop several times, her voice low and frantic. Then she covers her face with her hands, and sobs.

"I'm sorry, Cal," she manages in a ragged voice.

"Mim, it's okay," I say, panicked by her intense reaction. Out of everyone I know, Mim's the last person I expected to see crying over something like this. I would have bet even Dylan would start bawling before she did.

"No, it's not!" Mim exclaims. She drops her hands, revealing the tears dripping down her cheeks. "I've been ignoring you because I've been trying to do this all on my own. But the truth is..." She takes a big, sobbing breath. "I can't do it at all!" she finishes in a passion.

"What are you talking about?" Dylan asks.

"I'm talking about this!" Mim gestures to the hotel room. "I'm talking about the ghost. I've only seen her once, and it was only briefly. Like, a second or two. I haven't talked to her, and I can't even get a clear sense of what she looks like. They tell me she's broken-hearted, and I guess because I can see her she must be. But I can *barely* see her, and now I won't be able to release her. We'll all fail, and it's my fault!"

"You're not at fault!" Kornelía says, rushing to her friend. "We can't fail. This is for practice, not for a grade, remember? And we'll all help, okay? That's the idea, anyway. We'll work together."

"Yeah, Mim," I agree. "If we can't free the spirit, then so be it. But we'll do everything we can to help her. Okay?"

Mim sniffs, glancing up at me, tears tangled in her eyelashes. "Okay," she whispers.

Kornelía envelopes her in a hug, and Mim sobs a while more before finally getting herself under control.

"We need to get started," she says as she wipes the wet marks off her cheeks. "I'm not sure if we'll be able to make contact at all, but this is where she's been noticed the most. Cal, I can't remember what you told us. I'm sorry. What did you say the ghost's name was?"

"Isabelle Levasseur."

As soon as the name leaves my mouth, the lights in the room go out. Without warning, we're thrown into darkness, the temperature plummeting. I shiver, shaking my head as static fills my mind.

"I don't think we need to worry about making contact," Meander says in a low voice.

I search for him in the darkness and can just make out his outline. He's facing the corner of the room, and slowly I drag my eyes over to the corner as well. The static in my head grows louder, and soft blips of voice like an out of tune radio sound between my ears. A strong scent of rosewater hits my nostrils, and I try not to choke on the potent smell.

Across the room, tucked between the wardrobe and the curtained windows, a faint bluish light illuminates the spirit of Isabelle Levasseur as she flickers in and out of existence.

32

"YOU CAN SEE HER?" MIM ASKS, HER VOICE STRAINED.

I force myself to look away from the spirit, so I can answer. Only, Mim's not asking me. She's staring at Meander.

"Only vaguely," Meander replies. He sounds relieved, and I suspect I know the reason why. He studies Isabelle before glancing at me. He understands I can see her, too.

Mim follows the turn of his head until she lands on me, her eyes trained a bit to my left. Without Isabelle's faint glow, Mim must be having trouble seeing anything in the otherwise dark room.

"Can *you* see her?" she asks.

I turn back to the corner of the room where the spirit continues to flicker. "Yes," I say, confused. This is a broken-hearted spirit. So why can I see her? And Meander? I glance at Kornelía, her head bent low over an audio device. Her eyes are closed, and I wonder if she's seeing the spirit in her mind. Can all three of us see Isabelle better than Mim?

"She's here," Mim says with annoyance. She's trying to take control of the situation again. "Somewhere over here." She points in the general direction of the corner, and Dylan switches on his digital thermal reader.

"Woah," he says with a nod and a smile. "There's a huge cold spot there."

"Can you see her, Mim?" Kornelía asks. She opens her eyes and grabs a flashlight from one of the bags.

Isabelle's presence has used up the room's electricity, but our battery-powered devices don't seem to be affected. With the beam of light shining on an empty notebook page, Kornelía starts to record the happenings in the room.

"Almost..." Mim says, her voice wavering with uncertainty. "I... Can you two see her?" she asks again, eyes flitting between Meander and me.

I don't answer. I *can* see Isabelle. Her stomach is faded, but the rest of her appears in crisp focus, her outline transparent blue and the details of her body wispy and white like smoke. She's wearing a dress. She has a large nose. Nice eyes. I can't see them like I could see the eyes of a living person. They're less defined, more like smoky holes in Isabelle's face, but I'm certain during her life her eyes were her best feature.

Crackles of dark blue spread over her shoulders and along her wispy torso. Lingering shadows of broken bones—remnants of the injury which took her life.

Her words, harsh and desperate, come to me more easily now. My head hurts with the static, but every few seconds, a couple of formed words filter through.

"...ed me...illed...Ro...must know...can't get away... help me!" she pleads. As she becomes more focused, her words grow more frantic.

Rosewater swirls around me, blooming like spurts of musty perfume as her fury rises. I don't like her anger, but it does make her speech more sensible.

I have the urge to run away. It's instinct. The natural tendency to flee the scene and stop the ache in my head, the churn of my stomach, and the shiver of my limbs. But this is not like the other times. I'm not here to be afraid. I'm here to help Isabelle. I'm not supposed to be the one communicating with her. But turns out, I am. So, I'm going to have to deal with it.

I place a hand on my stomach, trying to calm the bucking about of the day's meals. I study the spirit and work to make sense of the odd words in her static-filled rant, but I can't focus. Bile gurgles at the base of my throat, and I want nothing more than to pass out to ease the pain behind my ears. I blink, swallow, and wipe sweat from my brow. I try to translate the static into plausible pieces of conversation, but no matter how I twist the sounds, I can't understand what she's saying.

"Meander, come here!" I'm not sure why I make the command. I can't think clearly through the noise in my head.

Meander stands and comes to me.

"Go sit in front of her," I say, my voice wobbling. I point to Isabelle with an unsteady finger.

Meander stares at me, his gaze probably questioning and possibly annoyed. I don't know. I don't look at him. I keep my eyes trained on Isabelle, and once a few seconds have trickled past, Meander does what

I've asked. He sits down in front of where Isabelle hovers. The spirit is not happy with the arrangement. Meander's presence infuriates her, and soon she howls at me.

"He pushed me!" she screams, her smoky face contorted in rage. She isn't furious enough to throw things, which I'm thankful for. Still, the sound of her shrieking voice is enough to make me rub my temples, my eyes watering with pain.

"What's going on?" Mim asks, frustrated I'm making decisions without her.

I can't deal with Mim's temper right now. I want to get to the bottom of Isabelle's unfinished business. I want to release her. I want to make the noise, the smell, and the pain go away.

"Quiet!" I demand, hushing everyone in the room. "Who pushed you?" I ask the spirit.

"What are you...?" Dylan begins.

I hold up a hand, and he stops.

"Who pushed you?" I ask again.

For a brief moment, Isabelle's whole body diminishes—her form more transparent and her features softened.

"He," she says, her voice less enraged. She's quiet for the space of three or four seconds, before her anger returns in a rush. "He *pushed* me!" she screams.

The exclamation is so loud Meander groans while I stagger backwards.

"I heard something," Kornelía whispers, her headphones pressed tightly to her ears.

"Who is *he*?" I ask. "What's his name?"

Isabelle falters again.

"I see her!" Mim calls while Isabelle's form becomes

less distinct to me.

"Robert," the spirit says, the sound nearly swallowed in static.

"I see her," Mim says again in awe.

My head whirls, and I have to crouch to keep from falling. I don't understand what's going on. Why can I see the spirit when Mim can't, and Mim only sees her now she's becoming less defined to me?

Meander makes her angry. Meander seems to make all ghosts angry, and the angrier the ghost is to start with, the more enraged and even violent the spirit can become in his presence. Isabelle's stronger with her anger, so I get why I understand her better when her temper's high. But why can I see her in the first place?

I close my eyes and try to recall any details from our research. The records didn't offer much. Isabelle was born in 1832 and lived in the village. No reason was given for why she was staying in the hotel when she died in 1857. Her parents lived nearby, but she was at the hotel, and she fell down the stairs. And that's how she died.

Unless.

Unless she didn't fall. Unless she was pushed down the stairs instead.

"Robert pushed you," I say, Isabelle's words connecting in my brain. I look up at her. "Did he kill you? Did he push you down the stairs on purpose?"

Isabelle stares at me, and all her anger comes flooding back again.

"Yes!" she screeches.

The pain is immense, and I hold my hands over my ears, desperate to block out the horrendous noise.

"She's gone," Mim moans in disappointment.

Yet, she is more solid than ever to me. I see spirits who have been murdered. And, now, I understand why I'm able to see Isabelle. But Mim, however briefly, saw her as well. So, Isabelle has to have a broken heart.

"Was Robert..." I begin, unsure of what to say. I feel pathetically bashful, but I force the words out. "Was Robert your...your lover?" I finish awkwardly.

"Yes," Mim says. Her answer is firm. She must be communicating with Isabelle at last.

"But Robert betrayed you," I continue, piecing the story together. "He betrayed you and pushed you down the stairs."

"Yes." Mim answers the question again.

"Mim, talk to her," I instruct, pulling my gaze away from the corner of the room. "Ask her what Robert's full name was. And ask her what she needs to move on. Meander, come over here and help me go through these records. Dylan and Kornelía, you two help as well."

This time, no one hesitates. Kornelía pulls off her headphones, and Dylan puts down his reader. Meander stands, and with shaky steps, joins us on one of the beds. Mim converses with the spirit in Spanish while the others grab flashlights and begin opening the books.

"She doesn't know his last name," Mim tells us after a minute. "She doesn't remember anymore."

"Then we'll have to do this the hard way," I say with a sigh. "Everyone take a record book. Search for anyone named Robert. Try to find a birthdate somewhere around 1832, although I suppose he could have been born several years before or after."

"Can we check the hotel logs?" Kornelía asks.

I shake my head.

"I'll skim over them, but I doubt we'll find anything there. Isabelle was twenty-five and unmarried. Her parents were living here in the village, but she was paying to have a room in the hotel. If Robert was here with her, I have a feeling he wasn't supposed to be. I doubt his name will be anywhere in those ledgers."

"So, we have to find every Robert born within what, a twenty-year span?" Dylan asks.

"At least," Meander replies.

Dylan lets out a moan. "No problem. We should be out of here in time for a midnight snack. You know, three months from now."

Kornelía messes his dark hair. "Stop talking and get to work," she says.

We flip through the books, calling out every Robert we find.

"Robert Alard, born 1823."

"No," Mim says.

"Robert Granet, born 1830."

"No."

"Here's a good one. Robert Robertson, born 1828."

"*No.*"

"Mim, do you know what she needs?" I ask after a while of calling out names to no avail.

"She's fading on me," Mim says in a panic, tugging on her braids. "Her words aren't making any sense."

"Hold on." I get up off the bed and stand in front of Isabelle again. Meander follows and stands beside me. His attention strengthens her.

"They must know!" she yells, her body swivelling towards us.

"Who must know?" I ask.

"They!" Isabelle screams.

Meander places a hand on his head, shutting his eyes against the pain.

"Robert Houdin, born 1824," Kornelía says through a yawn.

"*Yes!*"

The room is silent for a moment as I look at the others. Meander and Mim wince while Kornelía and Dylan stare back at me with wide eyes, giving me the impression everyone heard her this time.

"Kornelía, Dylan. Find out what happened to Robert. Was he ever married? When did he die?"

"Dead?" Isabelle asks in confusion.

Her figure fades, and Mim resumes speaking in Spanish.

"She doesn't realize how long she's been here," she explains to us in English. Her words are breathy, like she's taking extra care to swallow down sickness with each syllable. "She thinks it's still 1857. She wants everyone to know what Robert is like. She doesn't want someone else to suffer the same way she did."

"I'm seeing nothing in the marriage books," Dylan says as he rifles through the pages.

"Oh! Here he is," Kornelía exclaims. "Robert Houdin. Died 1860. My French is a tad rusty, but it looks like he died from, um…. Well, from drinking."

"Tell her, Mim!" I instruct.

Mim's voice is quick and low, a slur of foreign words. She tells Isabelle, and the spirit's bluish light begins flickering brightly. I've never seen this before. I watch the spirit, the pain in my head easing.

Mim finishes what she's saying, listens to words I can't make out, and then smiles.

"She says he always drank when he felt guilty about something," she explains.

"He must have felt guilty about her. So much so that it finished him." I nod.

"He's gone now," Mim tells Isabelle in English. "He's gone, and he can't hurt anyone anymore."

The blue light disappears with Mim's final words, replaced with a bright, yellow-white light flicking fast like a switch being turned off and on. The light fills the room, and Meander steps closer to me as Dylan and Kornelía crowd beside us to watch the brightness grow.

Isabelle's once petite form billows outwards, her light streaming in all directions. In a flash, she moves, coming at us. Her light surrounds me, and I'm sure it surrounds the others, too. The static in my head becomes a low steady note, and through it, I hear two clear, tinkling words.

"Thank you."

The light bursts, the brightness so intense I have to shield my eyes. The rosewater scent turns sweet and warm, and in a blink, it all vanishes—pain, sound, smell, and light.

"She's gone," Kornelía says in a weak but certain voice. The room is silent and black. Even the flashlights have been drained.

I take a long, deep breath, and let a smile spread across my face as I turn in the darkness to say something to the others. My body gives out before the words have time to form, and I collapse on the ground in sudden exhaustion, watching the shadows of my friends do the same before I lose consciousness.

33

I WAKE WITH A MUDDLED HEAD FOR THE FIFTH OR SIXTH TIME SINCE Isabelle knocked me out. The first time, I was confused to find myself back in my bed at camp. I thought I had had a vivid dream or was still on the hotel room floor, hallucinating.

I realized Robbie was kneeling beside me, saying something I can't remember now but that eased my nerves in the moment. Since then, I've woken several more times. Sometimes, Robbie's shaking my arm, offering food and water I devour before passing out again. Other times, I wake with a start because my bladder is full. Each time, it's like a living dream—eating and dropping back to sleep or shuffling to the bathroom and barely making it back to my bed before blackness surrounds me.

I'm not sure how long it's been since we set Isabelle free. A few days, I think, but I'm so disoriented I could be wrong.

This time, waking up is different, though. I'm still exhausted, and grey shadows try to draw me back into the deep folds of sleep. However, I know I'm not going to give in this time because there's a thought in my head I can't shake.

The spirit in the woods.

I sit up, pressing my palms to my eyes and trying to keep my vision from swinging. There are no windows in the room, but it must be night because, when I remove my hands and blink through the darkness around me, I can see my campmates asleep in their bunks. I shouldn't be getting up. I think it several times, but I still slowly work my way to a sitting position and slide to the side of the bed.

My feet tingle from movement, and I try to remember when I changed into my pajamas. It might have been a day after getting back from the hotel—if a day has even passed since then. But as hard as I press my mind, I can't remember ever taking off my socks. I stare at my bare toes for several long minutes, the inability to recollect unnerving.

The thought of the spirit in the woods strikes me again, breaking my stupor. I flex my toes and force myself to stand, my head dropping to my chest even while I grab my sweater from the end of the bed and shove my bare feet into my sneakers.

I don't know where the idea came from. Or rather, I don't know where it's coming from *now*. The knowledge of what's stuck in the forest outside has bothered me since the moment I discovered it. Now that I'm exhausted, drained, and don't even know what day it is, I can't push away the ridiculous urge to get up and investigate.

The sane thing to do would be to inform someone of the spirit's presence and then go back to bed. But I don't think that's what I'm supposed to do. I'm not a child who needs to get an adult to solve his problems. I'm no longer a total novice when it comes to spirits, and maybe I never was a novice at all.

I helped Maggie when I was little, and I've helped Isabelle now, too. I came here to figure out how to stop the pain of seeing spirits. And I've learned the only way to stop the pain is to rid our world of the spirit itself. I'm finished running away. I want more of what Isabelle offered. I want to stop hiding and make myself a useful Sender.

At least I think that's what I want. I'm so tired it's difficult to know for sure.

Someone shifts in his bed, and I pause, watching each bunk to make sure no one else is awake. When there's no other movement, I leave the room, my steps sluggish and drowsy. Like the last time I walked through the house in the middle of the night, the lounge and hallways are empty and quiet. But, this time, there's no late-night study group in the dining hall to halt my progress.

I rub my eyes as I leave through the back and head out to the shed in the garden. It's not locked. I slide inside the dark structure and find a shovel near the back. Something skitters by my feet, but I'm too tired to be startled. I grab the shovel, turn to leave, and notice a flashlight on a nearby ledge. Flicking it on, I head back outside towards the front of the property, so I can cross the lake and go to the woods.

I don't have a plan, nor do I have days of research and a team of campmates behind me. But Mim didn't have those things the first time she contacted Isabelle, either. I don't want to free the spirit tonight. At least, I don't expect to. But, if I let it out of its prison and make contact for a brief moment, I can start the research and get the proper Senders involved.

Or, maybe, I'm just an idiot mostly sleepwalking through a French forest. My head is muddled with memories of Isabelle and the lasting effects of her crossing over. I haven't had time to recharge yet, but I don't have the luxury of waiting. If I don't act now, I never will. Even if I wait until tomorrow morning, my resolve will be gone, and it will be too late.

I stumble over roots and slip on a pile of fallen leaves, slick with leftover rain from the last storm. I don't have any trouble making my way to the correct spot, even though I should. By all accounts, I should be wandering through the night, each aimless step making me regret my decision. But I'm not. I know where I'm going, either from memory or an auto-pilot switched on in my daze.

Whatever the case, I make it in good time. Cold sickness seeps into my pores as I approach the spot where I fell, but I'm too tired to register the pain like I normally would—the sharp prickle in my head is just another layer of cloudy discomfort. I push through the unfocused static and get to work with the shovel—my arms heavy, and my digging weak but determined.

The sky is overcast, and the trees are lush and full overhead, but I don't have trouble seeing. If I tried to peer into the distant shadows, I wouldn't be able to make out much, but the task poses no difficulty. With the flashlight on the ground and pointed where I need it, I am caught up in something like a trance—my head aching and my limbs sore. I want to drop off to sleep and snap myself into a frenzy at the same time. I want to turn around and go back to bed and call myself crazy come daylight. But I keep working, pushing the shovel into the dirt, dragging up clods of earth, and half-heartedly throwing them off to the side.

The mound is not deep, which is a small favor. It doesn't take long, even with my slow pace, to reach the hard, wooden board the spirit thuds against in response to my shovel's tap.

"I'm going as fast I can," I murmur as my head swells with pain, the spirit's impatience recognizable even without it being in sight. I don't think as I clear away the dirt to expose the full length of the coffin-sized box which has been warped by time and is moist with decay. I dig the shovel under the board, prying it away from the others, and rip up the makeshift coffin lid, breaking the barrier between me and the spirit.

My brain starts working when I see the dusty remains of a body and am pushed backwards by the spirit rushing out from the box. In a flash, I'm positive I've been somehow tricked.

"Damn it!" I shout as the whirling mass of a man swirls around me.

The smell of lavender trails behind him as he circles me twice, his incomprehensible mutterings swishing through my head. I grip my forehead and try to take stock of my surroundings. The exhaustion is gnawing at me now, and it's a wonder I ever managed to dig down to the coffin at all.

I shake my head and watch as the man, his shadowed frame long and weasel-like, dips towards the ground and skims the woodland floor before swooping up and swirling back to me. I've never seen a spirit so hyperactive before, notwithstanding the brief episode in the café earlier this summer. Usually they're still or close to it. They hover in one spot, most of the energy they possess dedicated to trying to talk. Some move, and one even managed to throw things. But that wasn't the spirit, only it's reaction to someone else's ability. This spirit now is flying about, fully of its own accord.

"*The nerve!*" the spirit howls, the words coherent and brimming with fury. "*The nerve! The nerve!*"

He flies at me, his body rushing against mine—through mine—like sickly cold vapour. I've always wondered what it'd be like to touch a spirit, and I'm not surprised to find the experience thoroughly unpleasant.

"The nerve of what or who?" I ask, ducking out of his way as he swoops low a second time.

His cloudy hands, with their long, bony fingers, try to grab at something on the ground. I feel like I've been doused with cold water. I'm more awake now than I've been for days, and my previous actions tonight feel like something I did while still asleep. Now the spirit is out, though, I should at least take a shot at figuring out his business. He clearly didn't just need an escape. He'd be gone by now if he only wanted out of his prison.

"*The nerve!*" the spirit shrieks.

My head aches, my eyes sting with weariness, and my stomach clenches in on itself with hunger and sickness. I don't know why I'm here. I don't know why I came. I want to turn around and leave, even if I don't quite know the way back to camp. I want to shove the spirit back into his hole in the ground and tell someone about him in the morning.

But I can't make sense of my surroundings enough to walk away and head back to bed. I can't make sense of anything outside of my aching chills and the spirit's incessant screeching.

"The nerve!"

The lavender scent should be sweet and relaxing, but it's putrid and thick like bloated, rotted stalks being shoved in my face. I bend over in a lurch, my vision swimming. My groan mingles with the static as my eyes veer up enough to watch the spirit somersault in the air. He's got no distinguishing marks of death, no real distinguishing marks at all. It curdles what little food might still be sitting in my stomach from the last time I ate.

The intuition kicks in, the nagging knowledge of the spirit's demise. This man was not buried after a quick and brutal murder. The burial *was* the murder. He was buried alive, left to suffocate under the earth, alone in the empty woods.

It's a tragic story, but he's not a tragic man. At least, I'm fairly certain he wasn't. The way he moves, shrieks, and slits his translucent blue shadow-eyes makes me think he did something to deserve his comeuppance. He probably shouldn't have been buried alive. Still, he's not an innocent bystander, this one. There's a reason he was left here to die alone.

"The nerve!" he says again, this time more a growl than a shriek.

He spins back towards the ground, and something in the coldness of the air shifts in my head. I hear rustling behind me, and I'm not at all curious to know who's come out here to join in my foolish endeavour. I don't need to be. I know, by the way the chilly air starts to burn icily against my face and the spirit's anger swells as it swoops low to the earth once more. I know by the way the ghost manages to pick up a rock, which it almost gleefully hurls at my head.

I'm too out of it to dodge the stone. It hits my forehead, cracking against my skull and sending black sparks into my line of vision. I tilt, stumble, and fall altogether—landing hard on my knees before falling farther forward and onto my face.

"Cal!"

I hear my name being called, but it's not Meander's voice, which makes my confusion worse. Footsteps hurry towards me, and a figure swims out of focus until he stops next to my face and kneels down to examine my wound. Only then do I make out Daniel, who is supposed to be in Argentina and not out here in the woods with me.

"Is he okay?" a female voice says from behind him.

The sound is familiar, but I don't know it well enough to give it a name.

"Cal, can you see me?" Daniel asks, but his examination is cut short when the spirit throws a clod of dirt at us, dust and pebbles raining down. Daniel lifts his eyes, his expression awed. He can't see the spirit or the way it turns back around and scavenges the ground, trying to find something else worth throwing.

"He's coming back," I manage weakly. I try to press myself up, to get off my face and at least back to my knees, but my attempt is useless. What inexplicable energy I exerted coming here to release the spirit from his grave has been depleted. It's hard enough keeping my eyes open. All I want to do is sleep.

"We've got to get him out of here," Daniel says. "Ada, can you see the spirit?" A rock hits his arm as he's finishing his question, and he clutches the spot, muttering something in Spanish.

"No, I can't, but I saw that," Ada replies in frustration. "You're right. We've got to get him out of here."

"Cal, can you walk?" Daniel asks.

I try to nod, but I don't think my head moves. "Yeah," I say, the word slurring out between my lips.

"He might be concussed," Daniel says.

I try to shake my head to tell him I'm fine, but I don't think I manage that, either.

"Shit."

The word is low and mumbled in an English accent that makes me smile, or at least makes me think about smiling. Meander's feet come into view, and it's a relief to know I wasn't wrong about the spirit's sudden intensity. It's nice to see something making sense on this out-of-sync evening.

"Get him back to camp. I'll distract the spirit."

"How are you going to—?" Ada begins.

"Hey!" Meander says, and the single word's enough to grab the spirit's attention and hush Ada at the same time.

I'm surprised the spirit stayed oblivious to Meander for as long as he did. As soon as he realizes where the heat of his anger radiates from, the spirit turns on Meander like a predator. He doesn't bother with dirt or rocks. He rushes at Meander like he rushed at me, only this time, he doesn't strike without impact.

Meander staggers back when he's hit, his steps unsteady. He's tired too. He must be, and it takes effort for him to stay upright. I want to tell him to be careful or to try to get the spirit's attention, so we can bounce it between us until we're able to get away. But Daniel and Ada are working to get me to my feet, and the effort of coordinating my limbs is hard enough.

Still, I don't look away from Meander, and second by second, my head starts to clear. I don't notice at first. For a moment, all I'm aware of is the spirit making another attack by hitting Meander squarely in the chest, rocking him on his heels, and making him cry out in groggy pain.

"He's going to get himself killed," Ada mutters.

"No," I whisper, blinking rapidly as I take in the sight before me. They can't see the spirit, so they can't comprehend what's happening. They might sense the rushing, and they must see the way Meander's shaking and losing consciousness. But they don't see how the spirit's attacks are getting less violent because he is turning from murky blue-white to a lighter white-yellow, his form brightening with each new blow.

"It's dis...dis..." I can't make out the word. My head lolls against my chest, and I take a gasping breath as I try to step forward with the others' help.

"Disappearing?" Daniel asks.

It's not the word I wanted, but it works well enough. I nod once and take one wobbly step before I falter and slump forward again. My head's swimming, less from the pain of the rock-wound or the static of the spirit, and more from the buzzing. It's like a small tremor in the earth, a miniature earthquake tingling up my legs and through to my fingertips.

Meander's still shaking, but he's not crying out anymore. I'm sure he feels the buzzing too. Probably, far more than I do. The spirit lunges back, and with a shrieking effort, heads for him again.

"The nerve of those sneaks. Those thieving idiots. Those damned fools!"

The words roar through my head, making me trip over my lackluster footing, slip out of Daniel and Ada's grasp, and fall back onto my knees. The spirit makes a furious rush towards Meander, and when he hits his mark, he explodes in a burst of white light that shakes everything around me and sends me into blackness as if the explosion happened inside of my brain.

34

I DON'T REMEMBER WAKING UP AT ALL THIS TIME. THERE ARE NO FUZZY recollections of returning to camp, crawling back into bed, taking a trip to the toilet, or getting medical attention for my head or food for my stomach. When I woke after Isabelle, I had a general idea of how long it'd been since the event. This time, I haven't a clue.

I don't wake up on my own, either. A woman's voice, firm though not unkindly, tells me to open my eyes. When I do, it's bright in the room. The lights are on, and most of the beds are empty. Mrs. Buxley stands in the center of the room, and Meander sits up in his bunk, looking as sleepy and as shaken as I feel.

The color, as subtle as it ever was, is gone from his face. He is drained like someone five days into a bad cold or someone who's recently donated a lot of blood and isn't reacting well. Hell, if this was a cartoon and not my actual life, I might say he looks like he's seen a ghost.

"Good morning," Mrs. Buxley says, her stature taller when framed by the three sets of bunks. Her purple-toed shoe taps against the ground as she considers us. "I apologize for waking you. You both could use more sleep, but you leave Camp Wanagi tomorrow, and I wanted to ensure we had a chance to talk first."

My head throbs where the rock hit it. I reach a hand up and feel the bandage stuck to a good portion of my forehead. If we leave tomorrow, it means that, between Isabelle and the spirit in the woods, I've slept through the entire last week of camp.

"What happened the other night," Mrs. Buxley begins, her words measured.

"We getting kicked out?" Meander interrupts.

Mrs. Buxley looks surprised by the question, but when she turns to him, her expression softens into one of sad understanding. Meander asked the question as if it's a situation he's faced before. Given his ability, it's not hard to imagine him getting blamed for some bizarre act of violence caused by a spirit only he could see.

"Of course not," our instructor says at last. "We would never expel someone for using their talents. What happened with the spirit outside of this house was unfortunate but also unavoidable."

"I'm sorry," I say, needing to own up to my part in the proceedings. "It's my fault. I should have told someone. I don't know why I even went out there."

"As I said, it was unavoidable," Mrs. Buxley says with a small smile. "You were under something else's influence, Callum. Nothing could have prevented you from undertaking that task."

"I wasn't... What do you mean I was under

something else's influence?" The words startle me. My heart picks up speed as her foot stops tapping against the ground.

"When did you first come into contact with the spirit?" she asks, her voice almost conversational.

I search my memory, but the dates are fuzzy. I'm not as tired as I've been the past few days, but I still can't make sense of the calendar in my head.

"I don't know...a couple of weeks ago, I guess."

"And how many times have you thought of that spirit since?" she asks.

"Every day," I mutter. "At least every day since the game in the woods. Every day since I got close to it." I thought about the spirit more than I thought about Isabelle, more than I've thought about most of the spirits I've encountered in my life. Even while unconscious, the unmarked grave in the woods continually crept into my dreams.

Mrs. Buxley watches the realization dawning on my face. "It impressed itself upon you, and when you were weakened after your assignment, it used you for its benefit. Daniel tells me it's not the first time a spirit has done such a thing."

Maggie was already in my head, and now her image hovers bright and vivid behind my eyes.

"Yeah, but that was...different."

Mrs. Buxley smiles again. "Every spirit is different, Mr. Silver. Every spirit and every situation is always unique."

"So, what...? I was possessed?" I ask, the worry I felt earlier this summer coming back now with tenfold strength.

"Not exactly," Mrs. Buxley says. "The spirit was

not inside your body. But it did guide your will. You resisted when you were well, but it was strong enough to pull you in when your defenses were low. And I'm sorry for that. We always try to clear the area before camp starts, to ensure no spirits are close enough to bother our students unless it's an active part of our study. Evidently, our search of the forest was not thorough enough.

"Wooded areas often prove troublesome," she adds with a sigh. "The natural fluctuations in temperature and abundant sources of noise make it difficult for Senders to take accurate readings of the landscape. But enough of my digression."

She takes a deep breath and shifts away from me.

"As for you, Mr. Rhoades," she says.

"I wasn't possessed," Meander begins.

"No," Mrs. Buxley agrees, "you were only trying to help, which is exactly what we like to see in a Sender. But once the spirit attacked you..."

"He released it," I say, remembering the sixty seconds or so of the spirit's release better than I can remember any other events of the night.

"Yes," Mrs. Buxley says, but she doesn't sound impressed or even relieved. "You did release the spirit, but it was a lucky chance things worked out so well in your favor."

"What do you mean?" Meander asks, sounding weary.

"This particular spirit was angry," Mrs. Buxley explains. "It's not an unusual emotion for spirits to retain. But for this spirit, anger was the only reason it remained here. When it attacked you, you absorbed its anger. And you were able to absorb it at a rate greater than the spirit could produce it. You drained its life force. Without the emotion, it had nothing left. It didn't seek revenge, and it didn't have a message to relate to someone. The spirit was angry, and when you allowed it to outpour all its grief, the hold was broken, and it was able to cross over."

"Isn't that a good thing?" I ask, running a hand through my hair, which is greasy after days of not showering.

"This time, yes, but the result could have been much different," Mrs. Buxley says.

Her eyes are trained on Meander's, and he holds her gaze, hardened against anything she might say next.

"You were lucky this spirit had nothing but anger within it, Meander. If it had more, if it was staying around for a specific purpose, the anger you allowed it to feel would have only made it stronger. That would have allowed it to harm you or worse."

Meander doesn't say anything. For a moment, the two just stare at each other.

Mrs. Buxley sighs, glancing back at me. "Normally, we encourage our campers to embrace what they've learned during their summers here. We want them to take on the task of confronting the spirits in their everyday lives, those they've encountered close to home. But for you..." She looks at Meander and then again at me. "For both of you, I'm suggesting the opposite. You should endeavour to stay away from spirits whenever possible if you're not here at camp. What happened this week is a testament to the danger you could face alone in a situation at home."

"So, I finally find a purpose for my massively inconvenient ability, and now you're telling me I can't even make use of it?" Meander asks with annoyed incredulity.

"No," Mrs. Buxley says. "Your ability does have a purpose, and one day, you'll be able to make wonderful use of it if you choose. But, for the next year at least, try to stay away from the spirits in your life."

"Yeah, 'cause that's worked so well up to now," Meander mumbles, shaking his head.

"Do your best," Mrs. Buxley says, her voice a no-nonsense reprimand of his angsty words.

I like Mrs. Buxley. She's kind but decisive. I wonder if she has kids of her own.

"You may not be able to avoid the occasional run-in, but stay away from places you know are inhabited. And absolutely do not try to seek any spirits out to test your newfound powers."

She says the last words with a mocking smirk on her lips. *Powers*. We're not superheroes, and everyone in this room knows it. But I bet Mrs. Buxley has dealt with kids in the past who did think their abilities meant they were destined to save the world.

"We won't," I tell our instructor. I can't speak for Meander, really, but it seems like the appropriate thing to say.

Mrs. Buxley nods and gives us a lingering glance before she turns to leave the room. "Get some more sleep. You'll be woken first thing in the morning, along with everyone else. The other Shades don't know what's happened. No one does, aside from the faculty and your mentors. Your sector mates think you were hit particularly hard by the release of your previous spirit. You can disclose the true story if you wish. But it's your story to tell, and only if you wish to tell it."

Despite what she says, it's unlikely the story won't be known. Even if speculation hasn't already started, the bandage on my head will be an immediate giveaway when the others see me tomorrow.

Mrs. Buxley doesn't wait for me to tell her the secrecy is nice but pointless. She walks out of the room, switching off the light and leaving the two of us in darkness.

Meander turns on his reading light, and I do the same. I'll sleep again, I know I will. But someone's left a tray of fruit and sandwiches on the dresser, and I want to use the bathroom and gulp some water before I fall back into bed.

"Sorry you got pulled into this," I say, sitting still for several long seconds before I feel stable enough to stand.

Meander shrugs. "Couldn't let you stumble out into the forest alone. I knew something wasn't right."

"How did you, though?" I ask, my stomach growling as I approach the dresser. "How did you even know where I was?"

"I heard you leaving the room," he says. He eyes the tray of food but makes no move to get out from under the mound of blankets he's somehow managed to collect over the course of the summer. "I suspected where you were going. So, I got up to get help. Couldn't find Robbie or Alex. Didn't have a clue where the instructors might be. But I found Ada, and Daniel came when he heard your name."

Of course. Mrs. Buxley said only the instructors and our mentors knew what happened. Ada was Meander's mentor this summer. That explains why she was there that night.

"Sorry I got you concussed," he smirks.

I smile, grabbing a bottle of water and a sandwich and walking over to hand it up to him.

"You released the spirit," I tell him. "Which was insanely impressive, whatever Mrs. Buxley says."

He wraps one of his blankets tight around his shoulders, the movement shifting a stray curl, so it dangles over his right eye. His expression is solemn as he takes the proffered food, but his pale cheeks twinge with pink, and the corner of his lips twitch in what I think is a forcefully suppressed smile.

I turn away from his bunk, amused by his modesty and sorry he needs to feel modest at all. Meander is not a menace, despite what I'm sure a few shop owners or school teachers in his hometown believe. His talent may be dangerous, but he is not.

Injury or no, I'm glad he was with me in the forest. When I'm back in Canada facing tormented spirits while bystanders roll their eyes or try to pretend my abnormality doesn't exist, the memory of our success will be comforting. This summer, a boy followed me to the woods in the dead of night, risking his own safety for no other reason than to make sure I was okay. No one has ever done that for me. No one has ever understood—ever cared—enough to help me out after a spirit knocked me down.

I've met a lot of interesting people at Camp Wanagi, but no one fills my head with curiosity and hope like Meander Rhoades. Guiding spirits and head wounds aside, I'm happy the two of us have a victorious ghost story of our own.

There's noise below us, the rest of the camp up and lively in the waking hours. I head to the bathroom, brushing my teeth and cringing at the bloodstain seeping through my bandage before I amble back out into the bedroom to get a snack and return to bed.

35

"CAL, CAN I TALK TO YOU FOR A MINUTE?" MIM STANDS IN THE HALLWAY across from the boys' room, her thick hair down and her head bent. It's a stance I'd be unsurprised to see on Kornelía, but it's odd—and wrong—on Mim.

"Yeah, sure." I step back from the doorway and retreat into the room I had been preparing to leave for the final time this summer. It's hard to believe it's the last day of camp. Most of the campers are already in the dining hall, waiting for buses to drive them to airports and train stations so they can go home.

I sit down on the edge of the bed which has been mine all summer while Mim lingers just inside the door. Her eyes are red rimmed and puffy, and her skin is peaked.

"What's up?" I ask, confused by her strange appearance.

"I..." Mim begins. She stops and gives me a small smile before letting out a shaky breath. "I wanted to say thank you. You know, for your help last week with...with Isabelle."

"We all worked together, Mim," I say. It's true. We each played our part in releasing Isabelle. I talked to her when she was angry and wanted the truth of her death to be known. Mim communicated with her when she despaired, broken-hearted over the fate of her beloved. Meander brought Isabelle's anger out, making her stronger and easier to talk with. And Kornelía and Dylan dug through books, finding men named Robert and learning how the correct Robert eventually died. If it had just been me facing Isabelle, I would have failed. I think any of us would have. We needed to be a team to be successful.

"I know we all worked together, but I didn't want it that way," Mim confesses. "I wanted to do everything by myself, and I couldn't have done a thing if you weren't there to help. Everybody did something, but you took control, and you talked to her when I couldn't. It was because of you we were successful, Cal. I wanted to make sure you knew I'm not mad about it.... I'm thankful you were there."

I haven't given Isabelle much thought since our night in Fos-sur-Mer. I've barely been awake enough to think, and what little musing I've done has been on the events in the woods. But I'm glad I was there for Isabelle's release, too. What happened with the other spirit more or less forced my return to Camp Wanagi. I need to figure out why spirits can guide me, and how I can stop them from doing it. But Isabelle gave me something nice to look forward to next summer. The night in the hotel felt right and important. It was overwhelming, but in a good way.

SHADE

My talent, ability, or curse—whatever it is—at least I now know it has a purpose.

"You did a great job, Mim," I say, standing from the empty bed. "And I'm happy to know you don't mind me tagging along on your projects."

Mim smiles, straightening her back and clearing the dark hair away from her eyes.

"I guess you're not *so* bad," she jokes, giving me a playful shove as we leave the room.

We join the other Shades in the dining hall. Mim sits close to Dylan. They don't say anything to each other, but they look comfortable together. I sit across from them, a space away from Kornelía. She's hunched over her sketchbook, working on a drawing. She won't let me see it, but I'm sure it's a picture of Isabelle.

The other members of my sector are spread over two tables, and Robbie and Alex stand by the edge of one.

"Well, campers, you've made it," Robbie says once Mim and I are seated. His mohawk, now frosted at the edges with blue, glistens under the light of the broken chandelier. "You've completed your first summer at Camp Wanagi. You've met others with abilities similar to your own, and you've begun your education in the world of the Oracle."

"We've loved being your leads, and can't wait to see you all again next summer," Alex continues with a smile, a pair of sunglasses sitting atop her head and pushing her long hair back from her face.

"If the place hasn't sunk to the bottom of the lake by then," Dylan says.

Alex and Robbie exchange amused looks.

"Didn't you know?" Robbie says innocently, like what he's about to tell us is common knowledge and not something he's managed to keep hidden all summer. "We won't be back here next year."

"What do you mean?" Lu asks.

Alex laughs. "Camp Wanagi follows the Oracle and their studies. Didn't you wonder why this place was so unkempt? Every year camp takes place somewhere different. And, sometimes, the only lodging we can manage is an old home in the middle of a renovation."

"So where are we going to be next summer?" Dylan asks.

I look up at the cracked ceiling while he speaks. It never did make sense that an organization willing to fly campers in from around the globe would be so cheap on accommodations. I wonder who owns this place and how rich they must be to tackle renovating this sinking, decaying disaster of a home.

"You'll find that out next summer," Robbie teases. "For now, take what you've learned this year, trust what you know, and enjoy your time back in the world of the living."

He grins at us, and I can't help smiling back. I'm going to miss Robbie and his cheerful optimism. I'm glad I'll get to see him again next year.

The buses arrive a few minutes later. There are three, all going in different directions. I'm headed back to the Charles de Gaulle airport, along with Kornelía, Dylan, Reed, Sefa, and Sabeena. Mim, however, is flying out of a smaller airport, which means we have to say our goodbyes while we're still at the camp. I give her a hug, and while she's hugging first Kornelía and then Dylan, I watch the other campers exchanging their own goodbyes. I don't see Daniel, which is a shame. I never got to thank him or Ada for their help, nor was I able to ask him how his final task went, either.

Not seeing Daniel makes me realize there's another camper missing from the groups crowding around the buses, though. One more important than my mentor.

"Has anyone seen Meander?" I ask, turning back to my friends.

Mim and Dylan are whispering to each other, and they ignore my question. Kornelía shrugs and points back towards the house.

"I think he's still inside," she says.

There's no point doubting her because, if I've learned one thing this summer, it's that Kornelía has a good sense of these kinds of things.

"I'll be back." I cross the pathway again, hopping over the stones more quickly than I've done all summer. When I get inside, I find Meander sitting at the far end of one of the long rows of tables, a book open in his hands and his eyes downcast towards the pages.

"Aren't you leaving?" I ask as I near where he sits. "The buses are about to take off."

Meander looks up from his book. He's still drained, but there's a hint of color in his cheeks again.

"Change of plans," he says, his voice a sigh. "I'll be taking the train back to Paris tomorrow. Going to spend a day with my aunt and see if she's okay after, you know, the *burglary*."

After the events at the apartment in Paris, Meander discovered his aunt had returned home to find smashed clocks and dropped knives in the hallway. She assumed there'd been a break-in, and Meander let her believe it. It was easier than trying to explain what actually occurred.

I don't like the idea of him being back in that apartment, especially not so soon after what he's gone through here. "Are you going to be okay going back there?"

Meander nods, though his eyes betray his uncertainty. "It's just one night. I'll be fine. I'm on the early train back to England the next morning, anyway. If I have to, I can stay up overnight and sleep on the ride home."

"Well...stay safe," I mumble. I want to offer him advice or at least a word of comfort, but I can't think of any decent sentiments to give. I shift the bag on my shoulder, and glance over to the front door. "Anyway, I've got to go. But..." I pause and turn back to Meander, wondering where the two of us stand. I'm not sure if we're friends or if he only tolerates me. But I don't want him to slip away, an outcome easy to imagine with his preference for keeping to himself.

I press my lips together, fishing a small slip of paper and a pen from my bag. I scribble letters and numbers with a nervous hand and offer it to him before I can change my mind.

"What's this?" Meander asks, pulling the page from between my unsteady fingers and staring at the writing as if he can't figure it out for himself.

"My email address," I say with a shrug. "Just...you know. If you wanted to talk, ever."

Meander studies the paper and fixes me with a sarcastic smirk. "If I give you my email address, you're going to email me, aren't you?" he asks.

I do my best to keep my expression serious as I nod. "Of course. Constantly. Like, every hour on the hour," I say. "But I promise I won't spam your inbox with chain mail. No 'send this to fifteen people or a ghost will haunt you tonight' messages."

"Well, that's good. I've heard it's not much fun being haunted by a ghost." Meander snatches the pen and grabs my hand. "If you smudge this, it's your own fault." He writes his email address on my left palm, his fingers warm against my skin. Whenever I hold a book for longer than a couple of minutes, my hands are freezing. For all the time he spends reading, I would have imagined Meander's touch to be permanently cold.

It's an analogy that sums him up well. The first moments I spent with Meander this summer gave me the impression he might be a cold person. But the more we become acquainted, the more I feel his warmth. If I'm lucky—and persistent—I hope someday I'll know him so well all the frozen moments of uncertainty and misconception are gone.

When he's finished writing, he picks up his book again and lowers his eyes back to his story.

"Thanks," I say, memorizing the address before I turn to leave the château for the last time.

"Have a good trip home," he murmurs, but when I glance back at him, he's already absorbed in his book once more.

When I'm back outside and onto the bus, I sit next to Kornelía. She doesn't even notice when I slide in beside her. I wish she'd let me see the drawing she's still huddled over, but I don't push. Kornelía's talent is her own, and it's up to her if others share in it.

Soon enough the bus is on the road, and on its way to the airport, which means I'm on my way back to Canada. I'm excited to be heading home again, and I don't even mind the fact school will be starting soon. But I will miss Camp Wanagi. Good and bad, there's something miraculous about the world of the Oracle.

I sink back into my seat with a silent sigh, touching the fresh bandage on my head and wondering what lie I'll tell my parents to save them from knowing how I really got the wound. So long as I'm on a different plane home than I was on my way over here, I'll have time to work out a story while I'm in the air.

For now, I fish out my phone, and slip in my earbuds. As Kornelía draws and the other kids on the bus talk about their upcoming trips home, I turn on my music and watch the French countryside blur past my window.

THE STORY CONTINUES
IN BOOK TWO OF THE ORACLE OF SENDERS SERIES

REVENANT

ACKNOWLEDGEMENTS

I would like to thank the Seven Sisters team for welcoming me to the family and helping me share my story with the world. In particular, Martina McAtee for taking a chance on my submission, Molly Phipps for designing my fantastic cover, and Catherine Stovall for using her amazing editing skills to help get my story into shape. *Shade* would not be the book it is today without you all!

I would also like to thank everyone who has read, promoted, and supported my writing. Stories are meant to be shared, and I'm thrilled you've chosen to join me on my writing adventure. And, of course, an extra huge thank you goes to my husband, for tirelessly listening to my story ideas and taking many long walks with me to brainstorm what will happen next.

ABOUT THE AUTHOR

MERE JOYCE is a Canadian author of books for young adults. Her writing includes contemporary tales, high-action mysteries, and her personal favorite—ghost stories. When she's not writing, Mere can be found recommending books as a librarian, or spending time at home with her husband and two sons. She's also been known to be a selective, yet highly enthusiastic fangirl.

Find her online at:

MEREJOYCE.COM

OTHER BOOKS
BY
SEVEN SISTERS

In the small town of Belle Haven, where the paranormal is normal, one girl must embrace her true self...

Or die trying.

www.7sisterspublishing.com/martinamcatee

CPSIA information can be obtained
at www.ICGtesting.com
Printed in the USA
LVOW11s0742080418
572676LV00001BA/2/P

9 781642 556520